A GOOD MAN

A NOVEL BY

LARRY BAKER

ICE CUBE BOOKS
NORTH LIBERTY, IOWA

A Good Man

Copyright © 2009 Larry Baker

ISBN 9781888160444

Library of Congress Control Number: 2009923032

ICP Books, LLC (est. 1993)
205 North Front Street
North Liberty, Iowa 52317-9302
www.icecubepress.com
steve@icecubepress.com

Printed in Canada

The paper used in this publication meets the minimum requirements of the
American National Standard for Information Sciences—Permanence of Paper for
Printed Library Materials, ANSI Z39.48-1992 (insert eco-audit at book's end)

For

 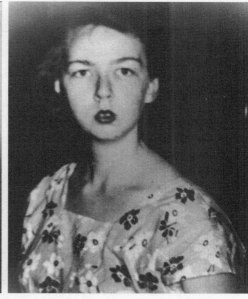

As much as mine, Harry Ducharme is their child.

A Note to Readers

This is a work of fiction. It never happened. I made it up. Any resemblance to any person, living or dead, is purely coincidental. If you think you see yourself in this story, you are wrong. However, if you see a wonderful person that reminds you of yourself, then it is you. Absolutely. I meant for you, and your friends, to see it that way. If you see an awful person that reminds you of yourself, you need to seek professional help. That being said, for the record, it is obvious that there are real people named in this story. I know some of them personally, some not. But I hope that every reader will agree that any use of a real person is done in a positive light. These people are real, as is my respect for them. However, if anybody who is real is still uncomfortable with being in the story, let me know and I will remove you from any future printings. Fair enough?

Also, this is a work of fiction that sometimes relies on the words of writers other than me. *That* is an important point of the overall story. Read the book; you'll understand. I have identified the sources for some lines, but not for others. Some lines are in the public domain, for others I got permission to use. If you think that a line or phrase was written by another writer, you might be right, and I will give them full credit if asked. For example, a cat named Pitty-Sing is a shameless steal. In that sense, I hope you have as much fun reading this story as I had in writing it.

Acknowledgements

First, Steve Semken. He got the manuscript on a Wednesday and told me five days later that he wanted to publish it. A good man doing good work in a good cause. He deserves much more success in the future.

Next, several writers have graciously permitted me to quote them at length. Thanks to Nathan Brockman, Stanley Fish, and Mark Morford. Their work is a valuable addition to the story.

Thanks also to Peter Guinta for letting me put his name on my words, and for his incisive comments as he read parts of the manuscript. In Iowa City, Jeff Carlson was an early and insightful reader. Bob Inman read the first version and, as expected, helped set me straight on many things. Haven Kimmel is on my thank-you list for, well, for being herself.

Mike Lankford, who knows most of my secrets, and Patty Friedmann, the best writer in New Orleans, are my two closest writer friends. We correspond almost every day. So far, the FBI has not knocked on our doors. So far.

Finally, singular love and thanks to Ginger Russell. Of all the people I have ever known, and I include myself in that group, only she is truly unique. The biggest mistake of my life was to not see that simple truth from the very beginning.

A Good Man

There are four irreducible objections to religious faith: that it wholly misrepresents the origins of man and the cosmos, that because of this original error it manages to combine the maximum of servility with the maximum of solipsism, that it is both the result and the cause of dangerous sexual repression, and that it is ultimately grounded on wish-thinking.
—Christopher Hitchens

It was, of course, a lie what you read about my religious convictions, a lie which is being systematically repeated. I do not believe in a personal God and I have never denied this but expressed it clearly. If something is in me which can be called religious then it is the unbounded admiration for the structure of the world so far as our science can reveal it.
—Albert Einstein

The Bible. That is what fools have written, what imbeciles command, what rogues teach, and young people are made to learn by heart.
—Voltaire

As to the book called the Bible, it is blasphemy to call it the word of God. It is a book of lies and contradictions, and a history of bad times and bad men. There are but a few good characters in the whole book.
—Thomas Paine

The Old Testament is responsible for more atheism, agnosticism, disbelief—call it what you will—than any book ever written: It has emptied more churches than all the counterattractions of cinema, motor bicycle, and golf course.
—A.A. Milne

God doesn't exist—the bastard!
—Jean-Paul Sartre

"With or without religion, good people will do good, and evil people will do evil. But for good people to do evil, that takes religion."
— Nobel Prize-winning physicist Steven Weinberg

"I have watched all things; I have endured afflictions. I have done the work of an evangelist, and I have made full proof of my ministry. I am now ready to be offered and the time of my departure is at hand. I have fought a good fight, I have finished my course, I have kept the faith."
—II Timothy 4:5-7

I

The Picture
April–1991
Dexter, New Mexico
Charles Yates

> *In dark ages people are best guided by*
> *religion, as in a pitch-black night a blind*
> *man is the best guide; he knows the*
> *roads and paths better than a man who*
> *can see. When daylight comes, however,*
> *it is foolish to use blind men as guides.*
> —Heinrich Heine, Gedanken und
> Einfalle

He was the only person he knew who had a video camera. It was a source of pride for him. He was going to record his life, the life of his friends, and they would all like him. He knew that most people liked to see pictures of themselves. Moving pictures would be better. All he had to do was learn how to work the damn thing. More than pushing a button, he needed to learn how to edit everything. If he was ever going to get out of Dexter, video would be his ticket. His girlfriend Sally was the first female camera operator for the ABC station in Albuquerque. She was his connection, and she was willing to do some private filming with him too. They were in love.

Yates practiced as soon as he got the bulky camera. He had one sixty minute tape which could be used over and over. Learn how to focus, to zoom and pan without jerking like a retard, film something and then tape over it again and again, an endless supply of subjects, until the basics were second nature.

He was hard on himself because he had high expectations. He wanted to be more than Dexter's best source of marijuana.

Sunday afternoon, a hot April, he put his camera on a tripod and pointed it toward a gulley stream that had become a swollen river overnight. Unexpected and inexplicable rain for three days had created flash floods all around Dexter. Yates had been as confused as everyone else. This was New Mexico, average rainfall for April about half an inch. Anomaly or not, the rain was also an opportunity. His friends told him they would be tubing down the rapids, would he tape them for posterity? He found a shady spot under an old two-lane bridge that spanned a drop of thirty feet over what was usually a dry gulley. Ten inches of rain had fallen in the past twenty-four hours, with temperatures fifteen degrees above normal. Today was suddenly cloudless, but the bridge blocked the sun as it traveled west this particular afternoon. The shade was an oasis as he waited for his friends. He framed his shot to include a leg of the bridge in each corner, as if they were an arch. He waited some more. His friends were nowhere to be seen. Just to be on the safe side, he switched on his camera, and then he lit a joint. Time for a nap soon enough, but a sixty minute tape ought to be enough. Yates knew they would shout at him as they passed. The camera would already be rolling. If they weren't there in an hour, their tough luck.

He was soon dreaming that he was at a job interview, a satchel full of demo tapes. The office did not have a roof, and the interviewer was bald and only spoke Spanish. But, as dreams go, this did not seem weird. Yates understood every word, and the bald man seemed very interested in him. But then the bald man started screeching at him, like tires skidding, and then his bald head exploded.

Yates was awake, blinking and confused, wondering if he was merely in another dream. A van was sinking in the water in front of him. Screams were coming from the bridge above. He looked up and saw people pointing down, then he looked back at the water, but the van was gone. "Holy shit!" he yelled out loud, but only he heard himself. He was a young man and a strong swimmer, but as soon as he stepped into the rushing water he knew it was hopeless. Wherever the van was under that maelstrom, he could not get there in time to help. He saw two men on the opposite shore waving at him, both wearing cowboy hats, but he could not understand what they were yelling. They were pointing. A hysterical woman was stumbling down the rocky embankment, and the two men chased her and held her back.

Yates knew somebody was trapped in the van, but he could not help. He was as lost as the others.

He would tell the story for the rest of his life. Waist deep in dirty swirling water, knowing that someone unseen was dying a few feet away from him, he started screaming at God, and then he was saved.

"Yes, yes, I know," he would testify to souls gathered in his presence, "It was a child who came out of that water. The baby who was saved by the black man. I wasn't in danger. I wasn't drowning, exactly. But when he handed me that baby I knew I was a different man. Call it what you want. I was saved. That's all I know."

The baby had come up from the water first, its arms pointed straight out from its body, its head limp to one side, a black hand under each arm. Yates immediately pushed himself deeper into the stream, the baby only a dozen yards away. The child was motionless, swaddled in a blue t-shirt, no further out of the water than it was when he first saw it rise. He had to fight the current, wondering how long the man under the water could hold his breath and still keep the baby above the surface.

"And then I realized that the baby was rising and coming toward me at the same time. You must see this as I saw it. Rising…and coming toward me…at the same time. Soon enough, it was full out and I could see the black man's arms holding that baby straight up. It was him walking out of the water, the baby over his head. All I can say is that I thank God that my camera was working, so you can see for yourself. This is proof that miracles happen."

The video was proof of something for sure. With three minutes left on a sixty minute tape, after almost an hour of just flowing water, the audio recorded tires squealing, a loud thump, and then a van dropped down from the top of the video frame and hit the water's surface in a splashy burst. Front down, the van was seen turning a circle, as if slowly drilling itself into the water, and then it was gone in less than a minute, with two minutes of film left. The eye of the camera never moved. Yates' "Holy shit" was audible, never to be edited out, and then he entered the frame. His back was clearly visible and then his body got smaller as it went toward and then into the water. A minute of film left, and Yates was waist deep in the current, his arms outstretched and both hands clenched into fists.

"And here it is, look to the right of the frame," he would tell his listeners. "The baby."

The child seemed to leap out of the water. It was not there, and then... there. Not merely rising, but soaring, its tiny arms outstretched, but once that initial leap was made, it did not move.

"See his hands, see his hands," Yates would say breathlessly. "The black man's hands. You gotta look close because the baby's blue shirt is so dark itself." And his audience would gasp. They had not seen the hands at first, their eyes always mesmerized by the risen child. Once they had focused on the child *and* the hands, as Charles had himself done at the original moment, it was as if their attention was the permission the submerged man needed to come forward.

With the child fully out of the water, the black man's arms were visible. If Yates had been on shore with his camera he would have zoomed in and recorded the face of the man as it followed the child out of the water, but it was not destined to happen that way. As the top of the black man's head broke the surface, just his dark hair, the tape ended.

"I was there. I saw him. The others did too. He exists. They'll tell you the same."

There was an explanation for everything. The van had stopped on the narrow shoulder of the bridge to fix a flat. It was a mistake, the mother admitted, but she was in a panic. She was alone with her baby. Smoke was coming from the shredding tire. She was not thinking clearly. She had to stop. She had not seen another car for a long time. She thought she was safe. Understandable steps toward a tragedy. As she stood behind her van, its side door open, she heard the horns blaring. A convergence of individually benign events. Her flat tire, two cars coming toward her from opposite directions, each in their own lane, the perception of one driver that the other was drifting into his lane, a swerve, the mother reflexively leaping to save herself. The universe of three adults and a baby reduced to a two lane bridge not wide enough to keep them safe.

Even the black man was explicable. The woman and one of the other drivers had passed him hitchhiking. A black man in the desert, they were reluctant to stop, and they admitted their shame to the press. He had not been too far from the bridge. The videotape did not show him going into the water, but he must have done it out of the frame. A minute or two under water for man and child would not have been impossible. Walking out of the water instead of swimming? The gully had a steep rocky slope. He was merely standing on the bottom, getting his balance, and slowly walking forward, pushing the baby up first to give it some air. But the current? If Charles Yates could barely stand in it, how could that man walk against it? Adrenaline, of course, thousands of examples of superhuman strength when somebody was in danger. Rational explanations for everything.

"But where did he go?" For Yates, that was the key question. "He handed me the baby, and he helped me carry that baby to shore, telling me to protect it. That was to be my job for the rest of my life. And then he was gone. But then the other stories, always the same. He appears, performs a miracle, and he disappears."

The press had an explanation. It took a half hour for the highway patrol to arrive. The rescuer had waited with everyone else for awhile, but then he said he had to go. The driver whose car was not damaged offered him a lift to Roswell. Everyone thanked him again, and the two men left. The driver told the press later that the man slept in the back seat until they got to Roswell, where he got out and told the driver to be careful. They shook hands. Nothing exceptional. Yates' insistence that the black man had "disappeared" was misguided.

"They say I'm crazy, but you tell me. You know the other stories. Who's crazy?"

It was a good story, the stranger who rescued the baby and left without becoming a media hero, and Yates' tape was shown on CNN. Compelling video, an inspiring human interest feel-good story. But it was not the tape that fueled the movement of the black man's believers. It was the picture. Yates' girlfriend took the tape to her television station and asked a film editor there if he could freeze one image and turn it into a photograph. *Easy,* said the editor, *but the more I blow this thing up the grainier it will look. The* editor surprised himself. The single image was a bit blurry, but emotionally precise. He sent it to the AP, and the image of a saved and risen baby, arms outstretched, its feet still dangling in the swirling water, was a one day sensation, front page news across the country, and then forgotten.

"But not by me or you, right?" Yates told his audience. "Am I right?" Everyone in front of him had their own copy, clipped out of the paper the very day they saw it in 1991. For a reason they did not themselves understand, the picture had value only if it had been saved from the very moment they first saw it. Their greatest fear was time. Their copies were turning yellow with age, the image fading, the paper itself crumbling. Possession of the picture had led them to each other, but it was only paper and ink. So, Charles Yates gave them hope. He told them that the black man was coming back, and the child was with him.

DOES YOUR RELIGION DANCE? BEHOLD, THE MOST DANGEROUS ISSUE FACING MODERN FAITH: ITS INABILITY TO EVOLVE, NAKEDLY.

by Mark Morford, Columnist,
San Francisco Chronicle, ©2007

It's a topic that jumped up like a stunned ferret from God's own hot plate three separate times recently—indicating, I think, that I'd better pay some sort of attention to it—the topic being the obvious but still desperately under-discussed idea that perhaps the most dangerous problem facing man in this modern age of radical technology and dazzingly scientific conundrum and other worldly raspberry vodka and ever-expanding notions of love and sex and human interconnection is the sad and treacherous fact that, well, religion and belief as we know them in America are, by and large, far too horribly stuck, limited, fixed in time and place and stiff karmic cement. Put another way: We as a culture just might be suffering a slow, painful death by spiritual stagnation, by ideological stasis, by cosmic rigor mortis. It has become painfully, lethally obvious in the age of George W. Bush and authoritarian groupthink that our major religious systems and foundations don't know how to move. They don't learn, adjust, evolve, see things anew. They don't know how to dance. And what's more, this little problem might just be the death of us all. It's a decidedly Tantric principle, that of a divinely animated, changeable universe, the idea that because we are fluxive and adaptive and ever-evolving species, that perhaps our gods, our doctrines, our belief systems should evolve and adapt with us.

November–2000
Harry Wakes Up in the Water
St. Augustine

Knee-deep in the Atlantic, squinting east toward a red dot on the horizon, Harry Forster Ducharme was trying to remember the first line of a story. The title and writer, that was easy. Stephen Crane... *The Open Boat*. Something about this spot reminded him of Crane. Harry's wasted education had not yet been erased by Popov. He could still retrieve obscure literary allusions at ease. As his mind cleared, he slowly remembered driving past a high-walled fort, across a bridge guarded by lions, past a lighthouse, past a liquor store, parking his Buick...well, that was still a bit fuzzy, *where* he parked it. "But here I am at last, in the goddam ocean," he mumbled to himself, "pulling fiction outta my ass."

To his left, north, was Jacksonville. To his right, south, was Daytona. In front of him, east, was a new day. Behind him, west, was sand. Harry was the center of his universe, asking himself important questions. *How did I get here? I know <u>why</u> I'm here. Character is fate, that's why I'm here. I learned that a long time ago, probably from a book. But I've lost track of the trip somehow. I give a Georgia stripper ... was it Cheyenne, or Sissy, at The Pony Tail? ... a hundred dollars to walk me to my car, she points me south, next thing I know I'm on I-95 headed to Florida. Go past the Savannah exit, been there, done that, see the signs for Jacksonville, but keep going, and there it is, almost hidden by a bigger billboard advertising some sort of World Golf Village ... best not to dwell on the meaning of <u>that</u> concept ... a billboard for St. Augustine ... "Oldest City in America"... and that sounds about right as a* *destination, so here I am, wondering if the tide is coming in or going out, and what's the first line of that Crane story?* The question was not rhetorical, nor meta-physical. He literally did not know how he had gotten to that spot. His last clear recollection was of him sitting in his car outside the *Pony-Tail* strip club in Atlanta; and then, as if teleported in a coma, he was knee deep in the Atlantic, alone at dawn. Two thoughts then occurred to him almost simultaneously after his initial confusion, one a question, the other a statement. *Where's my Buick?* and *I never learned to swim.*

Harry turned around and walked out of the ocean. He was hungry and hung-over. Standing on dry sand, he reached into his coat pocket looking for the aspirin he usually kept there. Then he realized that his mouth was cotton dry and the thought of putting the Bayer anywhere near his tongue...that thought made him gag. In his other coat pocket was a single Hostess cupcake, still in its plastic wrapper. Aspirin or cupcake, both would require some water to wash down, and, with that insight, he remembered the line he had been looking for.

None of them knew the color of the sky.

Four men in a tiny lifeboat, surrounded by water they could not drink, adrift in the Atlantic. Stephen Crane had seen this very spot, Harry realized. Crane had written about a lighthouse near here, surely the one that Harry himself had passed last night. A lifesaving station was mentioned in the story, somewhere near here, surely gone now, but the difference between the world of the men in the boat and the world of anybody on shore was the difference between land and sea, and translators were needed. The men in the boat were at the mercy of a God who was, at best, indifferent; at worst, hostile. A lecture was coming back to Harry, a lecture he had given the first year he taught, the only year he taught. A Master's in English, he had been twenty-four years old, parroting back notes from a graduate seminar he had taken the previous year, in front of his first classroom as a teacher himself, and four men in a small boat seemed very important to him. His students, however, were as indifferent as God.

Two semesters in front of a classroom were all he needed to convince him that he had made a mistake, a big mistake, with his life. Harry loved to read, and he had grown up admiring his teachers, so a BA and MA in

English were logical steps. Two semesters of teaching, six classes total, 150 freshmen, 1500 essays graded, how many hours of lecturing, how many hours of cajoling them to care. Some students made him happy, the minds of the others were somewhere other than with their bodies in class. *This is not for me*, Harry had told himself. *And it's not their fault. I'm just a lousy teacher. And as judgmental as I am about things, I hate grading papers. And, really, how much do I really know about this stuff? The world is going to hell, the country is in total denial, and I should expect these kids to care about this? Hell, I don't know much more than they do.*

Harry had quit teaching in 1972 but continued to read, happy that he no longer had to ask anybody else's opinion about a book, or dissect a story to justify his own education. He started looking for a new career.

None of them knew the color of the sky.

Harry studied the sky this morning. Red-orange across the horizon at dawn, and then, with the sun up, a cloudless blue sky sat on top of the grey wavy ocean. He studied that sky, memorizing the color of air and smell of water, the grit of sand, the warmth of his new world. He then remembered a moment from his past, one that had always come back to him at such points in his life. In an album somewhere was a picture of him and his two year old son on a beach. His wife had taken it as they were walking away from her. Harry was holding his son's hand and looking down at him. The sky was a postcard blue. And then it hit him this morning, *It was this beach. I was a good father in the beginning, and then it all went away.* But he shook his head and blinked, *Maybe not, maybe it never happened.* He stood up, brushed off the seat of his pants, and went looking for his Buick. It was all he wanted from his old world.

As much as a man can love a car, Harry loved his Buick. A black 1998 Park Avenue Ultra, sunroof, heated leather front seats, a car that even his stoic and frugal father might have respected, a banker's car, a solid Republican car, American-made, bought new and paid for in cash. *A man with a good car don't need no justification* ... another line from another story? Harry understood perfectly. The year he bought the Buick, he had a six-figure income. Walking on the beach in 2000, he had a hundred dollars in his wallet. The important thing, he told himself, was that *I don't owe nobody nothing.* He had zero debts, a zero balance on his remaining credit card, so he was a free man for as long as the hundred lasted. He wondered how much gas was in the Buick.

November in Florida, it was still warm. Walking barefoot, he found a beach access street, passed some restaurant called the Beachcomber, headed west, and found Highway A1A a block inland. He knew that his Buick was nearby. Teenage boys, wearing wetsuits and toting surfboards, passed him, headed east toward the morning waves. Harry resisted the urge to stop one and tell him, *You are one lucky bastard. Enjoy it while you can.* He had always resented the smugness of some adults when he was a boy.

This morning, oddly, he was not feeling sorry for himself. He knew he was not going back to Atlanta. For some reason, he was remembering, he had picked St. Augustine. *This is the Alamo for me*, he thought, *damn Mexicans can take their best shots. Or Cubans, or AARP-carders, whoever, whatever, this is my last stand.* And then he laughed at himself, *Damn, I'm channeling bad John Wayne movies now. I need breakfast.*

The Buick was parked at *The Shell Shop* on A1A, keys in the ignition. Harry took that as another good omen, but that positive was countered by the negative of an almost empty gas tank. Sitting behind the wheel, he found one more omen, significance to be determined. In a pocket on the visor above him were a Florida lottery ticket and a receipt. The lottery jackpot was thirty million, the receipt was for the cupcake. He had bought both at some place called *Harry's Curb Mart* on State Road 16. That name, surely, was an omen. Harry just knew that he was going to win the lottery, but he felt like he had to redeem the ticket at the store with his name. The serendipity had to be honored.

An hour later, after driving aimlessly around St. Augustine, omens were tripping all over Harry. Just as the low gas warning light started blinking and the Buick's alarm starting pinging frantically, he finally found his store. Painted across the front and top width of the building were the most profound words he had read in ages: *Through These Doors Walk the Finest People on Earth—"OUR CUSTOMERS."*

Harry walked in and became a finer person. The Curb Mart was a convenience store out of the Fifties...the southern Fifties. Hanging over the front counter was a rack of camouflage hunting suits for toddlers, complete with lace across the top. Behind the counter was a locked cabinet of assorted ammunition. Chewing tobacco and snuff were stacked neatly, and he could even see a butcher shop in the back. Behind the cash register was a peroxide blonde who smiled at him like he was a regular customer. As he handed her his lottery ticket, he felt a sensation that had been *awol* a long time. He was actually attracted to a woman who was probably as old as he was. She was obviously a smoker, a hazy odor of tobacco on her clothes, and her teeth showed a lifetime of coffee and cigarettes. But she had full lips and a firmly round figure, and, when she smiled at him it was sincere, and that smile made her teeth seem whiter. Harry told himself, *She's all the girls I lusted after in college, all grown up now, maybe even old, but, oh, the stories I bet she could tell.*

Harry was a winner. The ticket had four of six numbers. Five hundred dollars richer, he asked the smiling clerk to recommend a good place to eat breakfast. She told him, "Well, Nora got me turned on to this place just down the road, The Manatee, and I go there a lot. All you need to do is turn left out of the lot here, go a mile or so until you cross the railroad tracks, straight through the light and you'll dead-end on San Marco, turn right and go past the D&B school until you see a carousel on your right. The Manatee is directly across the street, but parking is a mess, so start looking early."

"Nora work here too?" he asked, not thinking it really mattered, just being polite.

"Lord sakes no. Nora's the radio woman. Knows everything about food and where to eat. I love her and her show."

Harry thanked her and was about to leave when she called after him, "You get there, you tell Cheryl that Polly Jackson expects a free breakfast for sending her a new customer. You do that, okay?" He nodded and gave her a thumbs-up as she added, "And you come back and see us. You seem like a lucky man. Bring some of it back to me, you hear."

Harry got to The Manatee in a few minutes. He soon found himself seated in the best organic and vegetarian café in the world, drinking a just-brewed cup of coffee. After eating his eggs and potatoes, watching the café quickly fill up, and sipping on his second cup of coffee, he admitted that Nora, whoever the hell she was, knew what she was talking about.

He was five hundred dollars richer, still had his Buick, had just finished a soul-warming breakfast, and the day had just begun. Harry was glad to be here. The how and why did not matter anymore.

Harry was smart enough to know what he was and what he was not. He was not having a mid-life crisis, but he was an alcoholic. He was too old for a mid-life crisis, he told himself, and if he was going to have one it would have been years ago when his son hung up on him, telling him to go to hell and never call again. That call had coincided with Harry's waking up in a motel room with two teenage girls, a 40th birthday gift from the two young ladies who had heard him joking on his program about turning 40 and spending the night alone. When he accepted their proposal, Harry had called them *Sisters of Mercy*, telling them how he felt like a Leonard Cohen song. "Leonard?" the prettier *sister* had almost giggled, "That's such a lame name." The other *sister* was confused, "And where was he going?"

He had accepted their charity and shared their drugs, and he left them sleeping like babies the next morning, wishing he could be sure which of his memories were real and which were simply fantasy about the previous night. In his coat pocket was a note from one of the girls: *Remember your promise.* Forty seemed a lot heavier age than thirty-nine, and he went back to his apartment in Tulsa to shower until he ran out of hot water, standing there trying to remember a promise he had made. He went to work that afternoon, and he forgot about the promise until the end of his three-hour shift. The last caller to *Harry Ducharme's Tulsa Talk, Home of Golden Oldies and Oil Town Gossip,* was a young girl whose voice trembled, "Harry, it's me, remember. Me and Connie have been listening for your whole show, waiting for you to do what you promised, and now you're signing off and you broke your promise. You are such a bastard." And then, the click of a connection severed.

Harry had sat there, going through the motions of his finale, looking through the studio window into the control room where his technician was giving him a look of *What the hell was that all about?*

The promise came back to him at that moment, and Harry understood, had to admit, that the sum of his life was a negative number. He had promised to wish the sister Connie a Happy Birthday. She was turning eighteen the day after he turned forty. Her sister friend, whose name he would never recall, had asked him to wish her Happy Birthday on the air, *make a big deal of it, say something nice to Connie and make her remember this day forever, make her feel special.* But he had forgotten. With casual absolution, Harry told himself that he would call his own son that night. If he could not make Connie happy this day, he would humble himself by asking forgiveness from his own son, whom he had ignored for almost a year. He was forty, time for a new direction in his life. His son hung up on him. He called his ex-wife. Her husband answered the phone and said she was out, *Would you like to leave a message?* Harry had run out of contacts. The next 364 days were as close as he ever came to having that much advertised "crisis" that other men seemed to be having. He was not interested in a sports car or trophy wife. He liked his job, but he knew he needed some sort of change. It would take him over ten years to get to St. Augustine. From Tulsa to Dallas to New York to Atlanta, to the ocean and breakfast at The Manatee, Harry had found his final gig. He was beyond a crisis, but not the bottle.

His gypsy days were over, and he would need a permanent home soon enough, but for his first day in St. Augustine Harry was still a tourist. He parked downtown across from the Cathedral and walked for hours. He had seen it all before, old towns which lived off their history. St. Augustine had more than most, but there were still the gaudy and borderline-tacky gift shops up and down St. George Street, the carriage rides along the bayfront, the locals in period costumes. But the core was genuine. It was a damn pretty town, he had to admit. Robber Baron hotels converted to colleges and office buildings, Tiffany stained glass windows everywhere, bouncy blond coeds, tanned the old fashioned way, but no longer a temptation for Harry, who surprised himself by still possessing a smidgen of self-respect. But, of course, he soon found a new favorite bar tucked between touristy shops on St. George Street. A small overhead sign with the key word: *Tav-*

ern. Noon, time for lunch, Harry walked into the dark narrow tavern and sat at the bar. He was surrounded by a dozen people, and none of them looked like tourists. In their own way, they looked like him. It was a familiar scene for him, and there was comfort in that, but he soon realized a major difference between this tavern, this small crowd, this moment, from all the comparable times in his past. There was no music in the background. Everyone seemed intently listening to a woman's soothing voice coming out of the speakers at each corner of the ceiling. She was describing a meal she had eaten the night before at some restaurant called The Gypsy Cab Company. Harry's first response was to glibly see the word *gypsy* as another omen of his own future, his decision to stay in St. Augustine until he died, but within a minute the woman's voice made him forget about himself as a free agent. He became famished. He could smell the glazed chicken on the woman's plate from the night before, hear the clink of raspberry tea glasses, taste the crisp lettuce on his tongue.

With the restaurant review done, the woman shifted into a history of apple pie. The crowd snapped out of its collective torpor and tavern talk resumed. Harry looked up and confronted a tailored and tooled black leather vest barely containing a set of breasts situated to suggest that with just the wrong move, the pressure would be too much and the snap of relief would be heard in heaven. Some early drunk would get the view of a lifetime and forget it happened by 4 P.M.

Harry wandered north of those breasts until he leveled eyes on the barmaid's face. An eruption of wavy dark hair was held back with a pair of sunglasses, and her long lashes made her eyes even brighter. Her voice was deep and cheerfully loud, and he noticed how white her teeth were as she pulled a cigarette to her mouth. She was beautiful, always a good omen, and she knew the right question to ask, "What'll you have?"

Harry's response was Pavlovian, a line used a thousand times in the past thirty years of bar ordering, delivered with as much residual charm as he could muster, "Two of you and a bottle of baby oil?"

The barmaid shook her head and laughed, saying without malice or sarcasm, "You're gonna have to do a lot better than that, mister. My five year old son can come up with smoother lines. And the little girls do love him so."

Harry was genuinely embarrassed, as if he had just heard himself clearly for the first time in his life. He averted the barmaid's eyes, but she did not let him wallow in self-pity for long. She reached across the bar and slapped him lightly on the top of his head to get his attention. "Hey, relax. My name is Michelle Remington. At your service. You don't look like a tourist, but you're new in town for sure. Tell me what you want, and then you can tell me the story of your life, okay? These other guys …," sweeping the room with her hand, "…are old shoes. So, tell me, you got any good news from the outside world?"

Harry ordered a Screwdriver and told Michelle his life story as she waited on the other customers. He took special note of how she handled a 50-something red-haired woman who was scribbling on a place mat with crayons. All of them, old and young, were on a first name basis with Michelle. Finally getting back her undivided attention, he even told her about his morning at the beach and his winning five hundred dollars in the lottery. Fifty-plus years of headlines. When he was finished, he had one question for her, "That woman you were listening to when I came in, how do I meet her?"

Michelle laughed and then shouted to a young blond-haired man in a booth behind Harry, "Kieran, how does a stranger meet Nora?" The young man had heard the question before, and his answer was always the same, "He doesn't." He then turned to the pretty blond girl in the booth with him and asked her, "Taylor, any hope for the old guy over there?" The young woman looked at Harry and shook her head, but her smile was itself an act of generosity.

Harry had turned around to face the couple behind him, who both raised their beer glasses and said together, "Good luck."

Looking back at Michelle, his expression gave him away. He was like a fly with one leg on a spider web, still free but not for long. Michelle nudged another leg on to the web when she said, "Nora's my mother." Harry leaned forward, assuming that Michelle would help him, but she merely pulled him all the way on to the web. "Well, she's not my real mother. I just feel like that, and she did deliver me, along with a few hundred other babies when she was a midwife, so I think I'm one of her babies. But then she stopped and just about disappeared, sort of." Harry waited. "So now all she does is her show for WWHD. Talks about food mostly, even cooks food on the air, interviews other women, anything to do with food or babies or female…problems, female problems…Nora talks about it all, but nobody sees her anymore."

"But you could introduce me, right?" Harry asked.

Michelle's eyes narrowed, suddenly suspicious of the new man in town, finally saying, "She wants to be left alone."

Harry sighed, and quietly apologized, "I'm sorry. I don't mean to presume too much. I just thought I'd like to meet her. I'm not sure why. A lot of omens for me today, and she…her voice…I mean I…dammit, Michelle… can you help me here?"

"You know, you are really wound up too tight, as much as you say otherwise," Michelle said calmly. "Trust me, you stick around long enough, you can meet her, if it matters all that much to you."

"But you *could* help."

"Nope, I can't. She wants to be left alone. She told me that a long time ago. You're not the first person to ask me, and you won't be the last one I tell no. I can tell you this. If you're lucky, one of these days it could happen. But she'll make *that* call."

Harry exhaled a deep breath and pushed his glass toward her for a refill, "Well, that's me. Lucky. Hell, I won the lottery, remember?"

Michelle took the empty glass and re-filled it with vodka and juice, "And that, Daddy Warbucks, is why I expect a big tip."

He left The Tavern and continued his sightseeing around St. Augustine, and all the footwork had had its toll by sunset. The next day would come soon enough. He would look for WWHD, find a room to rent, take a shower, start life fresh. He needed a job, and he planned on getting to the station at 10:00 AM, just as Nora began her show. He slept in his Buick the first night. Sleeping in that spacious back seat was old hat for him, and he always kept a blanket and a pillow in the trunk. Tomorrow, he told himself, was another day, a better day.

November–2000
To September–2001
Harry Settles In

Finding WWHD was not as easy as Harry had anticipated. He ate breakfast at the Manatee again, and the waitress told him that the station was within walking distance. "Go out our front door, turn left. That's May Street. Turn left on May and walk to Magnolia, turn right, look for a sign to the Flamingo Apartments, and WWHD is just around the corner from there. Should take you about ten minutes." An hour later, a panting Harry Ducharme knocked on the front door of WWHD, citing himself as proof of how out of shape the entire country must be.

At first, the walk had been pleasant enough. A mild morning, just enough breeze to cool the sweat slowly coming through his dirty shirt. From the Manatee to Magnolia was a fifteen minute walk all by itself. Not bad, really, and Harry had all the time in the world, or so he thought. But as he turned on Magnolia, Harry missed the sign pointing to the Flamingo Apartments. He kept walking, and the more he walked the more he felt lost in a fairy tale.

Magnolia Avenue was aptly named, its aged trees arching from each side of the street to meet overhead, forming a leafy green ceiling. Sunlight filtered through, but the street was still a shady forest, and Harry found himself walking slower and looking up more and more. Years earlier, *National Geographic* had named Magnolia one of the ten most beautiful streets in America. The *Things to See in St. Augustine* pamphlet put out by the tourist bureau always cited the magazine's endorsement, and made Magnolia a must-see destination for out-of-towners. Unprepared, however, Harry felt like he was the first person to have seen it.

He looked at his watch. It was 9:30. He would be late if he stayed lost. Reaching the end of Magnolia, he turned back and began looking for signs that he had missed. Walking faster, afraid of being late for a very important date, he passed a giant wrought-iron gate, the opening in a stone wall that lined most of the east side of Magnolia. How many more omens did Harry need? The day before, it was Harry's Curb Mart, and now this. He was at the entrance to *The Fountain of Youth*. The real *Fountain of Youth*. Open at 11:00, admission five dollars. He was only a few feet away from where Ponce de Leon had set foot in 1513, the spot where the Old World had first touched that green breast of the New World, seeking gold and eternal life. Harry hesitated, but only a moment. He kept walking, looking for the Flamingo Apartments and WWHD.

He found the road that passed the apartments and walked faster. Nora would be arriving at the station soon, and he had to meet her. And then he saw it, the tiny white building on the edge of the marsh, three cars in the small gravel parking lot. Harry had traveled a long time to get there.

He knocked on the station door, but, getting no response, he went in uninvited. It was a familiar scene: a disheveled entrance, posters tacked on top of posters, stacks of boxes full of tapes and paper. The biggest stack was a small mountain of cookbooks. Through a giant window, Harry could see the broadcast studio where a large man wearing headphones was waving his arms as he spoke. The overhead speakers were set to a low volume, but Harry knew the man in the booth and the voice overhead were the same. Captain Jack was winding down the morning show, "...and if the Democrats keep trying to steal this election we all need to hit the streets and head to Miami. Fair is fair, the dice are rolled, and the Gore-meister is a goner. Fat ladies are singing, barn doors are locked. More tomorrow, folks, as we can finally start flushing the stains out of the Oval Office."

Harry was fascinated, but not surprised. He had known hosts like Jack Tunnel all over the country. Right-wingers were spawning themselves, it seemed. But the more he listened to Tunnel, the more he thought that *this guy* ought to do comedy. It was a first impression that never changed as long as the two men were to know each other. Harry liked Jack Tunnel, and Tunnel would sometimes go into a rant in front of Harry only to have Harry remain silent long enough for Tunnel to hear himself, which usually led to him stopping in mid-rant and rolling his eyes, as if to say, "Hell, there I go again." And, of course, the other bond: Harry Ducharme and Jack Tunnel were drinkers.

Watching Tunnel wind down that first morning, Harry suddenly realized that it was time for the Nora James show but she was nowhere to be seen. Then, from the overhead speakers, he heard Tunnel do the segue to Nora, and then her voice floated down from the ceiling, "Good morning everybody. And good morning to you too, Jack. It's so nice to hear that you're not taking this election too personally. So, folks, if you must, absolutely must, go to Miami, let's talk about road food. As for you, Jack, you should stick to your diet."

In the studio, Tunnel was laughing as he picked up his newspapers with one hand and then reached for a large birdcage with the other. He looked though the glass and waved at Harry with the hand holding the birdcage, and Harry could see feathers fly out between the bars.

Newspapers tucked under one arm, Tunnel introduced himself. Up close, Harry thought he was looking at a heart attack about to happen. Tunnel had dark bags under his eyes, his flowery Hawaiian shirt was drenched in sweat, he needed to lose about a hundred pounds, and, unlike his radio voice, he spoke in gasps. Tunnel introduced his parrot too, "This is Jimmy Buffett, my co-host. Helluva lot less trouble than my last co-host."

Harry opened his mouth, but Tunnel kept talking, "Had a damn Jack Russell Terrier named Bobby Lee, but he kept having spaz attacks when I was on the air. Howling, then he'd go stiff on the floor and start pedaling his feet, then up and run around the studio bumping into equipment, pissing all over the floor. I'd have to deal with him and people would think it was me howling. Damn, I loved that dog, but Jimmy here is a lot less maintenance." Jimmy Buffett squawked. "So, stranger, what can I do for you?"

Harry told him about wanting to meet Nora James, and how he wanted to talk to the owner about a job.

"You want to meet Nora James?" Captain Jack laughed. "You and every other hungry soul in this state. Get in line, my good man."

"And to ask for a job," Harry added.

"And who the hell are you? Tell me again."

"My name is Harry Ducharme, and I've come down from…" Harry tried to explain, but Tunnel cut him off with another laugh.

"No way you are Harry Ducharme." Jimmy Buffett squawked again. "Harry damn Ducharme is a legend, my friend, and you sure as hell don't look like a legend. You look like Freddy the frigging Freeloader."

How do I respond to that, Harry asked himself. *A legend?* So he just stood there as Tunnel described the Harry Ducharme that was known throughout the ranks of radio hosts. The sum total of Ducharme's *legend*, evidently, was to serve as a cautionary tale about how to screw up your career.

"And you want a job *here?*" Tunnel concluded.

Harry remembered a scene from Dickens, some poor orphan asking for more gruel. All he could meekly say at that moment in his life, in response to a question that spoke a world about how far he had fallen, was, "Yes, please."

Tunnel put his newspapers on a table and set Jimmy Buffett next to them on a pedestal, which was evidently his home away from the studio, provoking another squawk and a response from Tunnel, "Cool your jets, Buffett. You work with me, but I ain't married to you." He motioned for Harry to sit down, then he slowly bent his knees and fell into a chair across from him. "I won't help you with Nora, she makes those decisions, but I'll call the Station Manager, he's out shopping for quill pens now, and tell him to get his sorry ass down here and hire you. We've got a spot opening soon, 10 to 2…at night, sorry…but the other plums are already taken. Don't let the manager fool you. He looks like that farmer in the Rockwell painting, you know, *American Gothic*, with the pitchfork and dowdy wife, but once he hires you he leaves you alone…"

Harry interrupted, only to anger his soon to be best friend, "It was Grant Wood. And the two people are not married. I'm from Iowa, you know. We learn that early, that…"

Tunnel blinked, tilting his head down just enough so that his eyes seemed to be looking up, and then he licked his lips before he spoke with an edge. "You liberals know everything, don't you?"

And then there was silence. Harry forced a smile, wondering how he should respond. Tunnel seemed to be reconsidering his offer. But then he shrugged, smiling with what seemed to be genuine affection, and said, "Hey, it's America. Free country, Rockwell, jockwell, go to hell. Grant Wood gets wood. You seem like a nice guy, Harry, even for a liberal. So, shut the hell up for awhile and lemme tell you how to float in this pond, okay?"

As Nora James whispered above them, Tunnel told Harry all about WWHD. As long as the FCC didn't fine the station, hosts could do what they pleased. But each new host only had a year to establish an audience. Tunnel's morning show had been an instant hit, and the ad revenue paid a lot of bills. The host salary was a flat ten thousand for the first year, plus an additional ten percent commission on all ad revenue in the host's slot, if the host had made the deal. Each host was responsible for filling 28 hours of air time a week. Twenty hours had to be live, and then the host could either do the other eight live, working seven days a week, or he could put some tapes together and pre-program a shift, but he was responsible for getting the ads in too. In a pinch, the Manager would contract with Clear Channel and hook into their programming, Golden Oldies or Top Forty, the usual suspects of generic AM music.

WWHD usually only had two people in the building at a time: the host and the Manager, who also acted as sound engineer. Tunnel called the Manager a ghost, "He's here when I arrive, and he stays until ten at night. I think he sleeps in a coffin somewhere. And he still claims he talks to the Old Man who owns the place, and *that* guy has been dead for centuries."

All broadcasting was done on-site, except for the Nora James show. She did a remote broadcast from her kitchen somewhere in St. Augustine. For that four hours, the Station Manager was alone in the building, doing the books. Tunnel arched his eyebrows twice when he said, "doing the books."

"You're going to fit right in, Harry. This station was made for you. You can offend anybody you want as long as you don't say *fuck* or *shit* or *cornhole* or *dickwad*, stuff like that, on the air."

Until Harry was hired, WWHD only had three hosts who had lasted more than a year. The other three daily slots were always in flux, but Harry would make a solid fourth. WWHD would eventually hire Carlos Friedmann, fourth generation Jewish-Cuban. who would anchor the late shift after Harry. Carlos loved to torment the Miami Cubans with constant, albeit insincere, praise for Fidel Castro.

If Jack Tunnel deserved a slot in a major market, Carlos was destined for even greater success, but not in radio. All he needed was some discipline to channel his imagination and talent. That was to be Harry's pitch to the Station Manager after Carlos applied for a job. The Manager merely shrugged and asked if Carlos would work for minimum wage and sell his own ads. On the weekends, Carlos's ratings were a tenth as much as Captain Jack's, but he was still having a wonderful time...having fun...being alive. For that, for his immunity from cynicism, for his happiness, Harry would come to love Carlos.

Captain Jack Tunnel would begin the day for WWHD with his self-described "morning machine gun of conservative news and wisdom, plus my own brand of liberal smackdown, sautéed with the Liberal Putz of the Day Award."

Harry would eventually become Captain Jack's biggest fan, but he kept his adulation to himself, like a guilty pleasure. Tunnel had genuine talent. An avid magazine and newspaper reader, a coffee addict, a free-verse mixed-metaphor free-association poet, a verbal wit and poison ranter, Tunnel belonged on a larger stage than St. Augustine, the Oldest City in America. But he had been at WWHD for twenty years.

From ten in the morning to two in the afternoon, Nora James covered a world of food and domestic insights. She even did call-ins, answering questions about stain removal and child-rearing. Tunnel was a regular listener, telling Harry, "I'll never forget the show where she actually delivered a baby on-air. She talked her audience through hours of labor, explaining all sorts of shit about how babies develop in the womb, and you could hear the woman moaning and cussing in the background, but Nora was like it was just another day at the office. But I'm telling you, Harry, I never want to hear the word *placenta* ever again."

After Nora's show, WWHD juggled the two to six slot, but the six to ten slot was set even before Nora had been hired. Toby Lankford had been a country and western dj for years, but then he had a conversion experience. Not religious, although that's how he described it. Lankford had merely encountered George Gershwin. He was being taken home one night by a designated driver, part of his contract with the mega station he worked for in Cincinnati. He would drink to excess; somebody would get him home. He had been distracted that particular night, he told his listeners, *drunk* he admitted to his friends, not really paying attention to the channel, but a clarinet wail had slapped his ears and he was hooked. He saw God, so he bought all the Gershwin he could find, then *knew* he had found God, *until* he heard Beethoven. Toby Lankford went polytheistic. Bach knocked at his door, pushed aside by Brahms, who was pushed aside by Mozart and Copland. The addiction grabbed his throat and he spoke in tongues about the gospel of classical music. The Cincinnati station fired him. Trouble was, as Tunnel told Harry, "Toby was a C&W jock. That was in his blood too. He only wanted to play the classical top forty shit, but his delivery was always C&W, always *yall gotta listen to this here fella and his buddies and this was down-home to the folks around Vee-inner.* Damn, Harry, it was a hillbilly talking about second movements of second symphonies, and WWHD was the only place that let him do that. You listen to him tonight. You know how those FM classical shows always sound? They got snoot to spare. But Toby sounds like his parents were first cousins, or he's a redneck from Arkansas. But, you know, it works. He knows all there is to know about that high-brow stuff, as well as music in general, and he can tell stories about Beethoven and those other guys like he went to grade school with them." The obvious fact that Tunnel not only seemed to like Lankford, but actually respected him, made Harry like Tunnel even more.

After his introduction to Jack Tunnel, and after negotiating with the cadaverous Station Manager for a job, Harry was then formally introduced to St. Augustine, with Tunnel as his official guide. First, Tunnel walked him over to the Flamingo Apartments and vouched for his good character to a skeptical manager who had been holding an unfurnished apartment for another couple who had called the day before. Harry watched as Tunnel wrapped his sweaty arms around the man and whispered some sort of promise in his ear that made the man look like his rich uncle had just died. Furniture? Tunnel whipped three hundred dollar bills out of his pocket and shoved them at Harry, saying, "I know a guy at a rent-to-own place, one of my sponsors. This'll get you started." The manager said something about "utility deposits" and Tunnel just glared long enough for him to waive the requirement.

"You got a car?" Tunnel asked Harry. "Park it out back. Walk to work. Don't give the damn Arabs a dime."

Harry said, "I left my Buick in front of a restaurant. If you give me a lift, I'll…"

Tunnel just pointed toward the door and motioned him out with a fluttering hand. Three minutes later, they were parked behind Harry's Park Avenue, and Tunnel looked like a child on Christmas morning. "*That's* your car? That black beauty in front of us?" Harry nodded, admiring his own freshly washed and waxed vehicle, his last treasure.

"Harry, I'll give you ten thousand dollars for that car right now, even without a test drive."

"I've only had it two years," Harry said, more as a matter of fact than a negotiating tactic.

"Fifteen thousand," Tunnel countered. "That is a goddam great looking car, and I'd love to have it."

Harry thought, *We're sitting in a brand new Cadillac and he wants my Buick?* An odd pleasure seeped into his soul. He had something that Tunnel wanted, who knows why, but his car now had even more value for Harry. "No, I love this car. I'm going to keep it. But, say what, let's go in it now. Give me the tour. I'll drive."

The two men spent the rest of the day driving around St. Augustine in the black Buick, its radio tuned to WWHD. Nora James talked about her experience at various highway eating places, from the Cracker Barrel near Melbourne to the Denny's off I-95 near Ft. Lauderdale. But she also talked about how to make even a surly waitress happy, and the most diplomatic approach to complaining about a bad meal. Overall, she insisted, everybody was better off not stopping at those places, but should instead pack a meal and eat slowly. Harry asked Jack one more time if he would introduce him to Nora, but Tunnel insisted that, "I've never seen her place, I swear to God." Harry knew he was lying. But Harry had had a good morning so far. Plenty of time to find Nora James.

Harry then told Tunnel about his experience at Harry's Curb Mart, how it was a good omen, how all his life he had attached an inexplicable significance to anything or anybody named Harry, ever since his Uncle Ronald told him that he was named after Harry Truman. With that knowledge, Harry had started to read about Harry Truman, noting qualities in the dead President that he looked for in himself as he grew older. It made no sense to anybody else, his insistence that he was somehow connected to other Harrys in the world, but it was a habit he internalized more and more after his parents disappeared. As some people counted mileage markers on a long boring drive, Harry would make lists of other Harrys to pass the time. How was he like Harry Houdini? *A clever escape artist?* Harry Belafonte? *Handsome and a good singer?* Harry James? *A trumpet player, and Belafonte a singer, so how come I have no musical talent?* Harry Winston? *A jeweler, a dealer in precious stones?* Harry Carey? *Closer to me for sure? A damn drunk?* How about Harry Chapin? *Another singer, raspy voice, but great story-teller, and my life is turning into a story, a story with a bad ending?* Harry Crews? *Brilliant, but more intense than I'll ever be. How many other writers were named Harry? And other singers too?* Harry Nillson? Harry Connick, Jr.? Harry Hopkins, FDR's right hand man? Harry Harlow, the monkey man. Harry Longabaugh, the Sundance Kid. Harry Thaw? Harry Angstrom, Harry Putnam? Harry Lime? Harry Shearer and Harry Anderson, the actors? Harry Reasoner, the newsman? Harry Reems, the porn star. Harry Bogen, *a character in a book whose title I can never remember?*

Real and fictional Harrys? English kings named Harry? And Harry Cal-lahan? That's me, the Dirty Harry of talk radio? And even a bar? Harry's Bar, where Hemingway and Proust drank, my kind of place, even if it was in Venice. Home of the Bellini, I'd fit right in, except for my lack of fame or talent.

Harry explained all this to Tunnel, who rolled his eyes and said, "You have way too much free time on your hands, Vladimir. You need a grip, and lunch. Let's go to my favorite restaurant, but you can't tell Nora…" seeing Harry turn his head toward him, "…*if* you meet her. She's not a fan of my place, but I love it. Turn around and cross the bridge over to Anastasia Boulevard."

As soon as Harry saw the sign for *Cap'n Jack's Restaurant*, he laughed, "Jack, never ever make fun of my name fetish again, okay?"

"Hey, guy, it's all part of my town. These folks get a lot of free advertising on my show and I get free biscuits. Helluva deal."

As soon as they walked in, Harry heard the shouts, "Captain Jack is here. The Captain is on deck." As they were led to a corner booth, Harry thought, *I don't think anybody has ever been glad to see me walk in the door. My parents, sure, but that was a long time ago.*

After lunch, as they stood near the cash register, Tunnel nudged Harry to make sure he saw the framed and signed picture on the wall: Captain Jack Tunnel in the WWHD studio, headphones around his neck, holding up a copy of the *Cap'n Jack's* menu. It was Harry's first clue as to why Jack Tunnel, as talented as he was, was satisfied to be in St. Augustine. More than satisfied, he was happy, and Harry envied him.

Tunnel then took Harry on the Grand Tour. Past the old Spanish Fort… "buy a ticket and go through there for sure, damn impressive"…past the marina…"and every year the Bishop comes over to bless the boats"… taking time to drive slowly around the downtown plaza which had been temporarily turned into a movie set…"some story set in St. Augustine about some sort of weird movie theatre"…past the Coast Guard station… "this is Marine Street, see that house there, big murder back in 74, right there on the front porch, blood all over the place…" past *Lake Maria Sanchez*… "ghosts, Harry, come right up out of the water, yes I'm serious…" and then through Lincolnville… "the black section of town, you know, your liberal base, Harry, but there's the Blue Goose Bar too…" and so it went. Jack Tunnel was the archivist of *America's Oldest City*.

The tour ended downtown, where Harry tried to interest Tunnel in a drink at The Tavern. Tunnel had other plans. "I like The Tavern, don't get me wrong, but it's not my place, you know."

"Don't tell me there's a bar down here called *The Tunnel of Love* or something like that." Harry was more thirsty than hungry.

"Oy vey, like I've never heard that one before," Tunnel sighed good-naturedly. "Nope, we're going to The Tradewinds. Everybody knows my name there." And *that* line sent Tunnel into a gale of laughter.

For the rest of his life, Harry called The Tavern his second home, but he still enjoyed going to The Tradewinds with Tunnel. Indeed, the first time they went in, although only early evening, everyone *did* seem to know his name. And his picture was on the wall behind the bar counter. The Tradewinds was much bigger than the Tavern, with room for a live band and a dance floor. Black and white promo photos of singers and bands, all of whom had played there at one time, sometimes early in their careers, were on the walls. The more times Harry went, he understood that although he saw a lot of the same locals time after time, some of whom he saw in The Tavern too, a lot of the clientele was out-of-towners, and The Tradewinds was as much local color as the old Fort was. A place to go when you're in St. Augustine. *If I live long enough, Harry told himself, I'll be a local too. I'll sit here and make fun of the tourists.*

That first night, Harry and Tunnel had barely settled in at the bar when an oozy drawl crawled over their shoulders.

"Why, Captain Jack Tunnel, as I live and breathe."

Harry turned around, but Tunnel kept looking straight ahead as he spoke," Why, as I live and breathe, if it isn't my sweet Scarlett O-Hora."

Harry tried not to have any expression on his face, but he had seen this woman's type before, in a hundred bars in dozens of towns. A once passably good body gone south, but this woman now obviously had a magic mirror in which she only saw the woman she was twenty years earlier, and dressed accordingly. Her tight white hip-hugger pants drew Harry's eyes to her exposed navel as well as her fleshy hips oozing out of the top of those pants. He knew that when she turned around that her ass would be round and firm…until she moved, and then the comedy would begin. But her face gave away the most. If her diet had worked anywhere, it was not her face. Too much sun, her brown skin tight around her eyes, but her cheeks looked like they had been injected with too much collagen. A few more years, and fewer still if she continued to drink, and she would have jowls.

Extending her hand to Harry, the woman said, "And who is your handsome friend, Captain, and why is he a stranger?"

As long as he lived in St. Augustine, Harry would never see this woman in The Tavern.

Without turning around, Tunnel introduced them. "Ashley Ass-Lick, meet Harry Ducharme. Harry, meet the writer Ashley, lovingly known by me as Ass-Lick, the belle da-la-ball of our fair community. A woman who takes a special interest in all artisans, such as yourself and myself."

"My pleasure, I am sure," Ashley said, ignoring Tunnel's abusive wit, her southern accent bordering between affectation and parody. "So you are a friend of the Captain, a friend named Harry, like Harry Potter, the wizard. Is that you, Mr. Ducharme, a wizard? A man with a magic wand perhaps?"

I wonder if this woman can say good morning without making it sound like a pornographer's bad script, Harry thought to himself as she held on to his hand too long. "No, my magic days are long over, I'm afraid. Right now, all I do is talk radio." And he immediately knew it was the wrong thing to say.

"So you must have much experience in oral communication, am I right?"

Tunnel started coughing at the bar.

Harry grabbed his answer out of a bag of irony he reserved for special occasions, "Yes, but I tend to stutter."

Tunnel began gagging, and Ashley just blinked furiously, unable to interpret the man in front of her. She nodded slowly and spoke slower, "I am…so…sorry to hear that. But…I do wish you…much…success in… your career. I will…certainly…be listening to…for…your show." Putting her hand on Tunnel's back, rubbing her fingernails down his spine, but not taking her eyes off Harry, she soon bounced back, "And you, Captain, you must come to my next party. You're such a favorite with my friends." And then she fluttered away.

"Jack...," Harry began.

"Don't ask. But I will tell you this. You put your pecker in that woman, I will never speak to you again. And, trust me, this has nothing to do with jealousy. She thinks she's a writer, and she's desperate for somebody, anybody, to read her driveling southern romance shit."

His first full night in his new hometown, Harry began learning all the gossip. Ashley and her writer-wanna-be friends were chapter one, but the St. Augustine novel had lots more, and Tunnel knew the dirt.

The two men sat at the Tradewinds for another hour and then walked back to the Buick. "You can spend the night at my place until you get set up over at the Flamingo. Not much room, but I'll find a place for you."

Harry had told Tunnel about sleeping in his car the night before. "Thanks, but I think I'd like to get started on my monastic life right away. A hard floor is exactly what I need tonight. Some incentive to get better."

Tunnel added to his offer, "Here, we're right near my house. Walk with me, see what you think."

Harry followed him across the street and over to the marina at the foot of the Bridge of Lions. Tunnel lived on a small yacht docked at the wharf, with a light at the bow, a light that bobbed up and down as the soft waves of the bay water rocked Captain Jack Tunnel's home, *The Tunnel of Love*.

As they stood on the wharf, Harry turned to his new friend and said, "The Tunnel of Love? I ask you about any bars named..."

"This, my friend, is *different*. You love your Buick. I love my boat. One of these days I'm going to sail around the world in this baby. Until then, take me back to my car, Harry *plunk your magic twanger* Potter, and come see me tomorrow at the station. We'll get your blood on a contract."

Alone in his empty apartment that night, Harry thought about Tunnel telling him that he was going to fit right in at WWHD, along with Jack, Nora James, Toby Lankford, and others to follow. A small world of people in their own comfort zone. But, in time, Harry *did* fit in, and he was happy. If resignation was happiness, or acceptance was happiness, or simply acknowledging reality …if those states of mind led to happiness, then Harry was happy in St. Augustine, at WWHD, from 10 at night until 2 in the morning. For the first year he was there, that happiness flowered, and he felt like he had a chance to make it last for the rest of his life.

He would go to work and talk about politics or other current events, with his own personal music favorites played to fill time. Soon enough to make the Station Manager happy, he developed a reliable audience, especially up until midnight, and he took call-ins from people who disagreed with him, but he never got angry, unlike the old days. He was helped from the very beginning by Captain Jack telling his own audience to take the time and "tune in to the new guy, the infamous liberal Trotskyite Harry Ducharme, come down to the Sunshine State to seduce our women and raise our taxes. Know your enemy, folks, and always remember that Harry is the love child of Teddy Kennedy and Hillary Ram-Rodham Clinton." Sometimes, Tunnel would tell his own listeners to tune in to Harry that night because he was going to call the late show himself and "give Harry hell about that comment he made last night about our Commander-in-Chief."

Harry Chapin's *W.O.L.D.* would become Harry Ducharme's new theme song, and not just in his mind. He would use it as the intro to his show but never entered it on the station's logs. Not feeling all of forty-five, going on fifteen, like the song said. Sing it, Harry. He was fifty-two, feeling sixty-nine, and his bright good morning voice had mellowed into a breathy sentence fragment. Not the morning DJ any more, now long past drive time. But, sure, he had played Tulsa and Boise. Sing it, Harry. A wife and child long gone. *Cat's in the cradle* gone. Dreams gone. A few more years, at this pace, in this direction, he admitted on those mornings when his mirror told him the truth, *I'll be a different Chapin song, all about some wasted taxi driver.*

It was to be his last outpost. Ten at night until two in the morning on WWHD, Harry talked. Eventually, he would turn the studio over to Carlos Friedmann, the twenty year old Flagler College kid who would be forever younger than his own son. Carlos was a stoner with an addiction to Salsa and disco music, a genre conflicted format that actually pulled in more listeners than Harry's old jazz, Sixties rock, book reviews, drunken poetry readings, and obscure guests. They both knew that their combined audiences were nowhere near as big as Captain Jack Tunnel, the morning man, WWHD's shock jock of A.M. drive time patter. Captain Jack was the star, screeching at 6:00 A.M. sharp, "We're taking out the trash and bringing in the cash. Wake up, my brothers and sisters, this is THE voice of the divine, sweetly *daaaa-vineeee* 69 on your AM dial. Need I say it again? Me, Captain Jack, Rush's evil twin, Hillary's worst nightmare, here to wake you up, get you straight, make you Right and bright. The man, the plan, and have I got news for you. But first, my legions and minions, a word from one of the smart people who sponsor this program…the folks at Rick's Muffler. Your heap sound like somebody is always pulling its finger? Rick's is the place. So pay attention and then stay tuned. You will NOT believe what happened since last we talked."

Harry and the other WWHD DJs often had to tolerate Captain Jack like children tolerated their abusive father. He paid most of the bills. They had nowhere else to go. Of all the DJs, only Harry, and Nora James, the "morning mother" (so labeled by Jack himself) for whom Jack was the lead-in, actually liked The Captain. *A life of quiet desperation*, Harry would say to himself, describing the Captain, *a loud man quietly desperate*. He himself could appreciate that desperation.

Carlos soon started calling Harry *The Cracker man…Galleta Salada*. Their home was 1169.1 on the AM dial, 100 watts of power, the last independent in north Florida, owned by a dead man whose estate had been in probate for enough time to inspire a Dickens novel. WWHD was the least valuable asset the Old Man had owned, a cinder-block building on the edge of a marsh, a single studio smaller than Harry's apartment kitchen. But the old man's heirs had divvied up the best lawyers in Jacksonville, and the fee clock had started.

It was not how Harry had imagined he would end his career, but it was okay.

September 11, 2001
New York City
Jane and Jean Norville

The trip was a gift from Jane to Jean. It was long overdue, they both admitted. Even though Jean was the older sister, by a full three minutes, she had always deferred to her sister's judgment. When Jane told her that they would go to New York City when they grew up, in spite of their parents' admonition that the City was not a safe place for young women, Jean was thrilled. They were twelve years old, forty years ago. In 1961, their Nashville parents were not even sure their own city was safe. Too many negroes coming too close to their own neighborhood, but at least Nashville was not like those ugly towns in Alabama or Mississippi, those towns which, as their father insisted, "simply fail to understand that the glorious war of southern independence is over, and we lost." In their father's mind, the negro problem was a matter of respect. Blacks and whites needed to "respect their differences, but that respect does not require integration."

The Norville twins went to Vanderbilt in 1967, itself not a hotbed of civil rights, but when they tried to explain their father's view to one of their history professors they were singled out in class as "the last surviving descendants of the O'Hara dynasty." Jean was perplexed; Jane was livid. In an affected and slow drawl, as she fluttered her hand in front of her face, she sighed, "My Lawd, Dr. Lewis, you have given me the vapors. I must get back to Tara and have my mammy tend to me. Would that meet with your approval?" The rest of the class waited breathlessly, reprieved only when the professor laughed, not from anger nor nervous insecurity, but from a generous appreciation, and said, "*This* is going to be a great class, probably my favorite." Jean wasn't sure about what had just happened, but she was nonetheless very proud of her little sister.

With the deaths of Bobby Kennedy and Martin Luther King Jr. in 1968, and filled with a sense that one's life ought to improve that of others, Jane Norville decided to become a teacher, a profession sanctioned by her parents and copied by her sister. Jean opted for elementary education, Jane for high school, and their first jobs were less than two miles from *Andalusia*, the Belle Meade estate on which they had been raised. They rented an apartment together, were separated by Jean's marriage in 1972, and then re-united by the deaths of their parents and Jean's husband in 1990. They moved back into the home in Belle Meade.

Jane and Jean were identical twins, but whereas every feature of Jean leaned toward beauty...the blond hair, high cheek bones, slender nose, and cherry lips...those same features in Jane were a half-note out of tune. Although Jane was assured by others that she was blessed with a sharper wit than her sister, a wit of intellect and humor, she knew the truth. Her sister was just as smart as she was, but she chose to let her looks intimidate people, not her mind, and as languid as Jean seemed, Jane knew that her sister was blessed not just with superior looks but also with that essence which eludes most people, Jane included, a predisposition to happiness. It was Jean's happiness, not her looks, that Jane envied.

Together on New Year's Eve of 2000, the sisters hosted a Millennium Party in Belle Meade. A new century was upon them, and the previous half century had passed too quickly. Toasting their guests and themselves, they praised the future. After midnight, as they ushered the last guest out, Jean turned to her sister and asked, "Do you remember your promise to take me to New York City?"

"Of course. Isn't it odd, after so much that has happened to us and to the world, you and I have never been farther than Atlanta. Good Lord, you're a widow and I'm a spinster. Is that what was supposed to happen?"

"And we're not getting any younger," Jean said, taking her sister's hand to walk back to the kitchen to supervise the caterers as they began cleaning.

"Well, it's settled. I am taking you to New York. A promise is a promise."

Almost two years later, Jane and Jean stood in the Trinity Church graveyard on a heavenly blue morning, looking down at the grave of Alexander Hamilton, when each thought she heard the other whisper, "Look up."

'OH GOD OUR HELP IN AGES PAST' – WORSHIP AMID THE BEDLAM (POSTED SEPTEMBER 12, 2001)
by Nathan Brockman

When the first 110-storey tower of the World Trade Center fell on Tuesday September 11, some of Trinity Wall Street's clergy were leading an impromptu worship service in the church building around the corner.

As Father Stuart Hoke began to sing, there was a tremendous, crackling report. The lights in the broad, high-ceilinged nave flickered three times and went out, and the sandstone church shook.

Later reports confirmed that the first of the World Trade Center towers had fallen, but the thought of many in the church was that a third plane had attacked. People ducked for cover, most under pews, but Father Hoke did not move from the podium. He began to sing again: "Oh God our help in ages past." He said later, "We were waiting to die."

The service began within an hour of the first plane hitting the center shortly before 9 A.M. Fifteen or so visibly shaken and mournful people gathered there. As Father Hoke, wearing a white alb, spoke from the reader's lectern, there were whispers of prayers. Some were there to pray. Others simply sought shelter.

"I'm going to read from the Beatitudes," said Father Hoke. "But first I have further news," and he relayed the news that the Pentagon had been bombed, too. "Jesus!" said one woman, whose prayers were whispered the loudest.

"If anyone strikes you on the cheek, offer the other also," read Father Hoke, as sirens sounded outside. He then read a psalm, with some reading along.

Smoke filtered in, high in the rafters. The diffused light coming through the windows seemed like the gentle light of dawn. The area between a set of internal glass doors and the main outside doors facing onto Broadway was filled with smoke.

It was announced that people should go to the basement, but then Father Samuel Johnson Howard, the Vicar, announced that the basement was far too filled with debris to attempt an escape from there.

THE WAIT

No firm information could be gleaned from inside the church. The windows lightened and darkened alternately, as dust and smoke and ash first lifted and then were blown back down again. One expedition attempted an escape, but those in charge came back covered in white, like ghosts, and said it was impossible.

There was no coming in, and there was no going out. People wanted badly to leave the church, first, and then, more importantly Manhattan.

Some prayed. Others, employees of Trinity, set about establishing some practical business. A radio was tuned to a news station and placed on the pulpit. "The building began peeling away," went one report.

Congregation member Nancy Nind wet cloth napkins from the sacristy and put them in a basket, handing them out to people who wanted to clean their faces and hands of ash, or simply to use them to breathe through.

David Jette, head verger, and Owen Burdick, director of music, brought out water bottles the kind used in office water coolers and placed them in front of the alter. Pastries left over from an earlier meeting were brought out too.

People were allowed to use the parish telephones, provided that calls were kept short.

"I was getting ready to leave the church then smash, the lights dimmed," recalled Melvin Fulton, who works in the congregational office. "Thank God they got the pre-school evacuated. The little ones were terrified."

There was another terrifically loud sound, although not as loud as the first, and the second tower came down. The dust thickened and the light dimmed again.

Jergens, a man who worked at 140 Broadway, recalled seeing a man jump from the Trade Center. "Are you religious?" he asked. The radio station began playing recordings of people screaming and sirens, made just after the first attack.

"That's not helping," said one man. The mood in the church did not lighten.

> Only time took the dust and ash and smoke upward and away, and finally the front doors were opened. I walked out with a wet handkerchief wrapped around my face, just below my glasses. The streets were six-inches deep in ash, frosted with a dark snow, and nearly empty. When I found sunlight near the South Street Seaport at the East River, my shoes caught my attention: they were covered in ash, white as a brand-new pair of sneakers.
> —Trinity News

"Sweet Lord, did you hear that?" Jean asked her sister, tilting her head back to look up at the Tower. Instinctively, she reached for her sister's hand. "Look, look there, that smoke!"

Within a minute, the sirens began. The two sisters looked at each other, each wondering if she was as pale as the other. Something bad was happening. The tips of their fingers were tingling, and their pulse climbed. They turned to see other people coming out of Trinity, all of them pointing to the north, some of them reaching for cell phones.

Jane and Jean would not remember all the details of that morning. Some memories were erased quickly, overwhelmed by the most disturbing, the most indelible, images. In their future recollections, as they described the day to their friends back in Nashville, they eventually told one seamless story, each sister given a scene to recall, but always in sequence, from beginning to end, as if their two voices were the same. Repetition, however, did not render their voice less emotional, nor did the constant re-telling fail to make their audience, many of whom had heard it before, weep.

"Look at the paper," she told her sister. "Like snow."

"No, more like confetti," the other sister said. "Look through these," handing her sister the small tourist binoculars they had carried with them. "You can see people in the windows. They're waving to us."

They were still in the graveyard. The quiet morning was gone, and the air was full of falling paper and the wail of sirens. A multitude of voices were streaming past the graveyard as tribes of refugees rushed away from the burning Towers. Intermittently, one of the sisters would look down and note the progression of debris filling the grounds of Trinity. Hamilton's grave was slowly being covered by the ashes and litter of American commerce. The irony was too obvious, so when the sisters later described their morning they left out that image. Besides, it was unimportant to the story they wanted to tell, a story with two versions, both truthful, but one meant for others and one meant to be kept within themselves. That private story had to wait for a special audience, an audience the sisters were yet to meet. "They're jumping, dear sister, they're jumping," one said, looking through the small binoculars.

It was the most horrific part of their public story, how they traded the binoculars back and forth, how they were, in their public words, "witness to the fall of dying bodies to the concrete earth…" The language surprised many of their friends. The sisters had not been the type to wear their faith on their sleeves, nor were they known for lyricism. But the line to follow dying bodies was more perplexing. How to explain their soft, no matter how many times told, their soft inflection of "….concrete earth, as their souls ascended." The sisters would admit it was not their initial thought at that exact moment, the horror had erased language itself. No, their public story was the result of time and distance and reflection, but as true as the moment itself. *How do you know their souls ascended?*, the skeptical members of their public audience would always think and sometimes ask. The sisters would only smile. The answer was in their private story.

"Did you see him too?" they asked each other, safe inside Trinity. "Was it just me?"

In the weeks that followed, they would search for any picture that was taken of the falling bodies, but the black man was not there. Some people were offended by their persistent questioning, their seeming macabre desire to see the death pictures, but the sisters could not reveal the real reason for their search. They simply wanted proof that what *they* saw actually happened, but there were no pictures of *their* vision. Eventually, it did not matter. They knew what they saw. They believed what they saw.

Through the cheap lenses of their tourist binoculars, they had seen the black man holding the hands of falling souls. They were falling together. Sometimes it was a couple, with the black man in the middle, each of his hands clasping the hand of the person at his side. If they had seen it only once, the sisters would have called themselves delusional, but it happened many times. The binoculars were too weak to show any face clearly, but strong enough to see color. Only one time did they look back in memory and think they might be guilty of glossing the past. The last plunge they saw, the black man between a man and a woman, they admitted that they might have imposed a image rather than have seen it, so they shared it only with themselves. As the trio floated down, their arms were raised straight out from their sides, as if they were three falling crosses. The sisters saw it, they were almost sure.

Their public audience would always ask, *Did you see the Towers fall. Were you terrified?* "No," they would say. "We were in the church praying when that happened. We heard them, we even felt them, but we did not see them fall."

"Do you still have the clipping in your purse?" she asked her sister.

They were sitting in Trinity with a small group of pilgrim tourists who had also sought refuge. The power had already shut down, and the ash clouds outside had dimmed the church, but it was not totally dark.

"I assume you're thinking what I'm thinking," her sister replied.

"I think I know why we were supposed to come to New York, if that's what you're thinking."

She reached into her purse and rummaged for the yellow and cracked newspaper picture. It had been folded four times, so she was very careful to unfold it slowly. She looked at the handwriting in the corner...*April, 23, 1991...* and wondered if it was hers or her sister's. They sat without speaking, and then, a minute before ten in the morning, as each held one side of the open picture, the church began to tremble and the stained glass windows turned dark.

September 11, 2001
St. Augustine
Harry Sleeps

Harry had no illusions about his relationship with alcohol. He was a drunk, a functioning, socially adept, but not subtle, drunk. He did not like the taste of booze, so his drink of choice had quickly become the screwdriver, vodka disguised as orange juice. Drugs were a phase of his youth, a youth that ended when he was fifty. Alcohol was his adult life, a life that began at thirty and had not yet ended. He worked drunk, he drove drunk, and he always went to bed drunk. But he was not drunk all the time. Seldom in the morning, but usually starting after five o'clock, and it was a routine that worked fine as long as he had morning or afternoon shows, but WWHD was a late-night gig, and old habits are hard to break. *But, hey,* he would tell his ghost, *nobody's listening anyway, right?* Unlike other drunks he knew, however, Harry knew his limits. He required a minimum of eight ounces a day, almost never more than ten. And he had been lucky, he knew that too. No drunk driving tickets, nobody hurt except himself. Or so he insisted. Nobody hurt, nothing damaged, except his reputation, and his memory. The great trade-off, as he told an incredulous Jack Tunnel one night at The Tradewinds, as they traded fables about each other and gossiped about the St. Augustine bar culture, through it all, Harry insisted, *I sleep like a baby on my mother's bosom.*

Harry had gone to sleep on his couch as soon as he got back to his apartment. In his sleep the morning of the 11th, he heard drums. Somebody was calling his name. A pounding thud, and then profanity, and then he woke up. Jack Tunnel was standing over him, his hands a spasm.

"You wanna answer your goddam phone, Harry! You wanna wake up! Goddam it, Harry, where's your television?"

Harry blinked, but he did not sit up. "Jack? Why are you…"

"You don't have a goddam television set? I've known you all this time and you never tell me that you don't have a television set!"

"Jack, I'm not sure I understand…"

Tunnel's hands threw themselves as far away from his body as possible, and he almost spun like a dervish. "You've got books all over this dump and you're sleeping on your goddam couch, but you don't have a tv? Are you insane? Do you have the slightest clue that we're under attack! We are under attack, for chrissake, and you won't answer your phone!"

Harry's first thought was that Tunnel was having some sort of drug flashback, some sort of *delirium tremens*, or that he had simply snapped. Harry wanted his mind to clear for a few more seconds before he answered, but Tunnel reached down and yanked him upright, almost spitting through clenched teeth, "Harry, we're at war!"

As Tunnel's hands gripped his shoulders, Harry saw something in Jack's face that turned the room cold and made him shudder. Whatever Jack was about to tell him, Harry was looking at a terrified man.

Of the millions of Americans who woke up that morning to start another normal day, who had their television pre-empted by special reports on all the networks, who saw the second plane hit, who watched as smoke and flames poured from the tallest buildings in New York, who then watched those buildings sag and fall to earth, pan-caking down and letting loose a Biblical cloud of ash composed of paper and plastic and concrete and steel and wood and flesh, Harry Ducharme was not one of them. He had slept through it all. That communal experience for most Americans was merely history to him. They had been part of that experience, he would remain a spectator, or so he thought.

Tunnel took him back to WWHD and the two of them sat in the small office watching replays of the earlier events. Tunnel talked to the screen and called dozens of people who were doing the same thing he was doing, but Harry kept quiet. At noon, he finally found the only analogy he could muster, a pale and tiny version of death seen live.

"You know, I saw Ruby shoot Oswald in 63, saw it live. I was...let me think...how old was I back then?"

Tunnel kept staring at the television screen, but he nodded in acknowledgement and said quietly as he exhaled, "I remember that. Everything was in black and white back in those days. I was younger then."

Harry sat with Jack for another hour, until it was obvious that the images of that morning had become a *mobius strip* on every channel, looping around and returning to the same spot, and the Towers always fell.

Back in his apartment, Harry thought about his show for that night. He could have opted to do what Nora and the others had done after ten that morning, simply let their time slots be filled by a news feed from a national source. No point in competing with them today. Nobody would care what he said tonight. But he called the Station Manager and made sure it was okay for him to go on as usual. The Manager agreed, but only on the condition that he keep a television going in the studio, even if the sound was off, just to be sure he was aware if anything important happened while he was on the air, and he better be sure to go to a national feed immediately. Harry appreciated the unintended irony. "...if anything important happened..." A small reminder of how un-important Harry actually was, but he did not mind. It was true. So he thought about what he would say at ten that night. All he knew for sure was that he wanted to find some poems to read, and he might talk about the time he worked in New York, his show then, about the city itself. But he wanted the poems to be first, perhaps a few short stories to read too. If he was lucky, he would go through his recordings of poets reading their own works and find something there, recordings he had packed and carried with him across the country in the whirlpool of his declining career, boxed in the trunk of a Buick, voices he had once described on air as "silent until called back."

Called back? Where had he heard that? Then it was obvious to Harry which poet he had to use for sure. *Called back*...the last two words of Emily Dickinson, a two word note, was it to her cousins? Or was it something about fog? Harry would consult Thomas Johnson later. All he knew at that moment was that he had the poem he wanted to start his show. He collected material for an hour, and then he lay down on the couch. He assumed that he would not sleep, all he wanted was rest, but he dropped off within minutes of his head hitting the cushion.

He awoke in the dark. His first thought was that he had slept past ten, but a quick glance at the digital clock across the room and he saw that he still had an hour. The only other light in the room was the blinking red dot on his phone answering machine. Then he remembered that he had turned off the phone ringer yesterday, which would explain why he never heard it ring this morning. He sat up, stood up, went to the bathroom, washed his face with cold water, and then he went back to his living room to sit in the dark and listen to his messages. The first dozen were from Jack and others who were yelling at him to pick up the phone or turn on his television. And then there was a voice he had not heard in years.

"Harry, this is Adam…"

He crossed his arms and started squeezing his chest, his breath leaving his body, nothing replacing it.

"…I guess I should have made this call a long time ago."

Adam was crying, and it was obvious that he was trying to stifle his sobs. He spoke louder and louder as his voice was being overwhelmed by a swirling roar in the background, and then the screams began.

"I wish I could talk to you for a second. I really do. I'm sorry. That's what I wanted to tell you. I'm sorry. I hope you can forgive me. I'm sorry I disappointed you. I wish it had been different. Okay? Please forgive me…"

There was more, another few sentences, and the beastly roar behind Adam's voice kept crawling toward him, and then silence.

Harry sat in the dark for a few minutes, rocking himself like a child wanting to sleep, then he went to the bathroom and vomited.

"I don't know how many of you are out there. Not a lot I suspect, but that's fine. I'm drinking right now, but most of you won't be surprised by that confession, right? Truth is, I bet I'm not the only one. It's okay. However you get through this night, straight or not, high or low, the important thing is to get through it. I won't tell you anything new tonight. I'll do the usual, let better people than me speak. My voice, their words, but tonight I have even found some people who can speak for themselves. I want to start with a poem by a dead poet. He drank himself to death. He was probably an unlikable guy, but that doesn't matter. Listen to him, let him speak for himself. I think he anticipated tonight a long time ago. Me, I think I could read this poem better than he does, but tonight, to begin with, this is his voice. It's his poem.

> Never until the mankind making
> Bird beast and flower
> Fathering and all humbling darkness
> Tells with silence the last light breaking
> And the still hour
> Is come of the sea tumbling in harness
>
> And I must enter again the round
> Zion of the water bead
> And the synagogue of the ear of corn
> Shall I let pray the shadow of a sound
> Or sow my salt seed
> In the least valley of sackcloth to mourn
>
> The majesty and burning of the child's death.
> I shall not murder
> The mankind of her going with a grave truth
> Nor blaspheme down the stations of the breath
> With any further
> Elegy of innocence and youth.
>
> Deep with the first dead lies London's daughter,
> Robed in the long friends,
> The grains beyond age, the dark veins of her mother,
> Secret by the unmourning water
> Of the riding Thames.
> After the first death, there is no other.

Thus, Dylan Thomas spoke first, and then Harry read the entire poem again, in his own cadence, making each word of the last line a poem all by itself. As he read, he looked at the phone switchboard, but it was dark. He was still alone.

"I know that most of you are Christians out there, and I know some of you have taken exception to some things I've said in the past about a few notable Christians."

This should get their attention, he told himself.

"But the god's truth is that I love the Bible. It's a better book than most of its preachers. And I was thinking I ought to read the Lord's Prayer, and it's wonderful verse, but you'll hear that a lot this week, I'm sure, so let me read something different, something I hope is true. I'm using the King James Version, my favorite, from Book 14 of John, and it begins like this:

> 1 *Let not your heart be troubled: ye believe in God, believe also in me.*
> 2 *In my Father's house are many mansions: if it were not so, I would have told you. I go to prepare a place for you.*
> 3 *And if I go and prepare a place for you, I will come again, and receive you unto myself; that where I am, there ye may be also*
> 4 *And whither I go ye know, and the way ye know.*

"See, listen to this again," and Harry repeated the lines. "Dylan Thomas and John are saying the same thing...," and for a second the alcohol betrayed him, "...and so a drunk and a Baptist walk into a bar looking for Jesus...," but Harry stopped himself.

Why am I doing this? He wanted to scream at himself. *Why aren't I home?* But, he answered himself, *And home is where? How many burned bridges behind you is home, Harry Ducharme?*

He took a deep breath and looked back at the switchboard. Three lines available. All of them silent. He knew he had made a mistake. He should not have gone on the air. Did he really think that he could find the right words to comfort *anybody?*

"So I'm wondering if anybody out there has anything to add. Is there a poem that you think makes sense of all this mess? I mean, I came loaded tonight..." pausing to wonder if anybody else caught the unintended double meaning, "…loaded with stuff to read. And then I want to tell you about myself. I was thinking about that today, this afternoon, thinking about my past. So I think I want to tell you about my parents, about Iowa, where I was born. Did I ever tell you that I was raised as a Quaker? Seriously, a Quaker. My parents went to the Friends' meeting every week. We worked on another man's farm in Iowa. Well, my parents worked. They never owned land of their own. I helped them, but mostly I went to school in a town called West Branch. That's where Herbert Hoover was born, and he's buried there too. Buried on a hill overlooking the house he was born in. I always liked that symmetry." *I'm babbling now,* Harry told himself. *This day is not about me, so I should shut up. I should shut the hell up.* "Okay, okay, let me tell you what this day is about in case you don't have a keen grasp of the obvious. This day is about grief, about pain, about loss, about holding on. You listen to this show anytime in the past, you know who my favorite poet is, and I knew she would have the right words. I want you to listen to this. Listen to this, and then I am going to say it again, slower, and then I'm going to tell you what I figured out about this poem and why it's almost perfect."

Harry reached for the orange drink in front of him, and then he began:

> *Pain has an element of blank;*
> *It cannot recollect*
> *When it began, or if there were*
> *A day when it was not.*
>
> *It has no future but itself,*
> *Its infinite realms contain*
> *Its past, enlightened to perceive*
> *New periods of pain.*

"Now listen to it again. Listen to me say it. *Pain has an element of blank*…the unspeakable and the ineffable…*It cannot recollect when it began or if there were a day when it was not*…no memory, no starting point, always there from before memory…*It has no future but itself*…more and more pain is all you can expect…*its infinite realms contain its past, enlightened to per-*

ceive new periods of pain. But, see, this is how you really read this poem…" and he began again, but when he got to the last word he immediately began again. "…enlightened to perceive new periods of pain has an element of blank." Harry read the poem again, and again, making the last word the first word, and the circular nature of the poem was made manifest for an audience that, Harry was sure, did not exist. "The beginning and the end, the first and the last, are the same, one leading to, the other re-introducing the other. And all you can do is endure the present."

The switchboard was still dark. The mute television was still pulsating, and Harry turned in time to see the Towers fall again.

"I don't think you understand, people. I need somebody to call me. I'm here. I'm ready to talk. I'll pick up the phone, I promise. I will talk to you. Please, call me."

The Towers were falling in slow motion. The phone never rang. Harry had three hours to go.

Near the end of his shift, he had one last poem to read. He was exhausted, and the studio had gotten so warm that he was rubbing ice cubes on the back of his neck as he finished his shift.

"Okay, folks, one last chance, one last poem, and I'll be truthful with you. This is not one of Dickinson's better poems, but I was in a hurry. It's probably too sweet for some of you, too sing-songy, maybe the opposite, too choppy. Hell, I don't know. I just opened the page and there it was. And it's not for you anyway. It's for somebody named Adam. For him, I hope it's true."

> I went to Heaven
> 'Twas a small Town
> Lit, with a Ruby
> Lathed, with Down
> Stiller, than the fields
> At the full Dew
> Beautiful, as Pictures
> No Man drew.

Harry keyed up the feed to Clear Channel, put WWHD on auto-pilot, and walked back to his apartment. 2:00 A.M., September twelve, 2001, a muggy night in north Florida. Once inside, he turned on the ceiling fan and opened all the windows. He could have turned on the air conditioning, but he wanted to listen to the world outside his apartment. Mosquitoes would keep him indoors, but screens kept them out. He had one chair near the front window, from which he could see the marshes in the daytime, the lighthouse at night, its beam shooting out and circling slowly around and around. He sat in the dark for an hour, wanting to go to sleep but wide awake. He listened to the message one more time.

"Harry, this is Adam. I guess I should have made this call a long time ago. I wish I could talk to you for a second. I really do. I'm sorry. That's what I wanted to tell you. I'm sorry. I hope you can forgive me. I'm sorry I disappointed you. I wish it had been different. Okay? Please forgive me. I've already called mom. Oh god, I guess this is it. I wish we could have at least been friends. Goodbye."

Harry re-played it, and even in the dark he could see the Towers fall again. *If I only had a gun and courage and an ounce of integrity,* he told himself, *I would know what to do.*

The phone rang. Harry shook his head, wondering if he was hearing things. The phone rang again, and he wondered when he had turned the ringer back on. A third ring, but not like the first two. *This is absurd,* he told himself, *the phone is not ringing.* But he picked it up anyway.

"Hello?" he said softly, prepared to get no response, to feel foolish hearing imaginary rings. He was standing in the middle of the room, and his eyes were finally adjusted to the dark.

"Harry Ducharme?" a woman said, a voice he knew. "Harry, this is Nora James. I listened to your show tonight. I knew you would have some-thing to say about all this. I listen to you a lot." Harry did not respond. "Are you there?" she asked.

"Nora...I thought you would...I thought we would never meet. I'm sorry, but I figured that if I hadn't heard from you by now then you weren't interested."

"Harry, you worry too much. And don't over-interpret me. A lot of men have done that, and it's boring. I'm just a woman who likes to cook, that's all. And I was wondering if you would like to have breakfast or lunch tomorrow. You can come to my house and sit with me while I'm on the air. I'll cook for you and tell everybody that you're my guest. We'll have a great time. Chances are, everybody will be watching television anyway, so we'll probably have the program to ourselves. Okay?"

Harry sagged and folded down to his couch, laying his head back on the cushion. "I'd like that very much. Thank you, Nora."

"Good. I'll call you around nine and give you directions to my place. Bring your appetite. Now, *right now*, Harry, go to sleep. You need some rest, so do what I tell you. Go to bed. Go to sleep."

Harry did as he was told. He stretched out on his couch and slept, and the only dream he had was of him and his son walking on a beach. The sky was postcard blue, and he was holding his son's hand.

September 12, 2001
Harry Meets Nora

A terrific and unique new cookbook: A TWIST OF THE WRIST: QUICK FLAVORFUL MEALS WITH INGREDIENTS FROM JARS, CANS, BAGS, AND BOXES by Nancy Silverton with Carolyn Carreno (Knopf $29.95). I know you're dubious, but I promise you can trust Silverton, a respected gourmet cook. Mixing packaged food with fresh items, she tells which packaged food to use to create delicious meals. Just my kind of shortcut cooking for these busy days.
—Nancy Olson, Quail Ridge Bookstore owner, in her email newsletter to customers.

You satisfy the hungry heart with gift of finest wheat, come give to us o saving Lord, the bread of life to eat. Refrain from "Gift of Finest Wheat" music and lyrics: Robert E. Kreutz

"Everything ends this way...everything. Weddings, christenings, duels, funerals, swindlings, diplomatic affairs—everything is a pretext for a good dinner."
—Jean Anouilh (1910-1987) Cecile

We haven't yet solved the problem of God," the Russian critic Belinsky once shouted across the table at Turgenev, "and you want to eat!"

Harry walked to Nora's house. In the year he had lived in St. Augustine, she had always been just a few streets from the Flamingo Apartments, perhaps a mile away. Michelle and Jack, the others he had asked, they must have enjoyed knowing how close he was to her all that time. *For us to know,*

Harry Ducharme, for you to find out, like the secret password to a children's club, and he was still new to the neighborhood. The events of the previous day had finally brought him over to their side of the street.

As he turned on to Water Street, he smelled her house before he saw it. Fresh bread, the aroma of bread fresh out of an oven, and, the closer he got, that aroma parted and then re-enveloped him in memories of his mother's kitchen in Iowa. Fresh bread, still warm, and more. Harry's nose twitched with the effort to name the other smell, and then it came to him as he finally stood in front of her house...cinnamon. Nora James was baking bread on Water Street, sprinkling cinnamon as if it were a magic powder. *Why would anybody on this street ever sell their house and move away?* He looked up and scanned her house from side to side. She lived in a huge three story red brick Queen Anne house with white railing on the porches and a turret at one corner. *How old?* he wondered. Not as old as St. Augustine itself, but surely from the nineteenth century?

It was 9:45, and Harry was starving. He straightened his shoulders, gathered his resolve, walked to the front door and rang the bell. Nobody answered. He rang again. Behind the door he heard, "Coming!" It was a man's voice, and Harry was instantly disappointed. The door opened and Harry was greeted by a young man who needed a haircut. The young man had a handsome face that was some mixture of races. Asian and Caucasian? "Come in, come in, my aunt's expecting you," he said, extending his hand.

Nora's voice came from another room, "Dex, show him in here and then go to work. You hear me?"

The young man rolled his eyes for Harry's amusement, and drawled back over his shoulder, "Yezzzzzzz, Aunt Nora." He then led Harry through the frozen-in-time interior of the house into a twenty-first century kitchen. Nora was just turning toward the door when the two men entered.

Harry did not see the woman he had expected. Nora was tall, not short, able to look him directly in the eye as he came forward. She was thin, not round, not earth-motherly at all. He had always imagined her as solid and attractive, not beautiful, but he now saw a beautiful woman grown old, almost a faded movie star quality, without the plastic surgery or desperate cosmetics. Her subtly-lined face had a long life behind it, for sure, but her green eyes could...Harry groped...*cut diamonds, could cut diamonds? Something like that?*

He walked toward her and then stopped. It was obvious that she was coming to hug him. Instant intimacy was not common in Harry's world, even before he got to St. Augustine. As she opened her arms to enfold him, softly shaking her head to loosen her long silver-streaked hair so that it would fall straight, she smiled and said, "Hello, Mr. Ducharme. We meet at last." And they embraced.

Stepping away from him, her smile seemed to turn into a repressed smirk, "That wasn't so bad, was it?"

Captain Jack interrupted, his voice coming from the speaker on top of a giant double-door refrigerator, "And this is going to be a test of us, folks, our resolve, and I just thank God that our President is George Bush. Can you imagine how bad things would be right now if..."

Nora never took her eyes off of her guest. "Jack is being himself this morning, but I have a feeling that he's more scared than angry." Before Harry could respond, before he had even said his first word, she added, "But let's not talk about that, okay? You're here, that's all that's important. And I promised you breakfast. So, let me get the show started. Feel free to take the house tour unescorted, and then come back and sit while I feed the masses," motioning to a couch on the other side of the huge room. The kitchen was also a den.

"I've been looking forward to meeting you," Harry said.

"So I've heard. From more than a few people." she said with a true smirk, picking up a wireless headset off the counter. "I just hope you're not disappointed. Now shush, Jack's introducing me."

Harry backed away, pausing long enough to ask, "The young man... your nephew?"

Nora flared her nostrils, pointed to the large clock over the counter, held up ten fingers to represent seconds, and spoke quickly, "Inside joke. He's the son of the man who owns this house. Now...GO!"

Nora James was on the air.

"Good morning everyone, as much as this can be a good morning. I suspect that a lot of my regular listeners are watching tv, and that's okay.

68

I'll be here tomorrow too. Always time to catch up. For those out there, I'm going to change my format just for today. I'm not going to take calls today. I'm sorry, but I think I'll do all the talking. And, I have a pleasant surprise for you. I have a guest this morning, the famous Harry Ducharme, WWHD's midnight host and Jack Tunnel's constant saddle burr. I'm cooking breakfast for Harry, and you're all going to listen in as Harry and I talk about…well, I think we should talk about Harry. He started talking about himself last night on his program, but I know there's more. So, stick around."

Harry had been standing in the door frame as Nora began her show, looking at her start gathering utensils and flip stove switches, listening to her speak in a voice that effortlessly disguised the motion of her body as she walked all around the kitchen, her arms seeming to go in opposite directions at the same time. She saw him staring, and, without tripping on a syllable, she waved her hand and banished him from her domain.

Harry walked through the house, no longer *hers* because she had told him that it was owned by somebody else. That fact explained a lot. The house's décor was certainly not what he would have predicted. It was antique, almost as if it was one of those restored homes on the National Registry of Historic Preservation. The kitchen/den was an aberration, as if from another house on another planet. The rest of the house on Water Street was a museum.

Then Harry found another room at the end of a dark hallway, a picture gallery room, a room whose walls were covered mostly in black and white photos. Some matted and framed, some small, some the size of movie posters, some as big as a door, and some of Nora from a time when she was young and youthfully beautiful.

Harry lost track of time, of the previous day's destruction, of this morning's walk to Nora's kitchen. The photos were their own world. *Why so many trains and train stations and cabooses*, he wondered, *so many graveyards and tombstones, so many of the ocean, water and waves?* So many variations of those three subjects, each of them more than a photo, but all eye-stopping, as good art was supposed to be. Three common subjects, and each photo provoked the feeling in Harry that *I've never seen this before.*

A picture of the Palatka train station, closed and boarded up, with a few elderly black men sitting on benches and smoking cigarettes, that would be his favorite of the train pictures. The graveyard pictures were more complex, especially in their lighting and camera angle, and Harry knew he would have to come back to look at them again. But his favorite picture in the room, the one he stood in front of the longest, was of the ocean. The water seemed to curve around upon itself, and the lines seemed to meet an invisible stone and swirl around it to meet on the other side. The colors of the water had a depth that no other substance, in Harry's mind, ever had, and under that surface there was another layer of line and color. But it was more than just the ocean that he saw. The harder he looked, the more he thought he saw a face in that water, but he wasn't sure.

The other pictures on the walls were not art. They were simply snapshots, enlarged and framed, amateur moments frozen in time. Two men standing next to a Corvair, one an Asian teenager wearing a Hawaiian shirt, the other a red-headed adult. Harry thought the boy looked somewhat like the young man who had answered the door earlier. Another: a stern looking older man, with a pretty young girl next to him, her head leaning into his chest and her right arm stretched across his stomach, him looking proud. Lots of pictures with a smirking young Nora playing around with other teenagers, but one in particular made Harry wish he had known Nora back then. Nora and a dazzling friend, a girl who looked like she could be the sister of the young man who answered the door, but, of course, impossible since the Nora in the picture was so obviously much younger than the Nora that Harry had just met. The person who took the picture had caught the two girls having fun and probably asked them to pose, but at the last second, as he must have pushed the button, the dazzling girl stuck out her tongue and Nora raised her middle finger. Snap and freeze. For as long as Harry was to know Nora, he would never see her as happy as she appeared in that picture from the distant past.

"Harry! Where are you?" Nora's voice had come from the kitchen and diminished in volume as it floated through the hallway to finally reach him in a whisper. She might have been yelling, but Harry had not heard it at first. Looking at her in the past, he grudgingly let himself be pulled back to the present.

Walking quickly back to the kitchen, he checked his watch. It was almost noon, and Nora quickly made him understand that he had missed breakfast. "For somebody so eager to meet me, Mr. Ducharme, you seem to have forgot your manners," she said, faking anger, her apron stained with a red juice that she was rubbing her fingers on and then licking. She was still on the air.

"I'm sorry," he stammered. "I was in that room with the photos..."

Nora stiffened and then reached over to flip a switch on the remote control panel, telling her listeners it was time for a word from the St. Augustine Public Library, then turning back to Harry, "Remind me to kill Dexter. He was supposed to keep that room locked. It's not open for visitors."

Harry's confusion was obvious, "Dexter?"

"My so-called nephew, Harry, and just about the most lovable, sweetest undependable child in north Florida. Dexter King Lee, son of Abraham Isaac Lee, the man who took all those pictures, the man who owns this house, the man who lost his virginity with me back when I was hot stuff."

Harry was speechless, and Nora was smiling again.

"I'm back on the air in thirty seconds. Breakfast is off the table, but treat me nice and lunch is possible. First thing, you put on this extra set of headphones and you apologize to my listeners for getting lost. Act like you were raised right, okay?"

Harry kept thinking about the picture of Nora that he had been staring at only minutes earlier. And then, in almost a tremble, he had a flash of recognition about one of the other pictures in that private gallery. A young and pouty blonde Lolita whose shorts were too small for her bottom and whose lips glistened even in black and white—it was that woman named Polly, the clerk at Harry's Curb Mart, who told him about Nora the first day he was in St. Augustine.

Nora began counting down, "Fifteen, fourteen, thirteen...and say, Harry, you see anything back there that you liked? Any profound epiphanies...eight, seven...and you are officially on notice. You now know a secret about me, and, fair is fair, before this day is over I better know a goddam secret about you, because the legal tender in this town is how much you know about the other person…three, two…and here we go."

"Welcome back, everybody. My lost soul guest Harry Ducharme is back with us, and I'm sure he has something to say. Harry?…"

And with that introduction, Nora punched Harry in the shoulder hard enough to knock him sideways a few inches, making him the happiest man in St. Augustine as he said hello to a daylight audience he could not see.

Every time Harry had asked about Nora in the past year, only to be rebuffed or put off, Captain Jack had always told him, "Always look for that first punch, my friend. She only punches people she likes. You get your first bruise, you're on the A-list."

For the next two hours, Harry and Nora talked on-air as she continued to cook or clean in her stainless steel kitchen. She teased him about his graying hair, and she teased him about his junk food diet, which was evidently common knowledge in St. Augustine. In that two hours, the Twin Towers never fell, and Harry began the story of his life, to be finished later that afternoon as he and Nora sat on the couch in her kitchen. She was his only audience.

Springdale, Iowa
Harry is Orphaned
His life, as told to Nora

I had just turned eighteen and was walking back from the store when I saw the Iowa Highway Patrol cruiser parked in front of our house, saw the cruiser before I saw the trooper sitting in the swing on the front porch, his smoky hat placed next to him. As I got closer, the trooper eased himself off the swing and put on his hat, stepped down from the porch slowly and took a deep breath. I can clearly remember that breath. He was a smoker.

"Would you be Harry Ducharme?" he asked me, extending his hand.

I had the feeling I would only understand years later when I finally re-read the poem. The hand was a snake.

Zero at the Bone, she had written, but at that moment I hadn't read enough Dickinson to make the connection.

I had always known I was adopted. It was never one of those secrets withheld until I was "old enough to understand." In my earliest memories, the word was used casually, but always in terms of how lucky my new parents felt to have me in their life. And so I heard my life story over and over from them. They never tired of telling it.

They had resigned themselves to childlessness, but God had blessed them with an orphan, they told me. The call had come from another Friend. A little boy...me... had been pulled from the Cedar River up north of West Branch. Well, not really in the river, as my mother explained, "But you were at the edge, and soaking wet, as if you had fallen in and gotten out, been saved, and crying like a baby. Well, who wouldn't, I mean, cry like that?" Those were her words, as best I recall.

My other parents, my birth but not real parents, known by everyone over in Ashfield, had been an abject example of Peg's Law: Pride, Envy, Gluttony, Sloth, Lust, Avarice, and Wrath. Social Services had a file, but not enough to rescue me. When I was finally found next to the Cedar, the sheriff drove over to Ashfield with every intention of arresting those other parents once and for all, but their parental rights had already been severed. The house was cinder and ashes, the bodies were charred bones, and I was free at last. Free at last? I don't know. I don't really remember them.

Of all that I learned about my early past, I eventually forgot everything, including my name. Don't laugh. I'm serious. I had been five when I was found, old enough for most children to have many memories imprinted forever, but I was a blank slate. My parents showed me all the newspaper stories when I got older, my birth records from the courthouse, even pictures of those other parents, but none of that stuck with me. I would look at the words on the page, the images in the photos, and I would calculate their significance at that moment, but then I forgot. I was told my other name, the name those parents had given me, but I forsake it. I was not that person, I was sure of it. People would tell me how those parents drank too much and were constantly yelling at the neighbors or at their only child, but it was all fiction to me. I was the true son of Joe and Marian Ducharme, farmers for hire in Springdale, Iowa. In the future, as much as I would parse the origins of my adopted name in countless bar-room conversations, the truth was simple: I was actually named after my Uncle Harry, Joe Ducharme's brother who had died at Omaha Beach on D-Day; not for Harry Truman, as my Uncle Ronald had told me.

My new family was poor, but I only understood it when I left to go to college. They were farmers without land, hired by those with land, especially other Quakers. Of all the questions that I wished I could go back and ask my parents...like all children who finally mature, but too late to appreciate their parents...I wanted to know, "How was it that you were the only farmers in Iowa who did not own even an acre of land?"

They owned no land, no car, no television. They rented a small house in Springdale, a town so small that going to West Branch down the road was called "going to the city." I never went hungry, and my clothes, worn and handed down from older cousins, were never ragged or dirty. My father would rise early and walk to a field to work. As I got older, I would rise with him and walk in the dark until we waited at a corner where I was picked up by the parent of a schoolmate and taken to the Friends Scattergood school in West Branch. In the summer, I would stay with my mother, helping her do the laundry she took in from other families, to clean and mend. My mother talked all the time, happy to have me as her audience. "The gift of gab," she would explain to me, "Your father never had it, but I've got enough for all of us."

My father was not a talker, for sure, but he was far from cold. He laughed at my mother's chatter, thought that any joke that I brought home was worth repeating so he could laugh again, and he was a man whose hands rested easily on his son's shoulders or around his wife's ample waist. His morning walks with me always ended with a hug as we went our ways. A big hug. I thought he was a giant. He was never angry, and seldom sad. He read his Bible every night, and I could see his lips move with each word. For the first ten years that I lived with them, my real parents, I had no bedroom. I slept on a lumpy couch, tucked in every night by my mother or father, and then I would go to sleep with the purr of their low voices in the kitchen. The light would slant into an otherwise dark front room. A certain slant of light, didn't Dickinson say that? Bits and pieces, words and parts of sentences, my father's grunty laugh, my mother cleaning the kitchen as my father sat at the table and listened to her day, punctuated by the clatter of dishes being stacked or tin pans being banged on the counter. The house was hot in the summer but warm in the winter. In Iowa, only the winter mattered.

As I got older, my school vacations were spent in a field with my father, and I learned more about corn and corn weevils than any of my friends. During the school year, school itself became my "chore." That was my father's term—chore. A responsibility, like a household chore. But I knew the difference. Reading books was a lot more fun than raking leaves. From September to June, my parents expected me to do school work first and then help around the house. On my tenth birthday, my father gave me a dictionary, "the key to your future"

I was told. And the older I got, the more that word "future" was heard. My parents would talk about my future, about the time when I would leave home and go out into the world, perhaps even to Chicago or New York. "You have to be prepared, Harry. Me and your father are happy here, but this is not for you. You've got your entire life ahead of you." I'd listen to them, but I wouldn't tell them my own feelings. They wouldn't have understood, or so I thought, how I didn't want to leave them, didn't want to leave my home, how I had some gnawing suspicion that I was safe only in Springdale with them. If anything appealed to me, it was working in West Branch, five miles down the road. I could get a job there and make enough money to buy my parents their own home, a large house in which we could all live. And they could use the car I would buy, so that my father didn't have to walk to work for other men. I didn't tell them all this because it was obvious that their happiness was somehow tied to my success in that nebulous and geographically distant future. But in the present time of my life, my routine was my comfort. Home and school for nine months, home and field work for three, the Friends service every Sunday morning in West Branch, books from the library, Scattergood school homework done before dinner, books to read on my own, odd-jobs for neighbors in Springdale for extra money that my parents insisted that I save for my future, regular visits from my aunts and uncles in Tipton and Cedar Bluff and West Liberty, nightly prayers with my mother and father, a Bible passage to be read aloud by me for their enjoyment, my father's own mumbled reading, and bed. When I was a teenager, with all that drama and angst, my rebellion against my parents took the form of a refusal to read aloud in front of them. That revolt lasted the first few months of my junior year. But it passed, my parents later assured me, "as we knew it would." Their peace irritated me, and I was pissy, "How could you know that? You've never raised any kids before." Right now, long past fifty, my list of "If I could take that back…" has that teenage snit near the top.

One of the threads of my comfort was the almost daily walk with my father, to be picked up for school or to go with him to a field. Silent walks most often, but chattier as I got older. Uncle Kennon, my father's bald brother, explained my father to me one Easter. "You look at your mama, Harry. First fifteen minutes of meeting her, you feel like you've known her all your life, that was my impression back then. But your papa keeps his own company a lot more.

Takes a long time to get to know him. Even when we were growing up, he wasn't much of a talker. But we could all depend on him for sure."

In those summer walks to a field to work, me and my father would pass by the small Springdale cemetery, and it was there that he talked the most. His own parents were buried there, and I absorbed his family's history as he talked. More than family history, however, my father, to my surprise, was a book of knowledge about the history of Iowa and America and the world. The lessons most often started when we stood near a grave on the east edge of the cemetery. The tombstone was not meant to be ironic: Uncle Tom. Thomas W. Jenkins. Called as a Slave, Richard Lewis. Jenkins had died in 1902, so he must have been a free man, but his slave past was part of his definition in death. My father thought that was an important idea for me to consider.

From my father, I learned all about John Brown and Harpers Ferry, how Brown had recruited and trained his men just a few miles from the very spot on which we stood in that cemetery, an Iowa connection. "Probably back in 1858, if we were standing here, we might have met the man. My great-grandparents might have known him back then. They worked the Underground Railroad over in West Branch and Iowa City. Think about that, Harry. We're walking historic ground, and history's all around us." I was young. When I looked around, all I saw were corn fields.

I understood even then that my parents had their own routine. As I got older and spent more time with my father, it seemed normal that he would talk to me when we were alone, but when the three of us, me and my parents, were together my father seldom spoke. My mother dominated any conversation. If I had a problem, I would talk to my mother, not my father, but I came to understand that she would then talk to her husband about their son, and then he would talk to me. It was indirect, predictable, safe, the way my world worked.

Nearing my eighteenth birthday, I became more and more obsessed with my parents, knowing that I was expected to leave them soon. As we sat together for dinner every night, a ritual unbroken from the first day I had come to live with them, I would will myself into becoming their true child, from my mother's body and procreated with my father's seed. I would study their looks, my father's chiseled face and broad brow, my mother's hazel eyes and thin lips. In the mirror every morning, I would see myself as some combination of those features.

Years later, set up for a blind date by a Station Manager whose sister needed company while visiting Tulsa, I was asked to describe myself to her when she called to confirm the date. That night at dinner, after enough drinks, she had told me, "Harry, you're nothing like how you described yourself. I mean, not in a bad way, but it's just that I was expecting something... somebody else."

I was not offended, and my response, more true than the woman would ever know, made her laugh, "Yeh, that's what my ex-wife said too. Except for the 'not in a bad' way part."

Christmas of my senior year in high school, I had resigned myself to the future my parents wished for me: college, my own family, success, grand-children for them. Going to college was probably going to be the hardest step simply because my parents had only been able to save a few thousand dollars in the past thirteen years. But it could be done. I had good grades, won some scholarships, could get some loans, and my aunts and uncles, whose own children had long been gone from home, would contribute. I had always been their favorite nephew. "Hard work and perseverance will get you through, Harry," my Uncle Kennon had said. "Dumb luck and spit," my Uncle Ronald had said. None of us understood Ronald. I had my own formula for success, learned from a history book in my junior year, in the chapter about monks in the Middle Ages: poverty, obedience, and chastity. I told that to my Uncle Ronald, who reminded me about the "spit."

All in all, whether the key to success was spit or hard work, it was the Great Mystery in front of me, my future. But before I left home, I made my parents accept my own gift to them. At the Christmas family reunion in 1965, I had asked my mother and father what they wanted for their 40th anniversary, which was to be a week after my graduation in May of the coming year. My father, as I expected, had insisted that no presents were necessary. All he wanted was mild weather. I had expected my mother to roll her eyes and laugh at what he said, as she usually did when he was being his usual stoic self, but this time she seemed genuinely hurt, and her face showed it even after she said, "Well, your father is right. You save your money for college. We'll have a good dinner for our anniversary, like we always do, and we'll be fine."

I remember focusing on her. Something about the tone of her voice. She looked very old, more lined than even my father. "Mama, dinner is fine. I'd like that," I started to say, knowing that the anniversary question had to be answered indirectly, so I asked, "But, I wonder, have wondered for a long time. When you were my age, was there something you wanted to do, something you still want to do?"

She looked at me as if I was some sort of beloved suitor who had finally proposed. Her breathing stopped, and she paused before answering, "I've always wanted to see the ocean."

My father stiffened next to her, remembering, he admitted later, a promise he had made her before they were married, a promise un-kept. I had never ever seen his face so stricken as he looked away from me. My gift to them became obvious to me right then. I had three hundred dollars saved. I would ask my aunts and uncles to contribute and swear them to secrecy. I would send my parents to the ocean.

A week after I graduated, I went to my uncle's house to get a long distance call from my mother. "Harry, I saw it just now, well, a few minutes ago, and you told me to call...," and she stopped. I could hear her sniffling, "...and I just wanted to thank you again. I wish you were here...but you'll see it soon enough, on your own." I asked about my father, and she laughed softly, "Oh, he's still down at the beach. He actually took his shoes off. I wish I had a camera."

Telling you this story now, forty years after the fact, I need to quote that Iowa trooper word for word. The "I'm afraid I have some bad news for you" part is easy to remember. It was what he said next that I had lost over time, but I think I can retrieve it for you. He said, "I'm afraid I have some bad news for you. Your parents are gone." And, see, not that they were missing, but that they were gone. He said they were gone. And that was it. Gone. Just like that. Gone.

Nora sat on the kitchen couch, her cat in her lap, as Harry sat on the other end of the couch. He had taken her through his childhood and his college years and his failed marriage and his career spiral, but he had skipped that day when he was told about his parents being part of a missing tour boat, a routine cruise a few miles off the Florida shore. Bits of the small boat were recovered, and then the bodies of two of the six people aboard, then two more a day later, but not his mother and father. They were gone.

"The ocean is funny, Harry. How it gives and takes. Two friends of mine, a long time ago, their plane crashed just off shore. We found one body right away, never found the other, the pilot. The ocean is funny that way. Sorry, no great insight here, and I'm guessing that the time is long past for anybody to offer you consolation for you losing your parents. But, still, I'm glad you told me."

Harry stayed at Nora's for dinner, and then he slept on the couch before he went to WWHD that night. He went to sleep with her cat curled up next to his stomach, and the sound of her cleaning her kitchen was the last thing he heard as he drifted off.

The trooper had stayed with me until my Uncle Kennon and my Aunt Betty arrived. The two older men discussed arrangements to be made with the Florida police, leaving me on the porch swing with Betty. Neither one of us spoke, and I kept both my hands in my lap even though Betty had offered her hand to me to hold. Uncle Ronald arrived, trembling, and soon enough me and the others were working to console the only bachelor Ducharme. Then, old Ethel Worrall arrived, our landlady, and a favorite of me and my father. Ethel was a retired school teacher, a woman who my father was fond of describing as someone who "would walk through heavy traffic to save a squirrel." Ethel had brought food. I suppose that was necessary, part of some sort of a ritual.

I finally left the adults and walked to the Springdale cemetery. I had walked the same gravel road a few weeks earlier with my father. As much as I tried to remember that particular conversation, I couldn't. Something about planting, that would have been typical, perhaps something about the Vietnam war, a topic which had come to occupy my father's mind more and more. He had seemed to let slip an urgent and repressed anger, compounded by me about to turn eighteen and having to register for the draft, but I wasn't sure this afternoon in June of 1966 of anything my father might have said on our last walk together. But I do remember this: I had been preoccupied with my own future earlier, resigned to the inevitable, but starting to absorb some of my parents' enthusiasm for that future. I had been thinking more about myself than anyone else, and I hadn't paid attention to my father as we walked.

I turned the corner of the cemetery and walked to the east fence, past my grandparents' graves, and found Thomas Jenkins. The wire fence was a few feet away from the grave. On the other side, the corn was only a foot or two out of the ground, but it stretched to the horizon, a rolling green carpet. In a few months it would be taller than me. I wanted to talk to Jenkins, as I had often seen my father do. "Mr. Jenkins, how are you doing? Fine weather today, and soon enough that corn behind you will give you some morning shade from the August sun that's coming. You take care, Mr. Jenkins, you hear, and we'll talk to you next time." I would tell my mother how my father would talk to a dead man, expecting her to be surprised, but she never was.

I looked around the cemetery. I looked for John Brown's ghost, tried to hear that prophet's voice. My father had always told me that John Brown was a zealot and a murderer, a man of wrath whose goal was pure. But my father had also said that, "Brown was a necessary agent. Somebody had to light the fuse." I was never sure if my father admired or condemned Brown. At that moment, standing over Thomas Jenkins, looking for John Brown, I thought I heard my father, but he was gone. The ground he had stood on before was still there, but he was gone.

September 13, 2001–September, 2003
Life in a Small World
Harry Finds His Audience

Harry had no illusions about his future. His son's death had merely confirmed a conclusion he had already reached. He was alive, and he would live a life of small pleasures until he died. He would talk into a microphone for four hours a night, five nights a week. He would eat and drink, and he would sleep. He would walk on the beach, and he would read books, but even those routines changed. He started walking on the beach after he got off work at two in the morning, instead of late afternoon. He would stop reading books about politics and history, and he would start reading more fiction, even going back to novels he had read thirty years earlier. The same books, but not the same Harry Ducharme.

It had not begun that way, his retreat into fiction. For the first year after 9/11 he had soaked himself in histories of the Middle East, all the views of Bernard Lewis and Samuel Huntington and even Edward Said. He surfed the web and read all the columnists, from Friedman to Krugman to Hitchens and even those like Sontag and Krauthamer and Cohen. He wanted to understand what happened. *Surely*, he told himself and his invisible audience, *if we know enough, then we will know what to do.* He would sometimes read an entire book chapter or newspaper column on the air. He called some of those writers and asked them to let him interview them on his program. Almost all of them declined because he had one iron-clad requirement. He wanted the interview to be live, not taped, so it meant they had to be willing to talk near or after midnight. Harry had also forgotten that he had a lingering reputation for abusive questions, zero credibility, and his audience demographics were undocumented. He was in no position to make the rules.

After his show on the night of 9/11, Harry never mentioned his son again. He no longer talked about personal life in public, but he entered the kitchen of Nora James over and over again, telling her the worst things about himself, unpacking baggage and putting away the soiled clothes he had carried around for years. Nora even forced him to burn some of it. For his WWHD world, he seemed to be the same Harry Ducharme. In that first year after 9/11, however, he seldom used the phrase "I think…," as he talked to his audience. Captain Jack spotted another new catch-phrase that seemed to appear more and more: "Is anybody wondering…," and Harry knew he was right. The more he read, the more overwhelming the facts seemed, the less sure he was. Not about 9/11 and the drum beat to Baghdad, which seemed like a song in which the lyrics of one song were sung to the music of another. Harry understood *that*. But he did not understand why nobody else seemed to hear the dissonance.

Uncertainty and dissonance were not Jack Tunnel's problem, and the two men had to reach a truce about the limits of any serious conversation. Tunnel went one step too far one night at The Tradewinds, suggesting that Harry ought to wear the American flag lapel pin that he had given him. Harry thought he was being funny when he said, "And my three listeners will see this come through their radios? My pin will give me some of your street cred?"

Tunnel had had more to drink than Harry, and his good mood turned red, white, blue, and then black. "Dammit, Harry, wear the pin. Stop acting like you're too good for the rest of us. We're at war with some Arab turd-suckers who would just as soon kill us as look at us. You, of all people, ought to understand that. You, you, you…" and he punched a trembling finger at him.

It had been Saturday night. The bar was packed, sweat and perfume and cigarette smoke flavored every breath and drink. Harry looked at his friend through blurry eyes, but he did not speak. He just sat in the booth across from Tunnel and stared at him.

"Oh, Harry, I just…," Jack started to say, not looking at him. But Harry shook his head, pushed his glass away from him, and walked out of The Tradewinds. He thought about going over to the Tavern, but he just walked around the downtown Plaza instead. He sat on a bench across from the Cathedral and called Nora, but it was late, she must have been asleep, there was no answer.

I don't have any illusions about changing the world, but none of this makes sense. All my life and all my books, and Jack and I are now living in different worlds? He's wrong. He has to be wrong. His world makes no sense to me. Who are the people who live in his world, his America?

Harry looked around the Plaza. Palm trees and cannons from the eighteenth century, a gazebo, and at the far end was the slave market block, certified by a bronze plaque. A line from Whitman, *time and distance availing not?* Something like that. Harry would look it up tomorrow. Something about the material world outliving us all? How, all around us are spirits from the past, past and present and unborn futures are sharing and will share the same material world. Who else sat in this same spot? Those people in the Towers, are they still there even though the Towers are gone? Build a new building there, will the dead still inhabit it? Harry would figure it all out tomorrow. Midnight downtown in America's oldest city, he got up and went looking for his Buick. He still had a pillow in the trunk.

The next morning, his head splitting and his mouth dry, Harry drove slowly back to his apartment. He had a message on his answering machine: "Jesus, Harry, I'm sorry. I was outta line last night. A damn fool. You gotta forgive me. I was a total butt-hole. Totally, just being myself. But I was wrong. Call me later, I'll buy your dinner. And no more talk about all this crazy shit happening around here. Okay? Please. Call me."

Harry kept talking. And life? His life? He and Tunnel remained friends, but the invisible line was almost always there. Politics had been their battleground, but Harry began to wonder if the issues were deeper. How to understand the world? How could two friends process it so differently?

Sometimes, Harry could listen to Jack Tunnel and wonder if he even took himself seriously. How could he be so mean-spirited on his program, and so gentle away from it? Vulgar for sure, but generous to his friends. So angry, and then apologetic? But never sorry on the air. Captain Jack did not back down, even when a caller trumped him on the facts of an issue.

Harry kept talking. He came to the studio five nights a week with a stack of articles he had printed out, a list of topics he wanted to cover, with specific quotes circled in red. He was trying to be rational, but he lived in St Johns County, Florida, where Republicans outnumbered Democrats three to one. But even the Democrats were not much better, in St. Augustine or in the rest of the country.

The crossroads came in early 2003, as Harry realized that the America he thought he knew...that country had disappeared. It went crazy, or it was kidnapped by aliens. Something beyond his comprehension, but it was still gone. Sitting in The Tavern among friends, he watched television as Baghdad was being shocked and awed. Everyone else seemed to be cheering, but all Harry could think about was the final scene of *Apocalypse Now*, the air-strike called in, the jungle turned into a fireball. But nobody in The Tavern was in the mood for Vietnam analogies. "Take that, pudsucker!" yelled a young man in his National Guard uniform, itself a violation of some military dress code, but he never paid for a drink again that night. The chorus began. "Stone age for you Arabs! Your ass is next, Osama! Red, white, and blow you away!"

Michelle was working the bar and she was kept hustling all night, but she made a point to keep Harry re-filled without him asking. She was also in charge of the jukebox volume, and as much as she tried to keep the music going the crowd kept yelling for her to turn it down so they could hear the television. So, she pumped up the volume on the three televisions, and the concussive thump of every cruise missile hitting Baghdad was like thunder in the Tavern. Harry was no exception to the feeling, the sensual vibrations of reverberating explosions. From a distance, it was a pleasure. *Too many books*, he told himself, *too many movies, something I read a long time ago, Tim O'Brien? Something about combat, if you could remove the danger, then combat was beautiful? An aesthetic orgy of color and sound, but O'Brien probably said it better.*

That was the night it finally changed for Harry. He stopped talking about the facts of the war, the right and wrongs of politicians and generals, the courage of war opponents and the duplicity of its supporters. He remembered how he felt within a few weeks of 9/11, as his grief for his own son was more and more internalized as his guilt surfaced. He and Jack and a lot more people around him all seemed to feel like they were part of something bigger than their prior petty disagreements, that the country he loved was going to change for the better. Evil would be punished. The issues were clear.

A single line from Michelle nudged him closer to his break, a line she shouted at the television as another building collapsed in Baghdad, "That'll teach you to try and kill George's daddy." Harry recognized the attempt at humor, and appreciated that Michelle seemed to know a little more background about the war than he would have guessed she knew. But the crowd was not amused. The paunchy man sitting next to Harry growled, "Michelle, you better watch what you say. This is serious shit."

Harry had glanced over at the man, and then back to look at Michelle, wondering if he should say something, but Michelle's middle finger, stuck in the man's drink and then pulled out and flicked at him, ended the conversation. The man eased himself off the stool and humped away as Michelle said to Harry, "He and me got history together. He knows I won't take his shit." Harry tipped his glass at her, his eyes still enthralled by her chest, "Michelle, will you marry me?"

She rolled her eyes and took his glass away. "Go home, Harry. I'll call you a cab. Or I can have Dex come pick you up. Nora told me to keep an eye on you, so maybe I'll just have him drop you off at her place."

"You didn't answer my question," he slurred, resigning himself to the usual rejection.

"Harry, go sleep it off. You're too old for me, as much as I like you grey panther types. Besides, from what I hear, you've got a crush on Nora," she grinned, wiping the counter as she lifted his half-full glass. In the background, somebody was shouting something about real men wanting to go to Tehran instead of Baghdad.

"Your sources must be mistaken," he said as he stood and handed her a fifty, motioning for her to keep the change.

"Harry, this is a small town. Never forget that," she said, stuffing the bill in her exposed bra.

September–2003
Harry on the Balance Beam

Harry almost went too far after the war started. He started drinking before his program as well as during, and sometimes he left the studio at two in the morning not remembering anything he said for the last hour. It happened too many times, until Captain Jack invited him over for dinner on *The Tunnel of Love*, catered by the A1A Aleworks across the street from the marina. Harry had been on board many times, but never for a meal. Tunnel swore him to secrecy.

"You do not tell Nora that I had A1A send a meal over. I told her I was talking to you, and she offered to do the cooking herself, to have Dex deliver it, but I said I was fixing my Chef Boyardee special. She thought that was a hoot, but she said okay. Her old line about crap in, crap out. Only thing worse than that in her world is chain restaurant food. Me, I like the food over there, and the waiters treat me right."

The two men ignored the outside world and let the boat rock them into amiability. After the beer-battered shrimp with black beans and rice, they sat on the deck and had their second drink. When Harry asked for a refill, Tunnel saw his opening,

"One more, and we call it a night, okay?"

Harry had already had two screwdrivers before he arrived.

"I know, I know," Tunnel stammered. "I'm hardly a role model here, but you and me are different, Harry. From each other. I drink too much, but I seldom get lost. A lot of people been worried about you…"

Harry interrupted, rattling the ice in his empty glass, "Why do I hear Nora's voice right now?"

"Shut the hell up, Harry. This is me talking. Even if Nora agrees with me...*which* she does...this is still me. And don't be going back to her pissed about me talking to you. She's the best woman in this town. She's helped me a lot. But this is still just me talking to you."

Harry did not disagree with Tunnel. He knew he was slipping closer to an edge, almost like he was back in Atlanta. He knew that St. Augustine was the end of the line for him, but he also knew that Tunnel would not understand his despair about the world around him. It was more than his son. It was more than his career. It was more than the war. But, especially about the war, Harry knew that Tunnel would not understand.

He was angry. He wanted things to get better, not worse. He wanted to do the one thing that his parents had told him was the reason he was born, the reason anybody was born. His father had said it first, but his mother made him remember it: "Harry, we're all here to make things better for somebody else. Sometimes how you make things better is by doing good things. Sometimes it's just being a good person, which makes things better for those around you. You're responsible for yourself, but everything you do is like a pebble tossed in water. You might not see them, but there's always a ripple." Harry could tell Tunnel what his mother said, word for word, and he would agree with all of it. But he would not understand how deeply Harry understood his own failure. That was the edge he was at. *I could throw a goddam boulder in a pond, and it would sink without a single ripple,* Harry wanted to say as his friend talked to him. *How to win friends and influence people was all I wanted, like that damn book I read in college, but a son and wife hated me, my bosses were glad to see me go, and I wash up on the beach here with a Buick and a hundred bucks. Good omens that day, some good times since then, but I haven't come much further, and a world without me in it will not be any different.*

Harry listened to himself whine while Tunnel kept talking like he was pitching himself for an appearance on Oprah.

"You need balance, Harry," Tunnel told him. "You don't need to stand up straight. Not the same thing. Hell, look at me. But you need to reach some sort of position and maintain it. You keep drinking like you do and your ass will fall completely over. Lean all you want, but keep your balance. Does that make sense?"

Harry almost laughed because he knew how hard Tunnel was struggling for the right words. Even though what Tunnel had, perhaps even intentionally, just said made perfect sense, Harry knew that his friend had not really heard himself. But they both soon stumbled into an agreement. They, and lots of people around them, were all a little off-kilter. All of WWHD probably needed professional therapy. But it was their home. And, so, what if? What if the inmates were running the asylum, so what if a parrot named Jimmy Buffett lived at the studio, so what if Toby Lankford screamed "Yee-haw" at the end of some Mahler symphony, or Jack Tunnel sang "God Bless America" at the drop of a hat, and Nora James seemed to be channeling Martha Stewart and Gloria Steinhem at the same time... who really cared?

"In the big picture, Harry, and you know my vision is sharper than yours so I see this much clearer than you, in the big picture we are little bitty pixels."

"You've been reading my mind, Jack."

"I thought I told you to shut the hell up and listen to me. You think you're the only loser who's rolling a stone up a hill? Get over yourself. More important than that, take care of yourself. We need to make a deal, because I want you to stick around as my punching bag. So, come on down, let's make a deal."

Harry heard the splash of a porpoise jumping out of the water near the boat. A hundred yards away, the Bridge of Lions was being raised to let a giant yacht sail under. The food from A1A had been as good as Jack promised. Harry looked at the lights across the bay as he spoke, "I want my old world back. Not the one I had before I came here in 2000. I want the world I had from 2000 until those planes hit the Towers. That was less than a year ago, but I was really happy then, those first months in town. The first time in a million years, I was happy. Go figure, eh?" Tunnel did not respond, so Harry continued, "How about this as a deal? Six ounces of vodka a day for me, all at once or spaced out, but no more, and you, *mon*

Cap-etan Stubben, you stop at two six packs a day..." Tunnel began nodding very quickly. "...and you lose fifty pounds."

Tunnel grunted, laughed, and broke wind almost simultaneously, "Screw you *and* the horse you screwed yesterday, Harry Ducharme."

"You want me around, Jack. I want you around too."

Tunnel cleared his throat and muttered softly as he stood to clear off the small table between them, "I'll try."

"One more thing," Harry said, rising to help clean the table and take the dishes to the galley below, "If that sonuvabitch Bush gets re-elected next year, all deals are off, and I start shooting Republicans."

Tunnel shrugged, a plate in each hand, "Relax, pardner. I thought you were a pacifist. Regardless, as sharp as we are, I don't think we can steal two elections in a row."

Harry Becomes a Local,
and a Dinner Guest

Tunnel did not lose weight, Bush was re-elected, but Harry still held himself to six ounces a day, measured out every morning in a plastic water bottle. Nora would mock him as "the very soul of self-discipline," but she did not try to convert him to abstinence.

Harry described himself as a stroke victim. Brain damage, near death, slow recovery, and a permanent limp on one side. He would never walk straight again, but he would not fall over. Isn't that what Jack Tunnel had prescribed? Regain some balance, keep walking even though your old self is gone. "All metaphorical," he explained to Tunnel, "the stroke analogy. But it's what you wanted, right?" Tunnel was pleased, but still talked to Harry like he was a personal trainer at the gym, "What I wanted? Me? Harry, you gotta want it more than me. You gotta do the reps. You, my liberal stroke victim, *there's* a metaphor for you, all you people are stroke victims, intellectual cripples, but you are still your own man."

If Jack Tunnel was a Gold's Gym of encouragement, Nora James was a Beverly Hills spa. Harry preferred her approach. The meals were much better.

He walked to her house several times a week for dinner, losing weight even though her meals were never low-fat. Sometimes he would go in the late morning and sit in her kitchen while she did her program. He wondered if any of her listeners ever knew that her cat Pitty Sing was walking all over the counters while she cooked. Nora was a messy chef. Sauces would drip or fly, her fingers would go in the dough or pot and she would wipe them on her apron or lick them clean, with the fingers going back all over the food. Harry did not care. He ate like a king. But he usually had to stay and help her clean the kitchen. And he was usually there when Dexter Lee showed up to claim any uneaten food, and there was usually a lot since Nora cooked in bulk, and he would take it to a homeless shelter or the St. Gerard House for unwed mothers.

Nora also introduced him to her private St. Augustine world. Dozens of people that Harry had known before he met Nora, all of whom had told him that they either never met her themselves or that they would not reveal her whereabouts to him. But 9/11 had been Harry's ticket to Water Street. Unlike almost everyone else, however, Harry was one of the few outsiders who had seen the photo room in Nora's house. "And that," she assured him, "won't happen again. And, if you're smart, you won't ever let Dex's father know you've been in there. Those are his personal pictures, not for gawkers like you, Harry."

"When do I get to meet his parents?" Harry had asked her. "Your mysterious landlord."

He had been joking, but Nora was not amused. "You will meet them when I want you to meet them. And you will be on your best goddam behavior, Harry, or you won't step foot in this house again. None of your sarcasm, none of your *the world is going to hell in a hand-basket* routine. The Lee family is sacred to me. All of them. Even Dex's Hollywood aunt."

It took time, but Harry would eventually have dinner with the Lees. Still, he always had the feeling that it would have happened sooner if he had not made that first remark about Nora's mysterious landlord. He told Captain Jack about his gaffe, and Tunnel grimaced. "Well, at least you didn't make any jokes about how Nora's program never has any commercials."

"She's always talking about restaurants or food products or cookbooks," Harry responded, "So I figured that she did what you and me and the others do, make it sound like it was just part of the conversation, not a paid plug."

"You did *not* hear this from me, Harry, but the Station Manager let it slip a few years ago that Nora's entire program is sponsored by Abraham Lee. Anything good that Nora says about something is strictly from the heart. And I got the feeling that old man Lee covers a lot of other station expenses too, just to guarantee Nora's spot."

"Have you met him?" Harry asked, remembering Nora's confession about removing Abraham Lee from the virgin category, assuming that Tunnel did not know, but wondering if Mrs. Lee did.

"Never," Tunnel replied, but he did not look at Harry when he said it.

Nora's dinner parties were St. Augustine urban myth. People heard about them, but evidently nobody ever attended. First rule of Nora's dinners? They never happened. People heard from other people who heard from other people who had heard about other people being invited. Until he met her, Harry had never gotten used to the idea that nobody would help him find Nora. They would talk about her, and a few, like Michelle and Jack and Polly, actually admitted knowing her personally. Even her appearance was a subject not to be discussed by the few who knew her. In the beginning, Michelle would tease Harry that he had been in the same room with Nora many times and never knew it, or that Nora had come to The Tavern "just after you left." Tunnel had heard that and just shook his head. "Michelle, lord love her and her bosoms, is yanking your chain, Harry. She knows how much you want to meet Nora, so she gets you all tingly with some sort of where's Waldo game. But you can take this to your Prosperity Bank… Nora James has not been out of her house in ten years, or more. Hell, for all I know, she might be a vampire, just like the Station Manager."

And so Harry waited for his invitation to an official Nora James "did not happen" dinner. It finally came, but a long time after he had breakfast with her on 9/12. Nora told him that he was to be the guest of honor at the first dinner to which he was invited. It was a coming out party that would make him part of Nora's private world. She knew about his obsession with his own first name, his fascination with comparing himself to other notable Harrys, so, except for Jack Tunnel and Dexter Lee, all the guests for his first party were named Harry. All of them already knew, or knew about, Harry Ducharme. Those that knew him had never admitted to him that they had known Nora all along.

Harry Jacalone, one of the Jacalone brothers who operated the garage on San Marco Avenue, where Ducharme's Buick was well known and lovingly tended. Harry Hellas, a photographer. Harry Upchurch and Harry Upchurch Jr., father and son attorneys. Harry M. Lage, a bookseller. Harry J. Hahn, a very short television reporter. Harry Reagan, from Jacksonville. Harry D. Andreu, Harry R. King, Harry C. Horner, and Harry J. Wilson, all professors at Flagler College. Harry J. Reardon, a County Supervisor. Harry Fleming, a retired postman. Harold "Harry" George, a librarian. Harry Nydick, from Jersey. Harrys to the left, Harrys to the right. But when Nora introduced the last Harry in the room, her guest of honor was speechless.

"Harry Ducharme, I want you to meet Harry Waldron," she said, repressing a smirk.

Harry looked at the smiling man, who appeared to be just about his own age, and then he glanced at Nora, sensing something in her tone of voice that made this new Harry special. As the two men shook hands, Waldron, who obviously saw the confusion in Harry's face, explained, "I own the Curb Mart over on 16. Nora tells me that you've been there, and I'm supposed to say hello to you from Polly too. You remember her?"

Harry nodded, flashing back to his first morning in St. Augustine, the morning of omens, and then he remembered the photo of young Polly and young Nora in the room only a few feet away from this covey of Harrys. Shaking Waldron's hand longer and more tightly than he usually did, Harry looked for Nora, to see her standing behind Jack Tunnel and looking over his shoulder toward her guest, an immensely pleased expression on her face that could only be interpreted as "who, *moi?*"

Other dinner parties followed. There was no pattern, except that Nora insisted that everyone dress up. No jeans or shorts, regardless of the weather outside. Sumptuous food, an alcohol buffet, and not to be repeated conversations—those were the Nora staples, and Harry always looked forward to another dinner. Soon enough, he was old news in Nora's world, and he always enjoyed those rare parties when somebody new, as he had been, was first invited and introduced. The house on Water Street sometimes had a feast for twenty in the Robber Baron dining room with Tiffany stained glass windows. Most of the time, however, the gatherings

were small, four to six, not including a few regulars that Harry could antici-
pate. Him, Jack Tunnel, Dexter, and Polly Jackson were often together, but
Tunnel once feigned anger at Harry because, "Ever since your loser liberal
ass showed up, I get invited less." Harry had wanted to tell Tunnel what
Nora had told him. Ever since 9/11, Captain Jack's morning show had become more jingoistic and bellicose, and Nora was tired of Lee Greenwood
music. Still, when Jack and Harry were together at Nora's there was never
a sign from her that she was irritated with the Captain. Harry pointed out
to her that Jack was almost a different person when he was in her kitchen,
more likeable, more calm. "Just like you, Harry," was her response. "But I've
already done all I can do with Jack. *You* still need some more work."

Harry's favorite dinners, besides the ones at which he and Nora were
alone, were those when Polly Jackson was a guest. Polly's presence made
it possible for Nora to totally relax. The two women evidently had a long
history, and Harry, like all the other outsiders, was privy to bits and pieces
only. The two women were like teenagers again, giggling and whispering,
acting as if any male in the room was an object of pity. Tunnel was their
easiest target. He would try to be funny around them, but they always
found a way to embarrass him. Polly had once complimented Harry on
his Buick, asking him when he was going to take her for a ride. Tunnel's
leering quip was, "You mean his Black Stallion, Polly-wolly. You want him
to give you a ride with his Black Stallion?" Polly hated being called Polly-
wolly, especially after Captain Jack had trained Jimmy Buffett to squawk
"Polly-wolly want a cracker?" every morning on his show, right before his
lead-in to Nora, when he knew that Polly would be listening. But as soon
as Jack started making Black Stallion jokes at dinner one night in front
of Harry, Nora chimed in, "Black Stallion? Isn't that what you call your
vibrator, Polly? So tell me, Jack, is it true that Harry has already given you a
ride with his Black Stallion? Was it fun?" Jack was more embarrassed than
Harry thought possible.

Polly was unique among all of Nora's guests. She was the only one
ever allowed to bring any food from the outside, and it was almost always
dessert, almost always chocolate, and always sinful. As one dinner wound
down, Nora had sat on the kitchen couch with Harry as Polly cleaned the

table. Harry was talking to Nora, but he was watching Polly rub her fingers on the dessert dishes and lick the leftover chocolate. She would let a finger linger in her mouth, or her tongue would wrap itself around a dripping tip, oblivious to her audience. Harry was thinking about the first day he had seen Polly back at the Curb Mart when Nora slammed her fist into his shoulder, "I expected better from you, Harry. You're not fifteen anymore." He felt a blush come up from his loins, but Nora would not let him off the hook. "You should have seen her when she went skinny-dipping years ago. A heart-breaking perfect body. Of course, here she is now, forty years and four kids later, and she still has you guys getting zipper burn. Life is so not fair."

Harry always thought that Nora was encouraging him to ask Polly out for a date. It was an attractive possibility, but Harry resisted. From the moment he had entered Nora's kitchen, he had wanted to take *her* out. To start over again. Nora was not interested. Ever. Harry had asked Jack if he knew anything about Nora's past love life, anything to explain her lack of interest in him, or anybody. Was there a *personal* explanation for why Nora had exiled herself into the house on Water Street, a house haunted with a locked room of photographs?

Tunnel told him to be nice to Polly if he wanted to know about Nora. "I've known Nora for about ten years, as long as she's been at the station, and that's as long as anybody else in town has known her, or about her. I came to work one morning and the Station Manager tells me about the new show that I'm supposed to do the lead-in for. And that's Nora. Me and the rest of town get introduced to her at the same time. But unless you've been to that house, as a guest, you've never seen her. Harry, I figure less than a hundred people actually know what she looks like, and as you know, they ain't talking or sending out Polaroids of her."

"But, Polly?" Harry had said, realizing that he himself had refused to talk about Nora whenever some stranger asked him about her.

"All I know is that she and Polly go back to the beginning of something. You want dirt about Nora, you gotta vacuum Polly," Tunnel laughed at his own pun, but then turned sheepish. "You don't tell Nora I said that, or Polly either, okay?"

Harry had gone to see Polly at the Curb Mart, trying to be subtle about his motives. Polly was happy to see him, but, as soon as she realized that he was there to talk about Nora, Harry realized that he had hurt her feelings. *I thought I had stopped doing that,* he snapped at himself.

Polly was more generous than he deserved, he knew that, as she smiled again and told him to meet her that night at the Blue Goose in Lincolnville. Harry had to ask for directions.

Lincolnville was the black section of St. Augustine, and the Blue Goose was the blackest bar there, even if the outside was painted blue. Iron bars covered the few windows, and "No Loitering" was painted in huge white letters on the outside walls. In smaller lettering was "Members Only." Walking into the dark interior, the first thing Harry saw was a faded, barely legible sign saying *No Guns or Knives.* Harry and Polly were the only white people inside. She had had a Blue Goose membership since Nixon had insisted he was not a crook.

It was early on a Wednesday, and the Goose was almost empty. The ancient bartender was barely tall enough to see over the counter. His head was mostly bald and he had bushy white eyebrows. He did not look at his pale customers, keeping his gaze level with the glasses as he poured their drinks. But he knew Polly, and she introduced Harry. The old man just nodded, never looking up, but he said, "Pleased to meet you. Heard all about you. My name's Pete. Any friend of Polly is always welcome here. You be our guest."

Harry looked around the Goose. A small stage, some floor space for dancing, lots of tinsel and streamers on the walls, reflecting color from the few overhead lights, a cracked mirror behind the bar, a pool room off to the side. It was not The Tradewinds, nor The Tavern, but Harry slowly felt comfortable.

He had wanted to talk about Nora, but Polly began to talk about herself first, and Harry found himself forgetting Nora for the first time in weeks. Polly's life was a combination of under-achievement but profound happiness. Four kids, two ex-husbands, and her first grandchild on the way. Harry's only disappointment in Polly was that she was a chain smoker. He asked her if she had ever thought about quitting, and she frowned, "A few times, but I'm hooked, I guess, even though it ruined my sex life with Mike, my second."

Hearing the word "sex" from her, Harry must have blinked, giving himself away. She smiled at him, resignation in her voice, "You don't smoke, do you, Harry?"

He shook his head.

"Well, that's the story of my life. All the good ones are gay, married, or non-smokers."

Harry tried to change the subject. "How long have you known Nora?" he asked.

Polly sighed again, "Gay, married, non-smokers, or they're in love with Nora."

"I'm sorry, Polly," he tried to apologize, but she waved her hand and proceeded to tell him as much as she was ever going to reveal for a long time.

"I've known her for a lot of years. We went to work at the same place at the same time. She delivered my last two babies, and she got me my job at the Curb Mart. She beat up my first husband, my first ex, when he came at me when I was carrying my third baby, and she has never ever passed judgment on me for any of the shitty dumb things I have done with my life."

Harry waited, but Polly merely turned back to the bar and motioned to Pete for a refill. Finally, she turned back to him and asked, "You play pool? Fifty cents a rack, loser pays. You up for that?" Not waiting for an answer, she walked into the pool room, her hips swaying. Harry followed, putting two quarters in the slot on the side of the table.

He broke, and scratched. Polly called solids and sank her first four shots. Harry admired how her bottom stuck out as she leaned forward to line up her cue. Polly knew he was looking. She beat him in less than five minutes, grinning as she blew the imaginary smoke off the tip of her hot fingers. She had one last thing to tell him about Nora, and then she told him to rack the balls again.

"Harry, anything important you want to know about Nora, even the stuff I know, you're going to have to hear from her. You might be special, who knows. But if you're like most people, you'll wake up without any of your own secrets still secret and you won't know anymore about her than you did before. My most true advice to you? As much as I love her, and you will too, Nora doesn't love anybody but herself. She will always keep her emotions, and her secrets, to herself."

Harry shot back, "You mean like how Dex's father lost his virginity?"

Polly rolled her eyes as she chalked the groove between her thumb and forefinger, "Jesus, Harry, I said Nora's secrets, not mine."

Harry almost froze in place, the tip of his pool cue resting on the felt surface of the table. Nora had led him one way, Polly was leading him another. Somebody was not telling him the truth. The Goose was filling up, and the recorded music was getting louder. Polly stood at the head of the table, leaning forward to break, a cigarette magically suspended on just her lower lip. Just as Harry lifted the rack, she rifled a stroke and the balls scattered with an explosive crack. The four black men at the other table turned in unison, each of them, like Harry, mesmerized as the balls caromed off side cushions, collided and ricocheted off each other again, and then, first the six, and then the ten plopped into the same corner pocket. Harry looked up at Polly in time to see her exhale smoke out her nostrils. "Since you think you already know so much about Nora," she said, her eyes concentrating on the two ball on the other side of the table, "maybe you can tell me what her real name is. Can you do that, Harry Ducharme?"

Fact Becomes Fiction
Harry Looks for the Right Word

The shift from fact to fiction had been subtle, even to Harry. There was no announcement. No new format advertised. No conscious decision. Harry's first clue came in the form of an advance reader's copy of a new novel sent to him by the Algonquin Press. "We hope you'll share this with all your listeners. With your permission, perhaps we can also use your comments as a future blurb? We'll be listening."

When he casually mentioned to Nora that he was starting to get review copies of new books, she asked him if he was so self-absorbed that he did not even listen to himself on his own show. "I mean, Harry, you even read the first fifty pages of a Graham Greene novel last week! You thought you were talking about Iraq, but you ended up talking about film adaptations of other Greene novels. And, excuse me, but how many times can you quote Emily Dickinson? You got a thing for her? I'm beginning to get jealous."

The clearest turning point was the election of 2004. After a week long rant about the failure of the American education system, the mass media's shallow and cowardly coverage, and John Kerry's head being up his rectum most of the campaign...all of which had led to Bush's re-election... Harry lost half of his invisible listeners, and more than half of the sponsors he had carefully cultivated over the years. The Station Manager was not pleased, especially after the bomb threats, and even Jack thought Harry had gone too far. "And if the Captain thinks you went too far, you are *really* out there."

Thus, it ended. A career of social and political opinions. Harry told himself, *The twenty first century can kiss my ass goodbye. Bush wins. The people have spoken. The bastards.*

But he also knew it was like a marriage gone bad, when one of the partners was still in love with the other. Harry had learned to love America when he was young in Iowa, and he had once told an audience that his father had "introduced" him to the country he would fall in love with. Walks around Springdale, conversations with Thomas Jenkins, stories of John Brown, Joe Ducharme had been Harry's matchmaker.

In the Seventies, he had met a woman who shared his passion for politics and history, married her, and "then she voted for Gerald Ford." It was a good line, about her voting for Ford and them getting divorced a year later, and it always got a laugh, but it omitted any mention of Harry becoming a major contributor to the campaign of Jack Daniels.

By 2004, Harry had switched affiliations, gone foreign, and started voting for Piotr Arsenieyevich Smirnov, but ended up electing his cheaper nephew Popov. His new listeners did not notice. When his political audience vanished, Harry barely noticed, except for him getting almost no call-ins on his show. He started reading books, calling himself the Dick Estell of north Florida. But he never read an entire book. A page, sometimes a chapter or two, and then he would turn into a teacher again, his first career, and he would talk about themes and plot and symbols and metaphors and characters, and then he would discuss an author's personal history. He spent a week reviving Fitzgerald, reading entire short stories and all of *Gatsby*, ending the week with *The Crack-Up*. "You lose points for lack of subtlety," Nora had told him Saturday morning.

He had to admit to himself his own limitations. He had little knowledge of world literature except for the standards of any undergraduate survey course. He was slow to appreciate poetry, but he worked hard to catch up. He knew more about nineteenth century American fiction than twentieth century, and even a patient invisible audience would only tolerate just so much Hawthorne and Melville and Crane. So Harry began reading more and more contemporary novels, more new releases, discovering writers he liked, choosing to simply ignore those whose work disappointed him. If a book got mentioned on his show, it was always good in Harry's opinion. He loved to find a new writer's first novel and rave about it. He fell for Haven Kimmel and John McNally and Andrew Greer and Elise Blackwell and Patrick Ryan and George Singleton and Keith Donohue, dozens of others. And then there were the writers who had been publishing for years, but always below the faulty radar of best seller lists, like Bob Inman, and Harry loved to introduce them to his listeners as if their fifth novel was their first. And that is when the review copies started arriving at WWHD.

Harry had an epiphany about writers the more he talked about them. Unlike politicians or political pundits, writers would talk on-air *anytime!* Two in the morning? No problem. Midnight? *You give me the station number, I'll call.* By 2006, as much as Harry insisted that nobody listened to his show, publicists would call him at his apartment and offer authors up for an interview. And the review copies piled up at WWHD. Jack Tunnel was bemused, "These folks must be desperate for attention. Especially if they think you and Oprah are kissing cousins."

Harry and Jack would go drinking together, and it did not matter if it was The Tavern or The Tradewinds or the bar downstairs under the A1A Aleworks, sooner or later somebody would yell at Jack to "keep giving 'em hell, Captain," while Harry's frequent greeting was, "Harry, you read any good books lately?"

His place in the small pond of St. Augustine seemed settled again, and he was forgiven for the politically indiscrete boat-rocking of his early years. His opinions now mattered, as long as they did not touch a political third rail. Guests at Nora's dinner parties would talk about the books Harry mentioned, agreeing or disagreeing with him, sometimes recommending titles for him to consider. Diana Smith, the owner of the last independent bookstore in St. Augustine, but out of business before Harry hit town in 2000, was a frequent guest of Nora's, and she was wistful, "I sure could have used you ten years ago."

Eventually, Harry talked about more than books, but never politics. He would read the obituaries every night from that morning's *St. Augustine Record*. Sometimes he would call the deceased family and get them to tell him more about that person, to share with his listeners, especially letters that that person might have written. Jack accused him of "getting too damn morose about people who croak," but he also insisted that Harry devote an entire show to Captain Jack himself when he died. "You can be my official audio biographer, Harry. Just talk to Nora first, she's got my papers."

Harry would interview local artists, musicians and painters in particular, getting them to talk about how they worked. He would advertise art walks on Friday nights, music festivals in the Spring, author readings at Rona Brinlee's *Bookmark* bookstore up in Jacksonville. He would even plug any gig for a local band of teenage E-Street wannabes, admiring and envying their dreams. However, he resisted the many invitations he got to do remote broadcasts. *Come down to our gallery early, Mr. Ducharme, and broadcast as our patrons arrive for the opening. Wouldn't that be interesting?* But, truth was, Harry was not interested. The bigger his audience got, the more he withdrew from St. Augustine itself. He parked his Buick at the Flamingo Apartments and could walk to WWHD. He could walk to Nora's house. Except for sorties out with Jack, Harry's geographic world shrank to the size of his broadcast studio. He became a night person.

After dinner one night, Nora asked him if he was finally happy again. The only other guest, as usual, had been Dexter. The young man was cleaning the kitchen, still juiced on too much espresso, listening to his iPod, seemingly oblivious to the well-fed adults on the couch. Harry had already told Nora as much of his life story as he had ever told anybody, sometimes without her even asking. This night, she had a more specific question.

"Talking about books, not the war, not politics, not the news, is that better? I mean, you *seem* happier. Certainly a lot calmer. Am I wrong?"

Harry had to be at the station in an hour. He was expecting a call from a writer in New Orleans, a woman who hated touring but who wrote wickedly funny books about her hometown. He had been thinking about the upcoming interview when Nora brought him back to her couch.

"Happy? Sure," he began, but knowing that Nora would expect more. "But, you know, it's all relative. I only had one way to go, right? Up. You get in a hole, you either get out or dig deeper. I'm getting out."

"That's it?" she said. "That simple?"

"Nora, what do you want from me? Do you want to know why I read so many books? And, tell me, is that a bad thing? I mean, there's no hidden agenda here. I'm not really trying to save literature in America. Too late for that, trust me."

Nora's cat Pitty Sing was curled up between them on the couch, its tail swishing back and forth even though its eyes were closed. "I was just wondering, that's all," she said, nudging the cat off the couch with her foot as she swung her legs up to lay both her feet on Harry's lap. He knew what she wanted. He began rubbing her ankles and the soles of her feet, deep massaging the flesh. As long as they had known each other, it was their only physical intimacy. "Just seems to me, Harry, when I listen to you on the air, that you are talking to yourself more than to anybody else. You're in Harry's world, and the rest of us are all just visiting."

He kept rubbing her feet as he looked over to see where Dexter was, and then he started to explain, only to stop himself. "I just think that..."

Pitty Sing was purring on the floor. Dexter was humming along with his music. Nora closed her eyes and waited. But Harry talked to himself, a low voice inside him that he was hearing more and more since his son died. *I think there's an answer somewhere that somebody else has figured out. That's all. Some combination of words that will make this world make sense. If I read enough, go back and re-read what I was too young to understand, if I do it long enough then someday I'll see how I fit in. Some "meaning" is out there, some design. Some connection to me. Somebody has already put it into words. And when I find those words I'll know why I'm here. That's all. I don't even need my own words. I'm not a writer, not creative. I just need the right words. It doesn't even have to be a sentence, perhaps a single word. Somebody has written that word. I just need to see it.*

He did not expect anybody else to understand, not even Nora.

Harry and Nora Adopt Dexter
The Peril of Parenting

The transformation of Dexter Lee after 2001 was to become the subject of much conversation among his parents, brothers, and friends. He had always been pampered by his parents, Nora had told Harry, but he was not a spoiled child. Sickly as a youth, hovered over by those parents, he had never seemed to grow up. He was not immature, but he seemed to, Nora's word...*drift*. When Harry had first met him at Nora's front door, Dexter had seemed a handsome young man, with the perfect combination of Asian and Caucasian features, but, in the following weeks, as Harry got to know him better, he seemed, Harry's word...*callow*. But the more that Harry knew him, more than weeks, into months and years, the more Dexter evolved.

Drift...callow...promising...Dexter King Lee had been a string of comparable adjectives, but he had become an enigma since 2002, with the most common description of him being prefaced with, "Who would have ever thought that the boy I knew had become so..." and the adjectives changed.

Nora insisted that some of the credit belonged to Harry himself. "You're his surrogate father, Harry. He listens to your show all the time, and he reads the books you talk about. And Lord knows he talks about you all the time around me." Harry would object, but not too much. It had taken a few years for him to see the change in Dexter, and in himself. Harry knew a lot about politics and literature, but the long curve of his life had taken him away from those things, what he knew best, and then back again. Any knowledge he had gained in his life had been rendered irrelevant by his character. That was his judgment upon himself. *Gifts squandered*, he told himself, and he compared himself to Fitzgerald, only to laugh at his own vanity. *At least Fitzgerald left something good, something bright and lasting*, he would admit to himself, on too many "mornings after," *and you, Harry Ducharme, will leave jack shit*. The lowest point was the night before he finally met Nora. Starting with the morning he met her, however, Harry had slowly crawled back to the earth's surface.

After 9/11 he had once pledged to become a dry man for the first time in thirty years, a possible transformation not cheered by Captain Jack, who did not like to drink alone. "You can stay on that wagon as long as you want," Tunnel had said as they had sat at The Tradewinds, "But you sure as hell better not get sanctimonious on me. I might be embarrassed by supporting Bush, but no form of penance you want from me about that will involve a change in my drinking habits. Hell, with him still in office, I might have to drink more."

When Harry had announced to Nora in her kitchen that he planned to quit drinking, she said, "I'd hug you, but then you'd fall in love with me. And how would we tell the children?" He knew exactly what she meant. In some ways, Dexter had become their child.

"I'll make you a bet, Harry," she had said, walking by him toward the sink, bumping him with her hip as she passed, "As soon as you tell Dex, he'll quit drinking too." Harry's expression was a question. Her answer was not subtle, "Not all your influences on him have been good."

Harry had protested, "You know, if you thought that all this time, you could have said something."

Nora had sighed, remembering a conversation from her past. "Dex's father, his original and, trust me, his real father, once tried to make me share responsibility for something *he* had done. I told him then what I'll tell you now. I'm just a tourist. An outsider, watching the local scenery. You've always been a free man, Harry, able to do anything you wanted. But, wrap yourself around this profound insight from a woman who lives in her kitchen...drink, or not drink, it was never just about *you*."

Harry kept drinking. Six ounces was his definition of abstinence.

Dexter had already graduated from Flagler College before Harry met him. He had also spent two years in the Peace Corps, teaching English in Columbia, refining his own Spanish. He had hitch-hiked across America, ignoring the absolute disapproval of his parents. He had informally apprenticed himself to a carpenter and plumber, and then taken those skills into Lincolnville, where he went door to door volunteering to do odd jobs for free. He also used those skills to work on his parents' rental properties. He worked at the Food Bank, the Free Medical Clinic, and he coached Little League baseball. He did all those things, but, except for the Peace Corps, he never did anything for longer than a few weeks. He was well known in St. Augustine, and well-liked, but the older he got the more his friends wondered, *Where's he going? And why is it taking so long?*

Nora told Harry all about Dexter as she prepared for her 2003 New Year's Eve dinner, and his first question was, "And his parents? Do they ever worry about his future?"

Nora shook her head, scattering flour out of her hair, but keeping her hands in the *crepe* dough, "God, no. Dex is their baby. His two older brothers will make their mark in the world. For sure. But if you left it up to Abe and Grace, he would never leave home." Anticipating Harry, she added, "Yes, he still lives at home. Yes, he's almost thirty."

The first extended conversation between Harry and the young Lee did not happen at Nora's house. Instead, Dexter had called Harry during his show a few weeks after 9/11. Harry had not thought about him since they first met, but it was late and Harry had felt himself merely going through the motions of a show. With Dexter as a listener, and then conversation partner, Harry's energy level rose. Mostly, Dexter simply asked questions, setting up Harry for a long answer or a rant, but he never ran out of questions. By the middle of 2002, Dexter was coming into the studio at least once a week and sitting down with Harry, sharing his orange juice, putting on the head-phones, telling Harry about an article that he had read.

At the Tavern one afternoon, in 2004, a meeting that Harry kept from Nora and Dexter kept from his parents, Harry had asked him if he even recognized the change in himself. Dexter had shrugged, looking down, but then he looked up and sighed, "I don't know how I was in the past. Who

I was. But something's changed, you know? I'll figure it out soon enough. Lots of time for that."

"You can't put time in a bottle," Harry had offered, enjoying his own allusion to Jim Croce, lifting his glass to get Michelle's attention.

"What do you mean?" Dexter asked, charmingly young in Harry's eyes.

"An old song lyric," Harry said, loud enough for Michelle to hear as she poured his refill.

"And that's you in a nutshell, Harry, an old song lyric, and you know *the* song" she laughed, reaching for Dexter's glass.

Dexter shook his head and put his palm over the glass. "No thanks. Two's my limit, especially since I promised Nora I would get Harry home safe...," seeing Harry jerk his head around, "...relax, she doesn't know we're here. I just made her a blanket promise about not letting you drive."

Michelle set the bottle down, reached into her apron pocket, pulled out two quarters and handed them to Dexter. "Go punch G-12, Harry Chapin sings about Harry Ducharme. Let's watch *our* Harry cry." Then she turned her back to the two men, singing badly, "Hello, honey, it's me. W-O-L-Deeeeeeeeee."

Of all the qualities of Dexter that Harry liked, it was the young man's curiosity that most appealed to him. Introduced to music that Harry or Nora had mentioned, Dexter would come back after listening to more by the same artists. If Harry discussed a book on his show, Dexter would read all of it and sometimes call in or come by the studio to question Harry. Eventually, the Station Manager let Harry train Dexter for his own show, eight hours on the weekends. Dexter's format was eclectic, so a listener never knew what to expect, but for that reason there was never a consistent audience. Harry and Nora understood Dexter's approach. It was like any other job he had ever had. He did something until he got bored, and then he found a new focus. Music mostly, from Swing in the Thirties to New Age in the Nineties, Big Band to Acid Rock (for one show only), Rock and Roll from the Fifties and Sixties ("You might be right, Harry. Good music died in 1973.") and movie themes. Dexter loved movies. If Harry thought that books held an answer for his own questions, he thought that Dexter was looking in music or movies for the same sort of key. But within six months of having his own show, Dexter announced that he was dropping off the air.

Thinking about his abrupt departure from WWHD, Nora suspected that Dexter's parents had expressed some sort of subtle disappointment about him working there. Harry was not sure about that, but, then again, he had not met the parents, so all he knew about their influence was what Nora told him. When he asked Dexter himself, he was told, "Harry, my parents love me too much to make me give up anything that makes me happy. It was my decision. I just thought I would like to get out more often. Something about the radio wasn't for me. Too much being alone in a tiny space. I guess I like being around people too much."

Harry told Nora about that conversation, and she grimaced, "You think he was talking about you, about turning into you?" Harry shook his head, but he found himself more self-conscious around Dexter anyway. Being aware of his influence on Dexter also made Harry more aware of himself. 2004 then proved it was all pointless anyway: the facts and opinions and history and logic and evidence. Bush was legally elected for the first time, and Harry slowly began to educate Dexter about the difference between *opinion* versus *interpretation*.

June 27, 1969

11:00 PM

Stonewall Inn

Peter Winston

He thought that this June night was to be no different. Even with all the whispers about police harassment, the trumped up arrests, the increase in patrol cars cruising up and down the street, he had still promised to be there for the bartender's fiftieth birthday party. As soon as midnight came, the hats and horns and giant strawberry cake were supposed to be delivered by a chorus line of men in Rockette drag.

Sully, the bartender, and a conscientious AA member, had told Winston, "I sure as hell wish I had a death wish just so I could drink myself into a stupor tonight." Turning fifty was not a milestone he had ever wanted to celebrate. Peter Winston had a twinge of doubt about whether the surprise party was a good idea or not, but the die was cast.

"Cheer up, Sully," he told him, "Alive at fifty is better than dead at forty-nine."

"Damn profound of you, Pete, coming as it does from a man who ain't seen thirty yet."

The two men laughed, and Winston raised his glass of water in a toast to a man soon to be older than his own father. "To you, Sully Crane, the stone sober rock of Stonewall."

Sully shrugged and muttered, his voice barely audible because of the music, "Head full of rocks." He turned to fill an order that had been shouted to him from the end of the bar, and then, a drink in each hand, he turned back to Winston, "Forgot to tell you, there was a man looking for you the other night, said he was your brother, said he would be back tonight."

Winston shook his head, "Must be a mistake. I haven't got a brother."

"Well, he sorta looked like you. 'Course, that is, if you got a negro brother."

Winston turned and saw the black man across the crowded room, over-dressed in a dark suit, surrounded by festive men who seemed oblivious to his presence. Winston blinked, and then the black man was gone. He looked around. The black man was talking to Sully, who was pointing in his direction. *So, at least he's real, if Sully can see him,* Winston told himself. The man walked toward him, and Winston recognized a charcoal version of himself. Sully had been right. The man approaching him could be his brother.

The man sat next to Winston and swiveled on the bar stool to face him, extending his hand, "My name is John Darby. I have heard that you are a good man, and I would like to talk to you."

Winston looked up at the Heineken beer clock over the bar. An hour to go until tomorrow. He realized that he felt very tired, that his entire young life had finally exhausted him. He felt older than Sully. "You want to talk, to me?"

Darby reached for a bowl of peanuts that had been sitting on the counter, took a handful, and then shoved the bowl toward Winston, "Are you hungry?"

Winston was defensive, "Are you selling something? Are you a cop? Did somebody send you? Did...," and he stopped himself, before he said his wife's name. "Sorry. I'm being rude. But, seriously, I don't know you. You're not a regular, and there's a lot of...stuff happening lately, some good people getting entrapped. You know what's going on, you do know?"

The black man nodded, motioning for Winston to send the peanuts back his way. At the end of the bar, Sully waved at Winston, pointed to the black man, and gave a thumbs up sign.

Darby reached inside his suit coat and pulled out a white handkerchief to wipe his hands and face, then he said, "I need your help. Not now, but in the future. Far in the future, when you think your life is almost over, I will need you."

"This is bullshit!" Winston said, thinking he was being set up for a practical joke, "You need my help? Gimme a break." He kept looking at the man next to him, waiting for him to respond, but Darby kept silent, until Winston tried to provoke him.

"Look, there's a party here in a few minutes, some good times, and then I'm headed out. If you want to sell me something, or enroll me in the Foreign Legion, whatever, you better get to selling, because I am outta here…," looking back at the clock, "… in two hours, and I'm going to be busy until then."

"You need to stay until closing, Peter," Darby said calmly. "Your wife Molly will be asleep until the morning. For the future to happen, however, you must stay here much later than you planned. Indeed, the future for you and the others here will begin in…," and then he looked at the clock, "…three hours."

Winston went cold, and then hot, and then quiet. This man knew his wife's name. He looked at his hands, and then around at men in a world that had never seemed larger than the room they were in. "You're not one of us, are you?" he whispered.

Darby turned to face him, "Of course I am. As your child will be, and his mother, and everyone else. We are all *us*, Peter. You came here with the news of her pregnancy, her joy and your great apprehension. You were going to tell the others. That news will wait. So, please stay with me here tonight and into the morning. Molly will come for you then. You will tell her the truth, and she will help you heal your wounds. She will not forgive you, as you will ask of her, because she knows that which you hide and hold in contempt about yourself does not need to be forgiven. You are not evil, nor are you sick, but you are hurt. As the world is. The future begins in a few hours, Peter, and it never ends. So, take joy in your life as you are, and when your child's child is born, you will see me again."

Darby's last words were drowned out by a drum roll and then the belching umpapa-umpapa of a tuba. The Stonewall doors had opened and in marched a Joel Grey impersonator, singing *Willkommen*, followed by a male Sally Bowles, who, just as he was about to announce that life is a cabaret, was punched by Joel Grey, who had come to an embarrassing revelation, "My God! We're at the wrong faggot party! Back to the limo, Dink, and…," with a bow and a flourish to a suddenly confused and quietly stunned Stonewall audience, "…and to you, my sweet princes, *adieu* and a good night."

Winston was as stunned as anyone else, and right before he turned back to the bar he had a feeling that the black man would be gone, but he was wrong. Darby was simply looking in the mirror.

"This isn't what I expected," was all that Winston could say, and, hearing himself, he muttered, "And that, I'm sure, is a giant under-statement."

Harry and Jack Have A Threesome
St. Augustine Listens
The FCC Sleeps

With his new emphasis on books instead of politics, Harry also began to like Jack Tunnel again. He had missed the friendship. Even though they had still talked almost every day from 9/11 to 2005, the two men had danced around the news of any hour. Jack had even stopped calling in to Harry's show to haze him. Fiction was neutral territory, however, so Tunnel felt free to give Harry a hard time, even when he could not totally avoid politics.

Only once did they go too far in the view of the Station Manager, and that was when Harry let slip his dream date. Jack knew just enough about writers to be appalled. He had to call the station as soon as Harry admitted that he wished he could take Emily Dickinson and Flannery O'Connor out for drinks. That would be his dream threesome, but he had not meant it sexually. He even said he would pick up O'Connor and drive her to Amherst if Dickinson still did not want to leave her house. He then got on the studio computer and map-quested a trip from Milledgeville to Amherst, telling his listeners the directions. Until Tunnel called, Harry had thought he was merely filling up air time.

"Are you drunk again, Harry?" Tunnel huffed into the phone at first. He was calling from The Tradewinds, so he soon had to yell. "Your wet dream date is two spinsters and you. A cripple and a bug-eyed recluse, and you?"

Harry was impressed, "Jack, I'm surprised you know that much about them. I figured…"

"You figured I was a goddam illiterate, right? Like all us conservatives?" he shouted happily, and the few listeners that Harry had at that moment began calling their friends to drop everything and tune in to WWHD. "I've read a few books in my life other than Bill O'Really and Sean Hammerty. And you *have* mentioned these women a few thousand times on your show, as if we gave a damn about their last words and curriculum V-ties."

"Jack, good to hear from you," Harry said, downing the almost empty glass in front of him and wondering if he had some back-up in the studio refrigerator. "But you gotta remember. I'm talking about conversation here. A *ménage a tres lingua.*"

"You are talking trash, friend. You cannot tell me that you would not hop in the sack with them if they dropped their drawers for you," and even Tunnel started to laugh at that image, choking himself for a few seconds. Still gagging, he told the Tradewinds bartender to shut off the recorded music and switch the overhead speakers on to WWHD. It was Tuesday, a slow night in every bar in St. Augustine.

"Wild nights, Wild nights…were I with thee…uh, uh…rowing in Eden… might I but moor…our luxury… the chart…, or something like that," Harry struggled to remember the exact words, laughing along with Tunnel, happy to forget the outside world, enjoying life again, so he asked what he thought was an obvious question, "Okay, Captain Limbaugh, if you could have a date with any two women who would you choose?"

It was the wrong question, but great radio. Tunnel did not hesitate.

"Oh, hell, Harry, I get my sheets in a knot every-time I think of me and Ann Coulter and Nancy Grace doing the wild thing on my boat."

Harry Ducharme, the few dozen patrons at the Tradewinds, and countless unseen listeners all over north Florida all had the same reaction, articulated by Harry, but only after a noticeable dead-air moment for WWHD. In the studio, the three phone line lights were blinking like a nuclear meltdown warning. Harry had a more comforting thought than six ounces of vodka and a quart of orange juice had ever afforded him. The answer to the big question: where's the sense in all this? It now all made sense. He was in a Manichean existential world. Not good or evil, but sane versus insane. Perhaps, profound versus trivial. And, down deep, pointless. All we could do was enjoy it. He spoke slowly.

"Jack, the mind boggles. The mind staggers. The mind is absolutely fascinated. Would you care to continue?"

The cat was out of the bag, the barn door could not be shut, the invitation was hand delivered.

For ten more minutes, all duly recorded on the WWHD master control, as everything was recorded, Tunnel described sex between him and Ann Coulter and Nancy Grace. Who's on first, who's on top, bony Ann and fleshy Nancy, with Jack in the middle. Nancy in the middle, rasping commands and critiquing performance. Ann with a bag full of sex toys, daring Jack to make her beg. Jack spanking Ann while Nancy was spanking him.

Harry tried to interrupt him, but he was also goading him on, and he had no defense the next day when the Station Manager reminded him that "all you had to do was hang up the phone."

Tunnel talked like he had the freedom of tenure. The FCC be damned. Ann Coulter and Nancy Grace were in his stable, and he meant to ride them. He ignored the occasional groans from his live audience in the Tradewinds. He ignored the leather-skinned swinger Ashley as she slithered toward him, as if a crone in heat. He ignored the beeping on his cell phone telling him that he had calls waiting. Pressed by Harry to change the subject, Jack delivered the line for which he was known for the next few weeks in St. Augustine, to be shouted at him as he entered any establishment. In response to Harry's admonition to stop, he said breathlessly, "I'm almost there. Don't stop me now." Instead of "Give 'em hell, Jack," his temporary entrance shout was to be, "Hey, Jack, you there yet?"

Back in his studio after that exchange, Harry kept quiet most of the time, punctuating Tunnel at times, hoping to slow him down, but not really caring. Looking at the clock in his studio, he realized he had another hour to go before Carlos came on duty. He wanted to go to the Tradewinds and drink with Jack, his self-imposed limit ignored for this special occasion, but he knew it would be closed and Jack would probably already be back on his boat. Listening to Tunnel go into more and more detail about his tryst with the blonde sirens, Harry always knew how to get Tunnel to calm down. When it came time, just as Jack was about to go gynecological, Harry interrupted him, "Jack, I thought Ann Coulter was a man. I mean, look at her hands and that jaw. She's an anorexic man in drag, isn't she?"

Tunnel was silent for a second, and then the tone of his voice changed, "This is girl/girl and me, Harry. I'm not into sharing. Especially with another guy."

Harry heard The Tradewinds crowd cheer in the background, but within a minute the conversation was over.

September–2007
Harry and Nora Go to the Movies
A Hurricane is Forecast
A Change is Coming

Harry wasn't sure he had ever been in love anytime in his life. He did not date in high school, and so avoided the usual initiations of adolescent drama, the certainty of a first true love. He dated in college, lost his virginity, dated a lot more, and had a serious long-term relationship with a senior when he was a sophomore. She graduated, but she did not wait for Harry. He remembered their last conversation. They used the word *love* as they had done before. But she left anyway, and he did not cry.

Evelyn, his first and only wife, was different. She was funny, and she thought Harry was funny, a trait he had never thought applied to him, but there they were…making each other laugh. She was smart, unlike a lot of the girls he dated, and the sex was the best he had ever had. Bed-breaking and bone-throbbing good. They were stoned when they first met, stoned when they got married, and, as she told him after their divorce, "our mistake was going straight." Too simple, he knew that, and the booze did not explain everything either. All he could figure out was that they must never really have been in love to begin with, and having a son together did not compensate for that. The mother loved the son, but not the father.

However, even as they grew apart they still had sex, and the less that she cared about Harry, the more Evelyn seemed to enjoy herself in bed with him. It was a contradiction that Harry noticed, but he did not analyze it. He simply enjoyed it. Even a few years after they divorced, with the right mood and situation, they had sex again. But then Evelyn met a man who was, in her cruelest truth to Harry, "all the man you never were." Harry would repeat that line a hundred times, and it always provoked a groan from whatever sympathetic audience he had, but he never admitted to anyone what he had said to Evelyn when she said that to him: "You're probably right."

She re-married and she never allowed herself to be alone with Harry ever again. It was not a fear of temptation on her part. She simply did not want Harry to have *any* illusions about her feelings toward him. In time, Harry understood. In time, he was glad she had met her new husband. She deserved to he happy, and that man made it happen. If he had never really loved Evelyn, Harry had always cared for her. But, Lord, he missed the sex.

When he started his radio career, Harry discovered how easy it was to get a woman in bed, as long as he was famous. He seldom heard "not tonight." Still, he had no illusions about his own sex appeal. He assumed it was the public Harry Ducharme that was so damn charming, not really him. And he always assumed that he would find the right woman and get married again, that love was finally going to happen to him for real.

"We are each the love of someone's life"—he had read that opening line in a wonderful book late in his life, and he wanted to call the writer and tell him that he was wrong. He wanted to tell that writer that he had a better line, a line that a naked woman had said to him as they sat in a hot tub in Tulsa, early December, on a porch that overlooked a yard that seemed to stretch all the way to Dallas. They were drunk in the tub, taking turns shooting her pistol at trees in the distance, naming each branch for a mistake in their past lives, and she said, pistol in her hand, "Harry, you're like a lot of guys I know. If you just shot your dick off, you'd be a happier man." Harry had considered that line the most profound he had heard in years, but he also knew that drunken wisdom was easy. He had liked that woman, and knew she would not be hurt when he answered, "You tell that to your husband too?" She had pointed the gun at him and smiled.

When he reached his mid-forties, Harry had his last serious conversation with his son, who was about to graduate from high school. Adam wanted his parents to sit together at the ceremony. Harry and Evelyn had compromised. Her husband would sit between them. Adam was satisfied, but then had asked his father the awkward question, a question that his parents thought they had answered years earlier: *Why did you divorce?* The official explanation, evidently, had not registered. Harry had looked at his son, seeing his and Evelyn's features looking back at him, and he was as honest as he could be. "I screwed up. I drank too much. I ignored your mother too much. I was a crappy husband and a pretty lame father. Both of you deserved better, and she had the courage to make it happen. And I owe you both an apology."

Adam had nodded, pushing his long hair away from his face, but he was still not satisfied. "But didn't you love each other?"

Harry had almost stammered his answer, "I don't...think...so."

"You're a bastard, dad," Adam had hissed, and then he stormed off.

The question had been unasked for a long time after that, and it only became relevant again after he met Nora. A question he first heard the Everly Brothers ask in the 1950s, on the radio at his uncle's house and on the car radios of his friends. *When will I be loved?* For a long time, Harry knew the answer—never. But it did not matter. Life went on. He always knew what love was *supposed* to feel like. After all, he had read about it in a book, lots of books. It had taken almost a year after meeting Nora, however, before he knew that he had been asking the wrong question. It should have been: *When will I love somebody?* And then the cosmic irony of his life became obvious to him. He had finally fallen in love...truly and deeply...with a woman who did not love him. Why?

"Harry, I need for you to take me for a ride in that big car of yours. Jack tells me that the mother of all hurricanes is coming, and there's something I want to see again before I get blown away. And, I promise, I won't bring Pitty-Sing along. I know you've never forgiven me for the last time."

The stories about Nora never leaving her house were not true, but it *was* true that nobody ever saw her out of her house. At least, nobody ever said they saw her. But her dinner guests, only when they were in her house, would tell each other stories about Nora doing something with them away from the Water Street house. She had even cooked dinner for Jack on his boat, disproving his earlier assurances to Harry that she was a ghost in St. Augustine. But, still, any life she had away from her house was, as Dexter told Harry, "Nobody's business except hers."

Harry wondered about the others. Did they love her too, as he did? How could they not? But wasn't that merely…*love*? What he felt had to be different, surely, because he had never felt this way before. He had once tried to talk to her about it, as they walked on the beach after he finished his show, but she had leaned into him and sighed, "You're sweet, Harry, but you don't really love me. You don't even know me." The walks had been their secret, not known even by Dexter. Harry would finish his show at two in the morning and then drive over to pick her up, and they would go to Vilano Beach. Full moon nights were best, but dark nights had their own mystery. They would look for the lights of shrimp boats and listen to the waves lap in on calm nights, the surf pound in on windy nights. Harry would talk, and Nora would listen. A few hours, perhaps only a few times a month, but five years of walking on the beach in the dark had convinced Harry that he must be different from the other people in Nora's life. *Surely, he told himself, I am different.* Some nights they would take folding chairs and just sit without talking. They never touched. The best nights were those when Nora finally talked. She never talked about her past, but she was generously insightful about the world that Harry shared with her in the present. She would "explain" the other "guests" in her life, and Harry wondered if one of the reasons that he felt he was different from the others was that she eventually shared secrets about those others with him. As if he were a co-conspirator. *Surely, this makes me different.*

She had told him that she wanted to take a drive up A1A toward Jacksonville, "I want to show you something, and then you can ask me any question you want, and I'll tell you the truth."

"Why do I feel like Diane Keaton in *The Godfather*?" Harry laughed. "Married to the mob, is that me? And we both know how that turned out."

"Harry, just pick me up after my show, and, please, vacuum out the Buick."

A1A ran parallel to the Atlantic. Where the dunes were low or the sawgrass was sparse, Harry could look over and see the ocean as he drove. He had been up and down A1A for years, but he had never paid attention to the spot that Nora wanted him to see. As they drove this late September afternoon, after her usual comment about how much she liked his car, she pushed the heat button for her side of the leather front seat, telling Harry that she was cold, turned and propped her back up against the passenger door, leaned back against a pillow she had brought along, put her feet in his lap, and went to sleep. Harry had not noticed at first, staring intently ahead because A1A was very narrow and the traffic was usually hostile to speed limits. But once he looked over, he had a hard time keeping his eyes ahead. Nora was thinner than she had been a few months ago, a goal she had told him about, and her face was closer to the face he had seen in the pictures of her in the Water Street house. She was an attractive woman, but she had been a beautiful young woman. Her sleeping face this afternoon was the younger Nora. Looking at her, he drifted over the center line of A1A, and was brought back to driving attention by the horn blast of an oncoming car.

"Stare much, Romeo?" Nora said without opening her eyes.

The road curved inland. How many times had he gone by without really seeing how much? It made no sense, a wide swing away from the ocean, probably a quarter mile deep, and a vast expanse of undeveloped ocean-front real estate, a prime location for more condos, but empty except for what seemed like a small shack at the north edge.

Nora had told him they were almost there, to slow down, and then she pointed, "There's a turn to the right, probably not marked, but it's there. Pull in and stop. And get my umbrella out of the trunk, please."

The few times Nora had been out in the daylight with Harry, she had always carried an umbrella to shield her from the sun. Harry had once made a joke about her being afraid to get as tan as Ashley Ass-Lick, and

Nora had visibly shuddered as she said, "That woman is toxic trash." It was an uncharacteristically uncharitable comment, but Harry did not disagree.

Harry was fascinated by Nora's fixation on this spot. She stepped out of the car and walked toward the ocean and then stood under her portable shade, not speaking. When Harry caught up to her, she still did not speak until Harry forced her, "When do I get my question?"

She said, "Stand here, do not move, while I go over there," pointing to a spot about two hundred feet away. Once there, she called back to him, "Notice anything odd about the spot you're standing on?"

Harry looked around and shook his head, so she said, "Head out of the clouds, Harry, and look down."

He did as told, embarrassed because he thought he had missed something obvious, but a moment of concentration still did not show him anything. He looked back at Nora, signaling his confusion, and then he saw it. The sand between him and her was oddly flat, and there was a noticeable drop-off to the ocean side and the north and south edges, but those drop-offs marked three sides of a giant rectangle, as if he and Nora were standing on the edge of a sand-castle stage and the distant ocean was…well, he thought, *what about all the hard sand between here and there? That quarter mile?*

"Dig down in front of you, Harry, just bend down and dig," she shouted at him from across the stage.

"I better find oil," he tried to joke, but he did as told. A few seconds of pulling sand up and tossing it aside were enough to hit something hard about a foot under the surface. Not oil, he found concrete. He was still down on his knees, looking toward her when she told him, "Now, come over here and dig right here."

More concrete was what he found at her spot, and then Harry could visualize how enormous the concrete slab must be beneath their feet.

"This is your dance ticket, Nora, I'll follow wherever you lead," he said.

She smiled at him, not a trademark smirk, but a smile that said she was glad to see the face in front of her. "Harry, this is all that's left of the world's biggest drive-in theatre. From here to that other corner, that's how wide the screen was, and a hundred feet high, and out there...," sweeping her hand across the empty space in front of them, "...was room for hundreds of cars."

"I don't believe you," Harry said, not as a prompt for more information. He just could not believe such a screen tower existed.

"Oh, God, Harry, this is the truest thing I'll ever tell you. Relax, enjoy the story."

She had worked at the giant theatre in 1968. Dexter's father had grown up living inside the screen tower with his parents and sister. Nora said that she had come to work for them the same day as Polly. There was also a mad dog named Frank who lived in the room above Dexter's father. And all the employees had apartments in the tower too. It was her first real family. Fireworks on the Fourth. A clumsy pilot named...*Harry* Lester. And she knew that Harry Ducharme would appreciate that small detail. A young man named Gary Green who had died years ago. A series of choppy details, all ending in a giant fire that had consumed the theatre, but Nora truncated the plot, telling Harry that she would say more later, but she was tired, the heat was getting to her, she was dizzy, she was thirsty, would he please take her back to the car and turn on the air conditioning. As he held her arm and helped her up the sandy slope to his car, he remembered what she had said that first morning they met.

"The thing you said about Dexter's father, the man who owns your house...," he started, but she anticipated the rest.

"Is that really the question you want an honest answer to?" she said.

"For chrissakes, Nora, you'll know THE question when we get there. This other stuff is just..."

"Just blanks to be filled in, I know. I'm sorry. I mean, I had this big scene all scripted out for us today, but it's not working. I really don't feel well. But I can tell you this. The only other person who knows the story is Polly. Be nice to her. I've made her my official biographer. She'll spill the beans if you ask her sweet, but only to you. I made her promise that."

Harry knew it was the obvious opening. They had finally reached the Buick, and the air conditioning was medicinal. "About Polly, I was wondering. She told me that it was her who was the first time for Dex's father."

125

Nora stifled a laugh. "And she believes it. But that was the public story I created. Abe's sixteenth birthday, I was twenty. On that beach over there, on the darkest night of June. Polly thought she was seducing him the *night* of his birthday. I set them up. But he and I were together a few minutes past midnight, as soon as it was officially his birthday. I was his secret first. And I told him to let Polly believe it was her. You have those mistakes, right, Harry, the things that seemed like a good idea at the time. I was a mistake for Abe. I thought I was so in control of everything around me. I wanted him as a trophy. I was a cliché, Harry, and I did the wrong thing. If I had been a good person, I would have helped Abe save himself for Grace. But I treated everybody around me as a game...," and she stopped, looked over her shoulder toward the ocean again, and for a split second Harry thought he was going to see Nora cry.

He reached for her hand, and she let him hold it, an act she had usually resisted in the past. "Well, this is more than I expected you would ever tell me. You're not exactly known for sharing yourself, you know. But there's lots of time, Nora. You don't have to tell me anything you don't want to right now...,"

She jerked her hand away from him, almost seething, "No, goddam it, there is NOT lots of time. There is never going to be enough time, Harry, not for me, not for you, not for any goddam anybody! And if you think that anything I've told you comes close to telling you the true worst things I've done with my life, then you're a fool." Harry stiffened, and her mood swung again. "Oh, here I go, Harry. I'm sorry. I'm a mess. I just wanted to show you this place because you are special to me. And I don't even understand why you are, but you're..."

"Different?"

"Sure, Harry, in a lot of ways. Does that make you feel better? Being different?"

He nodded, genuinely pleased to have her grant his wish, and then, just as he was about to ask her if she wanted to go back to her house, he was jarred by the sound of a loud tapping on the driver's window behind him. Turning quickly, he was almost nose to nose with an old black man who was motioning for him to roll down the window.

"You folks okay? Saw you parked up here, thought you might need some help."

Harry was trying to pull up the face, to remember where he had met this man, when Nora said, her voice noticeably happier than only a few seconds earlier, "Hey, Pete, how are you? And how come you haven't come to my house for dinner lately? Do you know…,"

The man extended his hand into the car for Harry to shake, "I certainly know Mr. Ducharme. He's a regular down at the Goose."

"Harry Ducharme, you tramp!" Nora was almost giddy as she feigned anger. "You *have* been seeing Polly, and behind my back, you've been cheating on me. But you know what, I bet you that even though you met Pete at the Goose you still don't know who he is," shifting her attention. "Am I right, Pete?"

"Yes, Miss Alice, he does not know me."

Alice?

Harry turned back to…*Nora?*

"Pete's the caretaker for this property. One of the original employees. If you look closely at the far edge of the property, you'll see his house. Well, his caboose. He lives in a caboose, and *that* is another great story. Me and Pete go back a long time."

"I'll leave you folks alone. Just wanted to make sure you were okay." Pete said, saluting with a finger to his forehead, and then he walked back to the beach.

Harry did not speak. He just looked at the woman across from him.

Alice?

She looked at him and sighed. "Park across the street, Harry. You still have a free question, as I recall."

He had seen a picture of the cemetery in the room at Nora's house. But the picture had had a tight focus, only a few tombstones. Parked at the rusty iron gate, directly across A1A from the old theatre site, he could absorb the entire lot, what seemed to be an abandoned cemetery. But that was only a faulty first impression. The stone fence was sagging, with shrubs like a greenish brown virus, all over the walls and obviously not trimmed in years.

But once he and Nora passed through the iron gate the scene changed. The grounds were immaculate, and the ground sloped up to a small peak, so that the graves near the top of the slope seemed to have a clear line of sight to the ocean, an unobstructed view of the sun as it rose every morning. Palm trees and cedar trees provided intermittent shade, and the manicured grass was un-typically lush for north Florida.

Harry started remembering other pictures back at Nora's house, specific tombstones with specific names, and here they were in real life.

"In case you're wondering, Pete takes care of this place too," Nora offered, but that was not the question on Harry's mind.

"Alice?"

"Nora," she said.

"But he said…"

"Nora, my name is Nora," she interrupted. "Alice is gone."

Harry looked at her, and then realized that the temperature around them was cooler inside the gates than on the outside. Almost pleasant. "But Pete said…"

"Pete, lord love him, is probably a hundred years old, and his mind is stuck in the past most of the day."

"So, who are you, really, and what is your real name? Even Polly told me that she knew your *real* name, so why not me? Why not tell me?" Harry persisted, "And why are we here?"

"You and your name fetish are a subject of much conversation among many of your friends. Do you know that? How weird you seem to them? Still, I'll make a deal with you. I'll tell you my real name if you tell me yours."

Harry blinked. It was not a question he could answer.

"I know your story, because I've heard bits and pieces every time we have dinner by ourselves. Your parents, the ones you adore, are real, but they're not the first, right? Those early years are gone. Isn't that what you tell me? The person you were is gone, and that person had a name, but it wasn't *Harry Ducharme*, and after all these years you still don't know, do you? It's probably in black and white in a hundred court documents, but you've chosen to NOT be that person. So who are you? You weren't born

Harry Ducharme and I wasn't Nora James…so what? A name is just a name. I might have been named Alice a long time ago, but she's gone forever. And thank god for that. She was miserable and she did awful things. Trust me, Harry whoever you are, you wouldn't have liked Alice as much as you like me. Trust me, sweet Nora James is a goddam saint."

Harry cocked his head to the left, and then he shook it as if he had just surfaced from the bottom of a swimming pool. Nora was waiting for him.

"So, I guess we're back to my other question. Why are we here?"

Nora laughed weakly, "Oh, there's a straight line if I ever heard one, especially coming from you."

Harry took her hand and led her to a bench under a covey of palm trees. Sitting down, they talked until the sun moved enough so that the shade disappeared, but long enough for Nora to tell Harry why they were there.

"This land caused a lot of trouble a long time ago. Dex's grandfather owned it and Grace's father wanted it for a cemetery. Old man West had his funeral home next to this land, but his sons sold the business years ago. The building is gone, the sons are in Jacksonville, but they kept this land. There and there…," she said, pointing to the top of the slope. "…Abe's parents are there, and next to them are Grace's parents. Grace's mother had been buried in Georgia, but when her father died she had her mother brought down to be with him…"

"And you knew all these people?" Harry wanted to know, knowing that Alice was part of that history.

"I know a lot of people here, Harry. I'll take you for the tour later. Show you the stone for that Harry Lester I told you about, a grave without a body. I'll even show you the stone for Frank the crazy dog. Abe's sister insisted that Frank have a stone too. She almost killed herself trying to save Frank from the fire, but…and you'll love this…that old fireman you interviewed on your program about Vietnam, Fred…he saved her life back then, running to get her right before she was able to rush back inside the tower to get a dog she loved but who everybody else hated. Just one of the stories about this place."

The more Nora talked, the more she seemed to feel better. Harry pointed out how her voice even seemed to get stronger.

"Oh, it wasn't all bad, life back then. Hell, except for all the death and destruction, it was fun. There were times, in fact, when I wasn't even miserable." She stood up. "Come on, I'll show you something."

She led him up the hill to look at the tombstones. The names were all part of the story she had just told him. Looking down at one, Nora noticeably sighed. Harry said nothing, not even when she asked him, "You want to know something about Alice?" She took his silence for a yes. "You'll keep this to yourself? Be my priest, hear my confession." He nodded without looking at her. "She wasn't as rotten as I describe her, and this story won't make sense to you, but it was the best thing she ever did for somebody else. That man right here, Abe's father."

"The father of the boy whose virginity you took?" Harry could not resist the gentle jab at Nora, assuming that her apparent good mood at this moment had smoothed over some of the anger she had felt toward herself earlier.

She stopped talking, and Harry thought he had made a mistake. Another example of him talking without thinking.

"Well, if you put it in *that* context," she finally said, but without an edge, "I suppose you can handle the truth unvarnished. I was Abe's first, and I was his father's last."

Harry's brain stuttered and stammered and generally short-circuited. He did not ask her to repeat what she had said even though he knew that it all had to mean something other than the obvious: whoever she was, this woman had just confessed to having sex with a father and son.

"Harry?"

He kept looking at the tombstone in front of him, and the one next to it, husband and wife, grandparents to Dexter.

"Harry, you still like me? Love me?"

He turned to look at her. "Nora, or whoever, why do you seem to want me to NOT like you? Why tell me things that you think will push me away? Isn't that what you're doing? We're both almost sixty. Why would you not want somebody to love you?"

"Somebody did love me, a long time ago, and I loved him…," she whispered, looking at the grave, and then barely audible, "… but I wanted more."

Harry got angry. *This* was it? The reason she had gone into a shell. He had no moral high ground to judge others, he knew that, considering his own mistakes, but he wanted to raise his voice, *You brought me out here to show me this? To make me feel even more foolish that I already felt? You think I would think this was…normal?…just water under the bridge?*

Nora looked up just at the moment that his face showed the most anger and confusion, and she quickly reached out to touch his hand, "Oh no, Harry, I'm not saying any of this right. You're not understanding. No, no, the man I loved, that was someone else. Far away from here. Not Abe's father. No, of all the things I did a long time ago that you might have hated, going to bed with…," and her voice slowed down, from fatigue, or perhaps a desire to be clearly understood. She began again, "I had gone away after she died, Abe's mother, and then, maybe ten years later, Abe found me and told me that his father was dying too. I came back to see the old man one more time because he and his wife had been very good to me that summer in 1968. Better than any adult had ever treated me. By the time I came back, his mind was going faster than his body. Oh, Harry, he thought I was his wife. I was like her in a lot of ways, tall, same hair, and I could talk about the past, but he kept talking to her, not to me, the Alice I used to be, and he was so happy to see his wife, so sadly happy, as if she had never died, and I became her for one night. A few months later, he was dead, and I was gone again. Still, it was the last good thing that I ever did when I was Alice."

Harry stopped himself before he spoke. In the past two hours he had learned more about Nora than she had told him in the previous six years. He knew that if he said the wrong thing now, he would never learn anything else. He stood next to her, seeing her get older again, not like she was as she slept in his car, and all he knew was what *not* to say. All he had were questions.

"Dexter doesn't know, does he?" and as soon as he said it he knew the answer. It was a silly question to ask her.

"Dexter doesn't know about me and his father, and Abe doesn't know about me and *his* father. You're the only one who's got the big picture."

"How about Polly, your official biographer?" he said, with genuine affection.

"I was kidding about that, Harry. She knows a lot of the dirt, but not all the important stuff. Polly put me on a pedestal a long time ago. Soon enough, I liked being up there. And for all her bed-hopping and assorted other bad habits, down deep she's a very moral person. I don't want to disappoint her. I mean, it took her a long time to forgive me for some other stuff. Why press my luck."

Harry had a hundred other questions, but he knew that she needed to go home. On his list, however, he added one more as soon as he decided to take her back to St. Augustine. Nora always referred to the house on Water Street as her "home," not the "house" that Dexter's father owned. It was her home. And then he realized that everything he had learned about her life, even the facts about Alice at the theatre across the street that no longer existed, all those facts began when she was twenty. It was as if she had no history before then, and there was still a gap from then until she returned to St. Augustine.

"Is this why you wanted me to bring you here, to tell me all this?" he asked as he helped her through the gate toward his Buick. Just as they reached the car, she finally answered him as she turned to take one last look at the cemetery.

"Not really. I was going to tell you a few things, mostly about the old theatre across the street, so you would know more about Dexter's parents. Pete showing up threw me off, but I suppose I would have asked you to take me here soon enough. And, no, telling you about my dirty laundry wasn't on my agenda. Shit just happens, Harry, isn't that true? No rhyme or reason."

He wanted to agree with her, but it would have contradicted everything he had been feeling for the past few years. Surely, shit did not *just happen*. If it was all just shit happening, then where was the sense of it? Harry wanted things to make sense. He wanted Nora to help him figure that out, but he was wondering now if she was just another lost soul, somebody like him. Clueless and blind in St. Augustine. Life had to be more than just shit happening.

"I suppose so," he lied. "But, still, why are we here?"

Nora smiled, almost the old smirk he had seen the first morning he met her, a smirk which said *I know more than you do and it's going to be fun watching you find out.* "Here's the deal," she told him, "Dexter's parents want to meet you. Better late then never, I suppose. I'm their rep, conveying the terms."

"Terms?"

"They're worried about their son, and they want your help. They know that you have a lot of influence over him. He'll listen to you more than them. And they know that you'll sit down with them if I ask you to do it."

"Dex has them worried? The boy is wonderful, everybody knows that. And he seems damn happy. Are they tired of him living at home, is that it? And why would they think I have any influence over him?"

"Well, Mister Angst and Anguish, as you are known by your fans, Dexter, for whatever reason, thinks you're the smartest man in town, and you've inspired him. Abe and Grace are holding you responsible, and they want to talk to you."

"Responsible for what, Nora?"

She cleared her throat and told him, "There's an election next year. The state House representative we've had since before Claude Kirk was governor is retiring. Open seat. Dexter wants to run for office."

Harry put both his hands on top of his head and muttered under his breath, "Jesus Christ, where did *that* come from?"

Nora would not let him off the hook. "Jesus Christ yourself, Harry, the boy hangs on your every word, reads all those books you talk about, and he believes the things you say. Come to think of it, Harry, have *you* ever listened to *yourself*? On the air, it's as if you are somebody else. Even Jack is impressed, but not about to admit it to you, that you seem so smart and that you make sense out of how you read those books and poems. And you think that nobody pays attention? All I know is, you did a number on Dexter, and his parents will be expecting you sometime soon. They're not happy about their son's plans, and you have a lot of explaining to do in front of them."

"They're not happy!? Nora, I'm not happy. That's a totally bad idea for Dexter. I don't need to have his parents convince me to convince him to drop those plans. I'll do it for free."

"No, Harry, you don't get off that easy," she said as he opened the car door for her. "You're still talking with them. And you *will* be on your best behavior. You will *not* use one obscene or profane word in their presence. You will respect them and their home. And you sure as hell will not talk about me at all. You know nothing about me and Abe, *capiche?* These people have their own story. Your story is different. The only place your stories overlap is with Dexter."

"And you?" he asked. "Aren't you a connection too? Or, at least, the person who you used to be?"

"Which is exactly why you're going alone, Harry. I have too much respect for Grace to intrude on her life."

"She knows about you and her husband?"

"Her heart knows it, and for that reason I will not ever chance hurting her again. This is a test for you too, Harry. If you hurt these two people, I will never speak to you again."

Driving back to St. Augustine, south on A1A, Harry watched Nora sleep again, her feet in his lap. The last thing she had said, as she was dozing off, her voice dying, "This is a great car, Harry."

Harry knew something was wrong with her, but she would not tell him. He had asked her point-blank, but she had just waved her hands and said, "I'm tired, that's all." He would have to ask Polly or Dexter, but he wouldn't be surprised if they did not know either. He knew that one person would know for sure, but he had promised Nora that he would not mention her at all when he finally met Abraham Isaac Lee.

The only question left to ask Nora was the question he had wanted to ask from the very start of the trip that early afternoon. Back on Water Street, he eased the Buick to a stop in front of the Queen Anne house and then hurried out to get around and open the door for her. He had to tap on the window to wake her, and for the briefest of moments, as she lifted her head off the pillow and turned to face the window, he saw a look that told him that she was happy to see...just him. The look of a woman waking up next to the man she loved, wasn't it? A minute later, standing on her porch as she stood in her doorway looking back at him, he asked, "Nora, are you ever going to tell me about the man you said you loved? I mean, was he the only one you ever loved?"

"Not now, Harry, but maybe sometime," she said. "But thanks for taking me to the movie, you know. Bye, bye. And don't forget that a hurricane is coming. You better stock up on the essentials." And then she shut the door.

Lincoln Motes
Iowa City, Iowa
February–2000

Hebrews 12

5 *And ye have forgotten the exhortation which speaketh unto you as unto children, My son, despise not thou the chastening of the Lord, nor faint when thou art rebuked of him:*

6 *For whom the Lord loveth he chasteneth, and scourgeth every son whom he receiveth.*

7 *If ye endure chastening, God dealeth with you as with sons; for what son is he whom the father chasteneth not?*

Jesus carried the Cross
I can carry this
Jesus carried the Cross
I can carry this

Lincoln Motes said it over and over, shifting the weight of his cross from one shoulder to the other every fifteen minutes. His first cross had been hollow, with a plywood veneer stained to look like oak, and its size alone made it impressive from a distance. But that cross was not heavy enough, six feet was not high enough, the burden too light, and Motes knew he was a charlatan. He crafted a new cross, genuine oak, eight feet tall, two hundred pounds, and if curious eyes looked closer they could see the red paint splattered at the center, where the two lateral branches joined the center trunk. Some would ask, "Why not at the ends, where his pierced hands would have been?" Motes was always ready. He knew the truth. "His heart was pierced as well, and this marks that spot." His questioners were always predictable, "You mean his side, don't you. Yes, that was pierced, but I do not recall any mention of his heart…" Motes would almost shudder with rage, no matter how many times he explained, "It was his flesh heart they pierced, and it burst at that moment his last words were uttered, ending the beginning."

February in Iowa, the test he wanted. Dressed like it was a spring day in Topeka, Kansas, from where he had come, Motes stood alone, ignoring the smirks and jeers of passing college students. He was sure that Reverend Phelps back in Topeka would approve. Reverend Phelps was a godly man, doing god's work, and Lincoln Motes was his acolyte. The calling was obvious to him. Surely he was not the only believer to know Fred Phelps and then see pictures of the martyr John Brown. Surely the same man, the same gimlet eyes, seeing the same sins, piercing the Janus souls of damned sinners and faint Christians alike. Brown died to free the slaves. Abraham Lincoln died *because* he freed the slaves. Lincoln Motes was born on April fifteenth, the day Lincoln died. His whorish mother told him how he was named. She was going to call him *Taxman* Motes because it was the IRS deadline. It was her constant taunt, him being the tax put on her by God, the five pounds of flesh ripped from her womb to punish her, to tax her. "Why else would you been born that day? God did it to remind me what I owed him," she would hiss at her son, "that you belonged to him more than me. I carried you, I bled you out, I suckled you, but you were never mine."

It was the same story every year, variations on a theme, but, as he turned ten and at last towered over her, he asked the obvious question, "So, why Lincoln?"

"It was the drugs they give me, to hide the pain, the drugs. I laid there and the pain went away, and I told them what I was gonna name you. It was the doctor who looked at me, I knew that look, seen it a million times from people thought they were better than me, and he thought he was so smart, I saw it, so smart to confuse me, talking to me without looking at me, him concentrating on you there between my legs, asking me if I knew why else the day was important, that it was the day Abe Lincoln died, a hundred years ago, to the day that very day. The damn drugs had put me out of my mind, and it come to me, you were Lincoln. After that, I didn't care. You were born. You were named. A name's a name."

Babies were dying across the street as Motes carried his cross. He had seen the whores go in, carrying their babies, but only the whores came out. If the Reverend Phelps had brought his flock to march with Motes, there would have been signs, images of the babies alive before and images of the mangled broken babies afterwards. Life and death. Life and murder. Posters and chants, promises of God's wrath from the Westboro travelers, and the sinning whores and jeering pampered college students would have turned their eyes away because the truth was not in them. They passed the charnel house every day, and they would be as Lot's wife, reduced to salt if they truly looked at the squatty red building and heard the silent screams. Reverend Phelps was right. They looked and did not see. They listened but did not hear. But Motes was alone this day. Phelps was confronting the sodomites in Oklahoma, his people on a newer crusade, pilloring those who chose sin. It was left to him to sanctify the deaths of those who had no choice. His cross was heavy, but Lincoln Motes was strong. *Jesus Carried the Cross. I can carry This.*

It was below freezing, but Motes still walked his block. If there had been wind, he might have faltered, he knew that, he knew he was merely mortal. He thanked God also for the sun, a cloudless bright day in Iowa. God was blessing him. Gratitude must be shown. He studied the sky, knowing how much light was allotted him. Another hour at the most. He kept walking. Soon enough, as twilight approached, he saw the black man.

Motes felt warmth for the first time of the day. He looked around. He was alone. There were no cars passing, no sinners walking. A convenience store at the corner looked empty. His cross was weightless. Across the street, the black man raised a hand and waved at him slowly. Was this a mirage? Motes turned a full circle. No cars, no people, no wind, no cold, still daylight, but no sun in the sky. The black man waved again and seemed to be shouting at him from across the street. Motes strained to hear, without success, so he motioned for the black man to come over. The black man motioned back, as if to ask him to come to that side of the street. Motes stood still, and he could see the black man look down at his own feet, as if in thought, and then he crossed over to Motes' side. As he walked, the air around him seemed to float in waves, as if heat were rising from the ground beneath him, as if he were walking across a desert and seen from a distance. The closer he got to Motes' side of the street, the blacker he became.

"Are you doing God's work?" were his first words to Motes.

"Jesus led me here," Motes said.

"Can you put down your cross for a moment? It must be a burden to you. You should rest, and we can talk."

Motes pondered this question. He was being tested. He knew the correct answer. "I am doing God's work. This cross is no burden."

The black man nodded, but he looked down as he did, so Motes was unable to see the true expression on his face as he spoke again, "Why are you here, at this place?"

Another test question, Motes was ready, reciting the scripture he knew best: "The Book says *'Rescue those being led away to death; hold back those staggering toward slaughter. If you say, But we knew nothing about this, does not he who weighs the heart perceive it? Does not he who guards your life know it? Will he not repay each person according to what he has done?'* Surely you understand this."

The black man nodded again, but this time, looking directly at Motes, said, "Proverbs 24: 11-12 can also be spoken thusly: *If thou forbear to deliver them that are drawn unto death, and those that are ready to be slain; If thou sayest, Behold, we knew it not, doth not he that pondereth the heart consider it? and he that keepeth thy soul, doth not he know it? and shall not he render to every man according to his works?*"

Motes was suspicious. Why would the black man distort the scripture almost into babel? "They mean the same, isn't that true? Unless your Bible's intent is different from mine." Motes' skin was warm, but he felt a chill going down his spine. He was not being tested by God. He was being tested by Satan. "Who are you? Why are *you* here?"

"I'm here to tell you that God has a plan for you, a purpose, and it will be revealed in the future. This…," and he spread both his hands as if to encompass the street they were on and the building behind them, "...is not your purpose."

"I am here to save the life of innocent children. There is no higher purpose," Motes almost shouted, sure that this man was Satan's emissary, if not Satan himself.

"Those that enter here do not lose their life, surely you understand that." The black man was stepping back as he spoke. Motes looked around. There were no lights in the buildings. No headlights from cars.

"This is my purpose," he shouted at the receding figure. "I'm not important. This work is important. I do it for God, so he will know me. I have no value. God doesn't see me...," and he became a child again, afraid of the dark, "...please don't go away. I wanted them to come with me, the Reverend and his people, but they laughed at me. Please come back. I don't want to be alone. I'm just a nobody. And nobody sees me. Please..."

The black man paused, and spoke softly, "Are not two sparrows sold for a farthing? and one of them shall not fall on the ground without your Father. But the very hairs of your head are all numbered. Fear ye not therefore; ye are of more value than many sparrows."

Lincoln Motes fell to his knees, but the cross remained on his back. The weight was crushing him. As he wept, he looked at the feet of the black man, who touched the back of Motes' neck, then leaned down and lifted the cross, whispering, "You are a sparrow, and God's eyes are upon you. As it was in the beginning, so shall it be at the end."

"I don't know what to do. You have to tell me what to do," Motes cried.

"You will come to me when you are ready. A Child of God will be here soon. Your purpose is yet to be fulfilled. You will not understand it, but it will happen. I will be at the warm water's edge, look for me there."

With a final touch, the black man stepped back into the darkness and disappeared.

II

September–2007
The Prophet Appears
Harry Asks for a Miracle

"That's not your real name, is it?"

Harry could still spot a phony a mile off. It had always been his forte, his style, his ticket to the big time. Years of practice not quite wasted. The slow foreplay of softball questions and feigned confusion, as if all he needed was just a *little more* clarification of the obvious, and then the pounce of a loaded question. His prey might dodge and squirm, but was, soon enough, *in the bear trap*, Harry would laugh to himself, *and the bastard either dies or gnaws his leg off*. But Harry's best shots were behind him, he had accepted that reality, except for the shots of Popov in the glass in front of him. His guests were no longer giants. They were now seldom more than average, except for the writers, smart men and women whose political opinions were irrelevant. The smart politicians began avoiding him years ago. After all, this wasn't New York. WWHD wasn't NPR. *Why bother?* Harry would mutter to himself that he was *talking to the lumpen-proletariat of America, and damn few of them.* He had wanted to be Edward R. Murrow, but, as Michelle had pointed out to him and Dexter that night at The Tavern, he had ended up being a late-night version of a Harry Chapin song.

"I mean, you've used more than one name, so why should I believe this one is real."

Here he was at midnight, a hurricane blowing outside, sitting across from a man who called himself Peter Prophet. Harry imagined Prophet handling snakes and quoting verse. But here he was across from Harry, not having said a word in twenty minutes. Harry had been working to fill the dead air, telling himself that he ought to win a Peabody just for doing a radio interview with a mute. He had once interviewed Prince Rainier and Princess Grace. Midnight tonight, he was interviewing a lunatic, and talking to himself. In the station office next to the studio, Jimmy Buffett was asleep.

"So, come on, just between me and you. What's your real name? I mean, who's to know. Nobody's listening. Who are you, really?"

A late-season hurricane was coming, or so the pros said, but hurricanes had been coming to north Florida for a thousand years, and they had always bounced up to the Carolinas. If he were still talking in South Florida, near the Keys, Harry would have packed his Popov and headed north or inland. He learned that with Andrew in 92. He had sat in a motel for a week after that one, his station down, his vodka stretched into potato vapors, and his core philosophy confirmed: *Mother Nature doesn't give a shit.*

WWHD's original bamboo roof had been blown off in 1972, replaced by tin, so Harry felt every BB ping of hard rain this night. The pros had predicted a storm surge of ten feet, but Harry knew what was happening. Katrina in 2005 had scared all the pros. No more half-hearted warnings. Tell everybody that End-Times was here, grab your kids and dogs and get out of Dodge. *You stay behind, don't say we didn't warn you. Your ass is your own.* Harry knew the routine. But he also knew he was safe. The WWHD elevation was five feet above sea level, but a five foot reinforced cinder block and concrete foundation had been had been added by the Old Man, who, legend had it, had predicted the Crash of 29 and Truman whipping Dewey, making a ton of money on both. If that surge came, it would be just enough to kiss the front door, and the 120 mph winds would be matched by a WWHD tower that had been double-bolted and double-tethered back in 1972. It had been the Old Man's promise to north Florida: *We Never Close.* When a storm in 74 knocked out power all over St. Johns County, making him break that promise, the Old Man added a room to the station and had a gasoline generator installed. *We Never Close.*

The only thing troubling Harry this night was the wind. Not that it could blow down WWHD, the walls were two cinder blocks thick and the tin roof had been welded as well as bolted down. Harry just hated the wind screaming. The slap of palm fronds against tin, or the yowl and thud of flying cats hitting the outside walls, those were merely entertainment; proof of the wind's power, not its soul. No, for Harry, the wind was more human than the water. It had a voice. He did not know the language, but he understood the tone.

Carlos Friedmann had called this hurricane *Diablo*, but Captain Jack was more creative. For the previous four mornings, he had grabbed the shrinking scrotum of his Republican dittos and twisted, "Hurricane Hillary is coming! Batten down your hatches. Freeze your semen and leave copies of your will with all your friends and relatives. Make sure your bullets are safe to fire another day, even if they have to use a turkey-baster. Hillary's coming and she's taking no prisoners. I've seen rain, and I've seen fire, folks, I've seen bad moons rising, and THIS windbag is the Tommy-knocker that's gonna scourge the Sunshine State. Run for your lives. Hillary's coming, but I'll be here to fight the fight for you. Captain Jack's ready to go down with the WWHD ship. That fem-nazi and me, right here at WWHD, main event, so stay tuned if you can. Pray for me. Light your candles. I need your love. And now a word from the Sally Walton Dance Studio, St. Augustine's door to Broadway. Cloggers and line-dancers, ya'll get to Sally and tell her that Captain Jack sent you."

"And tell me again, why are you here? You called me. You asked to come on my show. And tonight of all nights? But now you're not talking? This is starting to get spooky. I'm doing all the talking. So, tell me. *Are* you a spook? I mean, Halloween is a month away. Is this a trick or a treat, and what the hell is your real name?"

Harry froze in his seat. He had done it again. *But this is really it, he told himself, this gig was already the end of the line. I can't get any lower on the radio dial. And I just asked the blackest man in America if he was a spook?*

To his face? Please, god, tell me that, for once, I'm right, that nobody really is listening.

Two stations up the radio food chain, a six figure salary in the past, it was New York all over again. He had not been legally drunk then, merely oiled and careless. A conversation with a rabbi about Israel and the PLO, there had not really been a reason to use the word *Hebrews*, but he did, except that he had slurred and it sound like *Hebes*. Worse, he did not hear himself. He did not correct himself. He slurred it out and kept talking as the rabbi grimaced, and then the phone calls began. He was gone the next day, down to Atlanta, where he lost his temper in a conversation with Ralph Reed, implying that the boyish swarmy Reed was a money-changer in the Temple. From there, Harry had started walking to Damascus and ended up on the beach at St. Augustine just as Jeb Bush was stealing the state for his brother.

Except for the wind, silence. Harry stared at his guest, but the black man's face was indecipherable. Perhaps a slight tilt of his head, perhaps a squint, perhaps even a smile. Harry had a flashback: him back on the beach that first morning in 2000, still wearing his shoes, his feet planted in the sand as the ocean swirled around them and then up to his knees, coming in and pulling back, his shoes surely ruined and his feet sinking further into the sand, his pants soaked, his face looking east and the morning sun breaking over the horizon as he asked himself the perennial question of his life: *How the hell did I get here?*

Harry knew what he had to do at this moment. He had one chance to redeem himself. *I have to apologize. I have to tell this stranger that I'm a compete fool, and I need for him to forgive me.* Harry looked at his microphone and then at his guest. The two words...*I'm sorry*...were on his lips, but a simple motion of his guest's head stopped him cold.

Prophet looked straight into Harry's eyes and then slowly shook his head side to side. A slow shake that said what? Anger, or pity, surely disappointment? But unmistakable was the implicit command: do not talk.

Dead air in the studio, hurricane winds screaming outside, two men staring at each other, and then Harry's cell phone rang. He looked at his guest. Prophet nodded toward the phone. *This really is starting to get spooky,* Harry thought. He took the phone off the table and flipped it open.

Carlos Friedmann was frantic. "*Cracker Man!* I'm in deep *abano* and need your help! *Por favor?*"

Harry's body went limp. But then he looked back at Prophet, who almost seemed amused. "Carlos, I'm on the air, and in a bit of a mess myself, so you better be sitting across from Bin Laden right now."

"Worse than that. I can't get to the station tonight. My mama didn't raise no *adoquins*. You gotta cover for me. Can you do that? I'll be your best friend. Come on. Captain Jack was right. This storm is a *perra*. I'm staying home with Chickie. Come on. Four more hours. And it's not like you have anywhere to go yourself."

Carlos was right.

"Sure, I'll cover for you, but anybody calls for you I'm going to tell them that you were kidnapped by Castro."

"*Perfecto, Cracker,* but don't worry about any calls. Why you think I called your cell? Lines are down. But since you mentioned the Old Man, I have another favor to ask. And I am damn *pesado* about this."

Harry had given up pointing out to Carlos that, descended from Jewish Cuban cigar rollers or not, he was fourth generation and his first language was English, so his constantly tossing in cherry-picked Spanish was becoming a less and less endearing affectation.

"Carlos...," he started to say, wanting to get back to Prophet.

"*Mucho gracias, mi amigo.* I promised my people a big announcement tonight. You gotta deliver."

"Tell me, Senor Barnum, what should I tell your teeming *peons?*"

"You are THE man, *Cracker.* Here's the deal. Tell everybody that sometime near the end of the week, no advance warning, I am going to interview...you ready for this?...."

Harry felt good, his earlier *faux pas* almost forgotten, Hurricane Hillary somebody else's problem, his outlook on life improving simply by listening to Carlos get excited about his own ideas.

"You tell my posse that…you hear that drum roll, Harry, you hear it?… that I have arranged a secret phone interview with Elian Gonzales, straight from Havana. The little dolphin boy himself. Am I not a genius?"

When he finally heard who the guest was, Harry laughed out loud, and Prophet smiled with him. Harry then almost gagged laughing. "Carlos, you do not…"

"Oh, hell no, of course not. But you tell 'em anyway. Me and my amigo Steve Sapperstein have been working on this for a week. His Spanish is exactamento. And this will drive those Miami Cubans even crazier than they already are, 'cause Elian is going to tell everybody that he is being groomed to replace the Old Man himself. Tell me, Harry, is this going to be *muy placer*, or what? So, you and me, *socios*? This'll be bigger than Orson Welles and those Martians."

Their partnership sealed, Carlos had one last request for Harry, "Off the record, *amigo*, you got to quit drinking. You think we don't know what's in that big glass of orange juice in front of you? You've been talking to yourself for a long time on the air, even Chickie was getting creeped out, and with the phones down you won't be getting any call-ins, so you might want to take a break and play some of that old fart music of yours."

Harry and Prophet were alone again, and Harry remembered the thread he needed to pick up. Contrition was a breath away, but Prophet stopped him by leaning forward and touching his hand, speaking on-air for the first time, "You asked about my name. Let me tell you why it does not matter."

Harry had a revelation: *This guy is a pro. His voice changes when he gets close to a microphone.*

Prophet had arrived a half hour earlier. Harry had been airing a series of public service announcements while taking a bathroom break, and their introduction had been brief. The visitor's voice was different then, a low tenor, but as soon as he spoke into the microphone, it became clear bass. A slow bass, much slower and lower than private conversation, a bedroom bass.

"I am Peter Prophet now because I am about to begin the final phase of my journey. My work is almost done. I was John Bourne. I was Paul

Brand. I was Simon Goodman. I was James. I was Saul. I was all of those men, and more, and none. But now I am Peter Prophet, and I need your permission to use a poem of yours for my next sermon. That is why I called you."

Did I say spooky? Harry asked himself.

And then spookier. The black man in front of him became someone else. His face changed. All the hard edges around his eyes, the tight features in his face, they all softened, as if the man had become his own elderly father. Harry looked at the glass in front of him, blaming it again for every blurry vision of his life. The new old man across from him put his hand over the microphone and whispered to his host, "But you wanted the truth, right? You want my real name, as if that really mattered. But here it is anyway, Harry. I'm Bevel Summers. But, see, nobody wants to hear from a Bevel Summers. They want to hear from a Prophet, so I lend myself to that Prophet. And the Prophet supplies the other names that he uses in public. I'm the Prophet. That's the important thing. I'm the Prophet. I have been for a hundred years. I wish I was just Bevel Summers again. But my role is to be the Prophet. I was chosen a long time ago, and I'm soon to be released, thankfully, but not before I introduce the new Child. And I need you for that. Your permission to use your words."

Bevel Summers disappeared. The Prophet came back, took his hand off the microphone, and waited for Harry.

After another thirty seconds of studio silence, his cell phone rang. Caller ID: Carlos again. He did not answer it. Harry had never written a poem in his life, but Prophet was waiting for him to speak; that was obvious. Prophet, or whoever he was.

The goddam ball is in my court, Harry told himself, but he remained silent, riffing unspoken one-liners back at his guest, eyeing the glass of orange juice in front of him. At the beginning of his shift, the glass had had six ounces of Popov and twelve ounces of Florida's best pulp-free sunshine juice, an eighteen ounce drink to last four hours. Harry had always been a methodical drinker, proud of his pacing ability. Prophet kept waiting. The wind outside was louder. The cinder blocks of WWHD, to Harry's ear, were grunting, as if their shoulders were shoved up against a door that was too weak by itself to stand up to an assault of wolves, or barbarians. Harry smelled his own sweat. He was alone in a room with a shape-shifting madman, and the only moment in his life that was comparable was the time he had stood on his front porch, barely eighteen years old, and an Iowa State Trooper had walked toward him with news about his missing parents, Harry understanding that any news was going to be bad news, the sound of doors closing, and the present was about to become the past.

He looked at the glass in front of him, but all he could do was whisper, "I'm sorry. I have no idea what you're talking about."

Prophet shrugged and leaned closer to him, "Your spider poem, the noiseless patient spider poem. With your permission, I would like to use it as the core of my first public sermon at the Amphitheatre. And, of course, you are invited."

Harry was even more confused. "*A Noiseless Patient Spider*? But that's not my poem. I never claimed that. I always give credit. It was…"

"Walt Whitman, I know that, Harry. You told everyone when you read it last night. I had been listening to you for many days, but last night was the first time I understood you. And understanding you helped me understand myself and my ultimate purpose."

Harry was almost irritated. "You don't need my permission, whoever you are, to quote Walt Whitman. I didn't write that poem. I don't own that poem. I do not…"

Prophet ignored his protest. "As I listened to you, I felt that poem's essence, Harry. The *sense* of that poem, as you spoke, belonged to you. The truth of those lines. I have heard it before, with other lines and other readers, with music and singers, the work of one artist possessed by another. That was you last night, Harry, *possessed by* and *in possession of* that poem. Whether you understand this or not, I must now have your permission to speak those lines myself."

Harry's cell phone rang again. Caller ID: unknown. He ignored it. He then heard the explosion of something smashing against the metal roof. On the wall behind Prophet was a round white-faced clock, black hands and a red second sweep. Now past midnight, a new day, Harry thought about his feet on the beach that first morning in St. Augustine, how warm the ocean felt. He had wanted to keep walking out into the ocean that morning, to float away. Instead, he had gone to look for a job.

"Sure, why not," he finally exhaled as he looked at Prophet. "Go crazy. Knock yourself out. Lord knows, Whitman would be pleased."

"And you will be there?"

"I doubt it. I'm a little jaded about preachers, no offense to you, of course. I tend to be a little skeptical of motives, no offense to you, of course."

"No offense taken. I know your views on Falwell and Robertson and Dobson, the others. You are not subtle."

Harry leaned back, suddenly pleased and suspicious at the same time. "You're not offended?"

"I am never offended by the truth."

They talked for over an hour. Harry knew enough about Prophet to ask simple questions that could either lead to short truths or long evasions. He understood the first line of defense for all frauds, so he had to go beneath and around it. Prophet was a fraud, he was convinced of that, but a compelling fraud. Like the best frauds, Prophet believed everything he said. The longer they talked, however, the more Harry thought he might have been too harsh. If not a fraud, Prophet was surely delusional, and harmless. The acid test was money. Prophet never took a collection. He never asked for a donation. He had no church. He spoke in homes and fields, always unannounced, but his followers always seemed to know. He spoke at funerals and weddings. He had never spoken to more than a few hundred people at any one time. He spoke, and then disappeared. He had no address, no phone, and no friends, but he had followers, and those followers spread the word about his next appearance, and they avowed the truth of his miracles, lives and souls saved.

Harry was the first person who had ever formally interviewed him, and he was sure that nobody was listening. Past one in the morning, he asked about the miracles. Were the stories true?

Prophet paused before answering, cocking his head as if listening for something.

"You are an educated man, right?"

Harry nodded, suspicious again.

"You have read Flannery O'Connor, right?"

Harry nodded again, more suspicious.

"Yes, I know you have, because that is how I learned of you. Someone very close to me heard you one night. You read one of her stories, all of it, on the air. Do you remember?"

Harry slammed his fist on the table, his body quivered once, and he almost growled, "Hell, yes, I remember that night. I read one story. You know the one. Obviously. So, did your close friend also tell you that I got a call-in that night, some Christian who threatened to kill me for mocking God. And then an hour later somebody fired a few rounds into the WWHD building. All because I read a story, a piece of fiction. So you tell me now, what the hell does this have to do with me asking you about the miracles that others give you credit for? Am I going to get shot at again?"

"Harry, you were in that story. Among the many stories from which you come, you were the core of that story."

Full circle, Harry told himself, *We're back in bizarro world and I'm waiting for guys in white jackets to either come get me or this guy in front of me. One of us is crazy for sure.*

"You were once just a lost child from Ashfield, but now you are The Misfit."

Harry blinked and shook his head.

"But, you still have a choice. The Misfit told himself that he was the way he was because he had not been there when Christ was crucified. If he had been there, he would have seen the truth, he would know the truth, he would know how to act, he would not be the killer he was. You are like that, Harry. You want to *know* the truth, but you lack the *faith to believe* the truth. To believe is to know. It is a truth older than you or me. You are a Misfit, Harry Ducharme. You can do great harm, or you can..." Prophet stopped abruptly, cocking his head again, listening.

"The eye of the storm is almost here," he continued. "I must leave soon, while it is calm outside, but my invitation still stands. Come see me. Be in the crowd. Be my witness."

Harry looked at the clock. "I was asking about the miracles. You never answered."

Prophet was sitting straighter. "I am not God, nor the son of God. If you look closely at any miracle attributed to me, closely, you will find a rational explanation. Trust me on that."

"Well, I suppose I'm disappointed," Harry said. "I'd like to see a miracle someday."

"Harry, were you listening to anything I just told you?"

Outside, a horn was blasting. Harry realized that the wind was gone. The only sound in the studio was the hum of electronic equipment.

Prophet had one last request. "Before I leave, would it be possible to get a glass of fresh water?"

Harry plugged in a PSA tape and went to the WWHD refrigerator in the office next to the studio. He found an unopened bottle of Dasani and a clean glass. Back in the studio, he poured the water into the glass and set it next to his juice glass. As Prophet extended his hand toward the glass, he smiled and said, "You want a miracle?"

Harry answered quickly, trying to joke, "If that water turns red I'm going to believe in God for sure."

Prophet said, "The water is for you." With that, he picked up Harry's juice glass, still three-quarters full, and downed the contents with one long swallow. Then he reached into his coat pocket and handed Harry an old newspaper photo. "This is me in the beginning. Look at it. Drink the water. Come see me in a week or so. If you cannot be my witness, please be my guest."

The horn sounded again.

The two men stood and shook hands. Harry plugged in another round of PSAs and walked Prophet outside. WWHD was surrounded by total darkness. The lights of St. Augustine were out. Except for the sweep of the lighthouse across the inlet, the night was black. Prophet walked around to the front passenger side of the old VW van and opened the door, calling back to Harry, "Good night, Mr. Ducharme. Take care."

Harry stepped back as Prophet entered the van, and he saw the driver for the few seconds the inside light was on. She was looking directly at him. Harry sucked in a quick deep breath, frozen in the vision of a stunningly beautiful child. Long wavy silver-blond hair, her eyes piercing blue, milk-white skin, surely no older than a teenager. The door slammed, the light went out, the girl's face disappeared. Absorbed in that face, he did not notice the men and women in the back seats.

Harry watched the headlight beams lead the van away. He was alone, and he had four more hours to fill. He took a deep breath, looked around one more time, and then went back inside to discover that the PSA had finished and WWHD was broadcasting silence. Sitting down, putting his headphones back on, he noticed the red flashing light of his cell-phone. He had a message. The untouched glass of water was next to the microphone, but he did not reach for it. Plugging in a commercial tape for his favorite garage in St. Augustine, he listened to the message.

"Harry, you were wrong about one thing," Prophet's voice told him. "In the beginning, you thought that I handled snakes. That is not true. I never touch them. So, my offer still stands. Come see me. I promise, no snakes. And something else. You and I met a long time ago at the River of Life, when I was Bevel Summers, but I am sure you do not remember. I was a teenager, you were a child. I was white then, but now I am black. You were about to be an orphan, and now you are lost again. Me then, you then, me now, you now, we are still the same people. And we have always been connected."

Harry sat in his studio and tried to remember, but it was hopeless. His memory only went back to his parents in Springdale. Peter Prophet was nowhere after that, and any time before that had been erased. He finally picked up the glass of water and drank, wondering how a white man could be black.

The Black Man Speaks
December–2007
The Amphitheater
Noiseless and Patient

"*When looking to explain the conditions of political life and political judgment, the unconstrained mind seems compelled to travel up and out: up toward those things that transcend human existence, and outward to encompass the whole of that existence. ... The urge to connect is not an atavism.*"—THE STILL-BORN GOD: Religion, Politics, and the Modern West. *By Mark Lilla.*

Peter Winston stood with the other five and walked to the stage as the sun was setting. His knee was acting up again, and he was still angry about the argument he had had with Lincoln Motes the day before. It had been pointless. The Prophet had chosen each of them for a reason. Who was he to judge? Rather, as was explained to him in the beginning, each of them had chosen the path themselves. They were called, but they did not have to answer. The great irony for Winston was that he had been the first called, but the last to respond.

The Amphitheater had been closed for remodeling for over a year. Folk music festivals and historical re-enactment pageants had had to find another venue, and Harry was surprised that Prophet's appearance would have been the first event to mark the re-opening. So was the Amphitheater manager. When Harry called to confirm the show, the manager told him that he must be mistaken. "Hell, man, we don't even have the sound and light systems installed. The seats are in, but not the concession stands. You must have misunderstood your friend." Harry checked the newspaper—it had not been notified. Indeed, there was not a public notice in any form anywhere. In the days leading up to the supposed date, Harry would go on the air and ask Prophet to call him to confirm the details, but nobody called.

The afternoon of the gathering, Harry went to the Amphitheater and concluded that he had been the victim of a hoax. The main gates were locked, and the only people inside were two black men on a hydraulic lift, working on the Teflon tent roof. They were from Louisiana, out of town contractors, and they insisted that nobody else had been inside the fences for the past week. Harry was about to leave when he had an urge to stand on the stage and speak to the empty seats. The men from Louisiana looked at each other, as if to say, *Always thought that Florida was full of loonies, and this guy proves it.* Harry knew what they were thinking. No big deal. He was just seeing how far his voice would carry. About to speak, however, he felt foolish. He did not know what to say, even if nobody was listening. It had never stopped him on air, imagining that nobody was listening, but this was different. The 4000 empty seats in front of him were too much proof that he did not exist.

"I can hear you fine."

Harry blinked himself awake. One of the Louisiana black men was standing at the top level of seats, waving his right arm, saying, "Just fine. You got a good voice, mister."

I should be embarrassed, Harry told himself. But he just waved back and said, "Thanks." The man nodded and gave him a thumbs up. *One thing for sure,* Harry thought, *whoever designed the acoustics in this place ought to get a bonus.*

He stepped down from the stage and then climbed back up the three levels of steps to get to ground level again, convinced that there was not going to be any show that night in that place, but then he walked through the main gate and saw proof of…something? Prophet had said he would speak at nine that night. It was five in the afternoon, still a warm and muggy Fall day in Florida. There were at least fifty cars in the parking lot.

Harry saw children playing as their parents were setting up tables and chairs and umbrellas. An old school bus arrived, full. In the distance, small groups of people were walking toward the soon to be locked gates.

Harry pulled out his cell phone and called Carlos Friedmann. "Can you cover for me tonight? Remember, you owe me. I've suddenly got other plans."

Carlos had been sleeping. "You wake me up for what, amigo? I'm just about to do my first appearance on the primo tiempo sonar channel, with Gloria Estafan no less, and you wake me up to cover your sorry show. You don't think I got standards?"

"Carlos, I know it's short notice, but…"

Carlos laughed, "But you no got to apologize, vieja. I know what you're doing. You're going to that traveling salvation show, right? Hell, man, even my Chiquita is going to that show. I'd go myself if I thought I needed saving, but me and Fidel are going to live forever. Si, I'll cover your show. But I warn you, I'll tell all three of your regular listeners that you are on la rua to Damascus, looking for amor in all the wrong places."

Harry looked at the lot filling up, seeing a fire truck turn the corner and drive slowly through the lot toward the spot where he was standing. "Carlos, how do you say *You are full of shit* in Spanish?"

"Tu es bag de crap? Hell, I don't know, but I'll get my book and look it up for you. Meantime, you have fun tonight. Put a good word in for me to your spooky diablo friend, okay? And if Captain Jack wants to know who killed Jimmy Buffett, you act like you are shocked, totally shocked. Man, I hate that *pajaro*, and tonight's the night he dies."

Carlos had threatened to kill Jack Tunnel's co-host for a long time. It was WWHD lore, and Carlos had even held a contest on his own show asking for suggestions about how to do the deed. The Captain had complained to the Station Manager, but he had refused to take Buffett home with him after his show. "Not doing that," the manager had told Tunnel, "Jimmy's blood will be on your hands."

Harry called Nora James next, wanting her to be with him tonight, but Dexter answered the phone. "She's not feeling well right now. Me and my dad are here, and mom will come later. But I was going tonight, so maybe we could sit together?"

Harry was pleased. "Yeh, I'd like that, We can talk some more. But you might want to get here sooner rather than later. I'm thinking it will be standing room only. Tell Nora that I'll come see her in the morning and give her a full report."

"One more thing," Dexter said. "Nora wants you to invite the preacher over for dinner, and tell him to bring his *disciples* with him." Harry could sense that Dexter was using Nora's own emphasis on the word "disciples," and he could hear her skepticism channeled in Dexter's voice. "She's got lots of menu ideas, and we'll use the dining room. She even said to tell you that she would use the good china. And, yes, she'll put Pitty Sing in the basement."

Harry was glad that Dexter was coming to stand with him in the dark tonight, to hear Prophet announce the impending arrival of *A New Child of God*. There would be much to discuss tomorrow morning as they ate breakfast with Nora.

The stories about Prophet were consistent. He only spoke after sunset. He never advertised, but word was spread. *Somebody* always knew when and where, and the people came. Usually outdoors in an open field, near a stream or lake. He always wore black, but never a coat, even in winter. He never used a microphone. He never collected money. He was always accompanied by his six disciples, three men and three women. He never laid hands on a convert. He never touched the flesh. His disciples performed baptisms as he invoked a Holy Ghost, but he never entered the water himself. He just appeared. And then he disappeared. Witnesses proclaimed that he departed in an old van with three of his disciples, a woman driving. But he had no address, no phone, no intersection with this world except for his appearance in the dark. Not everyone who came to his sermons was saved. Some skeptics came and left as they had come. But others became followers, sometimes hearing of an appearance and traveling hundreds of miles to see him again. St. Augustine was different, his followers knew. Too many enemies would know, and the followers feared for his life because all of his sermons had hinted at his own death. The time was drawing near. And the word about this appearance in St. Augustine was that Prophet would actually reveal the next Son of God, forgetting that he only promised a *Child*.

Harry assigned himself a role; his skepticism required it. He watched the parking lot fill with pilgrims and their children, and then the fire truck arrived, followed by a sheriff's car, ordered there by the Amphitheatre manager, who had been alerted by a reporter. Harry found an analogy he liked: Tennessee 1925, Scopes, Bryan, Darrow, Darwin, monkeys. And H. L. Mencken, who was Harry's first choice for his own role, the acid-souled observer.

As soon as Dexter arrived, Harry tried to assign him a role too, but Dexter told Harry that his Aunt Nora had predicted that he would try to invent parallels, but she had already designated Harry as Prophet's successor, not his hostile interpreter. "Too many speeches from you, Harry, that's what she said as I left her house tonight, too many calls to arms for the Golden Rule and a progressive income tax." Harry laughed. Tourist or not, Nora had once described herself to Harry as having become "the string on the kite of your life." It was her self-classification, told to him in some form at more than one meal, "Somebody has to keep you from floating off to the moon."

"How about Billy Sunday for you and Elmer Gantry for me," Dexter offered, as he and Harry watched the crowd move toward the locked gates of the Amphitheatre.

Harry looked at him and said, "Not bad. You been reading books again? I warned you about that." He was watching a group of small children in the parking lot run around his Buick, thinking to himself, *Little bastards better not scratch my car.*

Dexter never took his eyes off the larger crowd, sighing, "Harry, *you* made that comparison a week ago on your show. So how can you be surprised that these people are here. They heard about it from you."

Harry disagreed, "Nobody listens to me, Dex, and if anybody does listen to me…"pointing to the parking lot, "…it's not *these* people. I do *not* do family radio."

The crowd was beginning to press against the fence, and some were climbing over, pulling others up with them. Another sheriff's car had arrived, and Harry could see men in uniform going through the crowd, telling people to go home, that the place was closed, and then a deputy got a bullhorn and began shouting, "You must disperse. There is no event tonight. You must go home."

"This is going to get ugly," Harry said, but Dexter was already pulling him toward the fence. "Come on, old man, I want a good seat."

Harry resisted, but the younger man led him anyway. At that moment, he heard his name. Turning back, he saw the sea of people part. "Harry Ducharme," the commanding voice said, and the split widened. Walking toward Harry, striding between the stilled waves of humanity, was a St. Augustine fireman in full uniform, a bullhorn in one hand and his helmet in the other. "Harry Ducharme," the fireman said as he approached.

"That's me," Harry confessed, but then he was confused. He knew this fireman; this fireman knew him. Harry had even interviewed him about his experience as a combat medic in Vietnam. It was Fred Tymeson, a tall broad-shouldered man so handsome that Nora James had insisted that women set fire to their houses in hopes that he would rescue them.

Fred tried to be angry. "Harry, this is your fault, and the Amp manager will be calling your boss tomorrow, fair warning, so you better hope that what I'm about to do works, or both of us are in deep shit."

"Fred…," Harry began, but he paused, realizing that, in the midst of a thousand people, there was complete silence as he and Fred spoke. "…I would apologize, but I'm not sure for what."

Tymeson handed him the bullhorn and pulled a ring of keys out of his jacket pocket. Behind Harry, Dexter snickered, "Watch out, Harry, he's got the keys to the kingdom."

Tymeson was not amused. "What I have are keys to a lot of businesses and most public buildings in this town. And I'm about to keep this new public arena from being torn down. I'm going to open all the gates…," seeing Harry about to speak, "…and yes, I told the Amp manager I was going to do this, and, no, he is not happy, but I told him that WWHD would be liable for any damage on the inside, and, no, I did not call your boss about that. And, yes, I am getting too old for this aggravation, Harry. I should have taken early retirement when I had a chance."

Harry thought, *This man has brass balls. No wonder he has a Silver Star.*

"So, for this to work, your role is to take this bullhorn and tell these people what I'm about to do. You're going to tell them to calm down, to take their time, to move slowly because there are women and children, and a lot of cripples, in the crowd. No pushing, no shoving, the show ain't starting until everyone has a seat. You tell them that the St. Augustine Fire Department is here to serve and protect. You tell them all that, and then you follow me to the biggest gate over there, and we better hope like hell that they follow you."

Harry felt Dexter nudge him in the back as he raised the bullhorn and began speaking.

Harry and Dexter did not sit down, opting to stand on the concrete mezzanine level at the back of the Amphitheatre. Then, with all four thousand seats below them gradually and quietly filled, with the sawdust littered stage empty except for six chairs, Harry and Dexter waited for the sun to go down.

Unlike a theatre crowd, most of the people sat in silence for Prophet's appearance. Children were hushed, adults would whisper. Those who had seen Prophet before quietly re-assured those who had not that all was as it was supposed to be.

With the last of the sunlight, but not yet in darkness, three men and three women rose out of their seats, where they had been scattered throughout the crowd, and walked to the steps on each side of the stage. Those who had seen Prophet before knew this was the announcement that he was nearby. His disciples walked up on the stage and stood in front of their chairs. No robes, no special clothing, except for the blue cape of the young woman, they looked ordinary. But most eyes were drawn to the youngest, that teenage girl whose first appearance as Prophet's driver had transfixed Harry with her beauty.

Then, as the disciples sat down, Peter Prophet was revealed to be standing behind the row of chairs. He walked to the front of the stage and spoke.

"Welcome, my friends. I am blessed to see you tonight, and I bring you good news. A new Child of God is coming."

A single pop of light exploded off to Prophet's right, and Harry shared the collective flinch of the crowd. But he knew the source. He had seen the *St. Augustine Record* reporter earlier. The camera flash was not really a surprise. Harry was more surprised that nobody else was taking pictures.

"And we gather here tonight to celebrate that arrival."

As Harry's eyes adjusted to the dark. Prophet's shape could be clearly sensed, if not seen. His body, however, was embodied in his voice, and Harry heard the radio voice from a month earlier, deep and smooth, but without a microphone. The crowd was mute.

"But first I must tell you why the child is coming. My time here is short. My presence delays its arrival. Indeed, I must die before the child is born. My death is its birth."

Harry heard Dexter almost groan, as did most of the crowd below them. A few murmurs of "No" and "Not so." Bodies shifted in the plastic seats.

"You must not worry, my friends, for I have known this since the beginning. My travels have brought me here to share this with you, so that you will go forth and spread the good news. Tonight is a new dawn. Tomorrow is a joy to possess."

Harry looked for the reporter, and then he looked for Fred Tymeson. Neither was visible. Turning to glance past Dexter, Harry stopped to study the young man's face, itself suddenly older. Dexter was not the same man he was an hour earlier.

"You will hear a story of the new beginning, and I will soon leave you a truth which only one of you will understand. But it will be enough. So, please close your eyes and let me first tell you a story, a story about spiders."

Harry knew what was coming.

"A speck of God, this spider. A noiseless, patient spider, on a little promontory, a ledge overlooking infinity, where it stood, isolated. You must see that spider now, you must shed any fear you have of that spider, you must keep your eyes closed, but you must see that spider, as I did, as I do now."

Harry's eyes were wide open. He was beginning to see in the dark, but the crowd below had its eyes closed, seeing a spider that Harry had already encountered. Next to him, Dexter's eyes were closed as well. Harry blinked, and he saw more. Even without electricity, the Amphitheatre was lit. And then a shiver swept through him, as if he had been gradually freezing and his body was just beginning to notice. At that moment, Harry understood that Prophet had always been misunderstood. *His followers always talk in terms of the Second Coming, Christ returning, the Son of God coming back.* Harry was thinking to himself, and he wanted to shake Dexter and tell him too, but Dexter was gone where the rest of the crowd had gone. *The Prophet never says son or Christ. He has always been precise. A Child of God was returning. A Child. A Child, but not necessarily a son.* Harry jerked his eyes away from Dexter and looked toward the stage, looked past Prophet, looked directly at the young girl behind him. She had been Prophet's driver, and Harry remembered the first time he had seen her, the long wavy silver-blond hair, her eyes piercing blue, her milk-white skin. Down below him now, she was at the end of the row of chairs. In the world of the Amphitheatre at that moment, she was the person most distant from Harry. Between them were thousands of people, all of whom had their eyes closed. Harry stared at the young girl. She was staring back at him.

"And I marked how, to explore its vacant, vast surrounding, the spider launched forth filament, filament, filament, out of itself. Ever unreeling them—ever tirelessly speeding them. That was the life of that spider. That is your life too. You are a soul, a soul standing on a high promontory, surrounded, surrounded, alone in measureless oceans of space, ceaselessly musing, venturing, throwing, seeking the spheres, to connect them. And you will labor, throwing yourself ceaselessly into that void, until the bridge you need be formed, until the ductile anchor hold. The gossamer thread you fling will catch somewhere, and your soul will connect and mesh and become part of all souls. You have been alone, but you will leave here tonight wovened and webbed into a design that stretches across time and distance, which avail not."

Prophet talked in the dark for another half hour, and Harry kept glancing toward the young woman on stage. She had closed her eyes, and as much as Harry looked at her, trying to will her into looking at him again, her eyes remained shut.

"The beginning now ends. You will go forth awake. You will forsake your old churches. They have lost their ways. Their preachers are lost. They offer chains, but not threads. They offer a dead Word. Soon, you will know the living child, but the child must know itself first. With that knowledge, the child will then sacrifice itself so that another may live. And so I leave you with this truth..."

Harry shuddered, a dread from long ago, that zero at the bone when he was told that his parents were gone.

"…That new child of God is with us tonight. The child is here and walks among us. *That* is my good news. I do not announce the spirit of that child. I proclaim its flesh and blood body and un-born soul walks among us at this moment, in this theatre, to be revealed when the child itself sees and understands the great design of God."

With that last word, Prophet's deep voice was replaced by the soft and tremulous acapello soprano of a woman singing. It was Prophet's driver. As the crowd opened its eyes, Harry closed his. He grasped the railing in front of him and leaned toward that voice as it took him back to the Friends church in West Branch. "How Can I Keep from Singing?" was the hymn question. From the moment his parents had disappeared, Harry had known the answer.

"Harry?"

He was being shaken by a strong arm.

"Harry? Planet earth to Harry Ducharme."

He opened his eyes. Hundreds of people were still milling around him, and dozens of beams of white light were directing the throng to exits, but nobody seemed to be in a rush. Fred Tymeson had called for more firemen, and he told them to bring all the four-celled flashlights they could. The Amphitheatre still had no power, so Tymeson made sure the flashlights were passed around and lit up as soon as the crowd rose to leave, guided out by a host of volunteer ushers. Harry's first thought after he opened his eyes was, *Everybody seems too normal. Is it just me that knows what just happened?*

A beam of light hit him in the eyes, blinding him until he yelled back, "Get that thing out of my face."

"Calm down, Harry," Tymeson yelled back at him from a distance. "You're dragging up the rear. But you ain't leaving until you and me make sure this place is empty so I can lock up."

Harry looked around for Dexter, but he was nowhere to be seen.

RELIGION WITHOUT TRUTH

By STANLEY FISH
New York Times

The truth claims of a religion—at least of religions like Christianity, Judaism and Islam—are not incidental to its identity; they are its identity.

The metaphor that theologians use to make the point is the shell and the kernel: ceremonies, parables, traditions, holidays, pilgrimages—these are merely the outward signs of something that is believed to be informing them and giving them significance. That something is the religion's truth claims. Take them away and all you have is an empty shell, an ancient video game starring a robed superhero who parts the waters of the Red Sea, followed by another who brings people back from the dead. I can see the promo now: more exciting than "Pirates of the Caribbean" or "The Matrix." That will teach, but you won't be teaching religion.

The difference between the truth claims of religion and the truth claims of other academic topics lies in the penalty for getting it wrong. A student or a teacher who comes up with the wrong answer to a crucial question in sociology or chemistry might get a bad grade or, at the worst, fail to be promoted. Those are real risks, but they are nothing to the risk of being mistaken about the identity of the one true God and the appropriate ways to worship him (or her). Get that wrong, and you don't lose your grade or your job, you lose your salvation and get condemned to an eternity in hell.

Of course, the "one true God" stuff is what the secular project runs away from, or "brackets." It counsels respect for all religions and calls upon us to celebrate their diversity. But religion's truth claims don't want your respect. They want your belief and, finally, your soul. They are jealous claims. Thou shalt have no other God before me.

December–2007
Arthur Poynter
Red Word of God Church
Jacksonville

And it was good. All that he surveyed was good. And he was pleased. From his office, behind the one-way mirror, his silent world below was motionless. *His* office and *his* auditorium. That was his secret sin. The possessive pronoun. *This is my world*, he would think to himself, but he never let his pride be seen in public. Arthur Poynter was a humble man.

His church was the Red Word, and he had been its founder. A few dozen converts when he was twenty years old, sweating under a tent in Palatka. He still had the Bible he used then, and he carried it with him every Sunday morning as he entered, nodding to the congregation of three thousand, their own Bibles open and in their laps, their souls primed earlier by the lyric exhortation of his assistant, Pastor Rick, himself destined to have his own church, endowed by Red Word and sanctified by his mentor, Pastor Art.

Red Word was a church in the round, its stage surrounded on all sides by cushioned seats. Smaller stages were at each front corner, where the Christian rock band would play on one and the organist on the other, depending on the time of the service. Above the congregation, on the opposite side of the auditorium from Pastor Art's upper office, was a loft for the choir. Discreetly across from the choir loft, and adjacent to his own office, hidden behind its own one-way mirrored wall, was the Red Word radio and television studio. Tiny remote cameras were at each corner of the great hall. Spread around the walls were four large screens, so that the relevant power point presentation could be seen clearly from any of the three thousand seats. Three services every Sunday, every seat filled for every service. Traditional music for the early service, organ and choir as the engine of those older voices. Christian Rock for the late service, another inducement to the young people, who preferred to rise late.

Poynter had mastered his universe by simply knowing his limitations. He had no ambition, he told himself. *This is my church, and it is all that I want.* From the time of his earliest sermons in Palatka, he had visualized the future Red Word. He had even made pencil sketches of the building he imagined, calculating budgets for a maximum of ten thousand congregation members, even using his education in Finance in an attempt to calculate future inflation. His inability to do that was a personal failure, as he told himself, *actuarial rather than spiritual.* And, of course, the spirit was all that mattered.

Poynter had begun preaching in 1982, a year after his political conversion. Ronald Reagan was responsible for both. Forsaking his New Deal parents, angered by the Muslims in Iran, repelled by Jimmy Carter's whiny faith, and buoyed by the light of Reagan's inauguration, Poynter was a born again Republican before he was a born again Christian. He considered his own run for political office, to ride the wave that seemed to be sweeping the country, but then Reagan was shot and Poynter knelt in his real estate office within minutes of hearing the news. He prayed for the President's recovery; prayed, he knew, sincerely for the first time in his life, prayed because he was genuinely afraid of the world and its potential, its proclivity, for evil. His real estate boss walked in on him praying, and knelt with him. The two men held hands in the beginning, but the older man then put his hand on the back of Poynter's neck, kneading the stiff flesh, and Poynter was touched. Reagan lived. Poynter bought his first Bible that afternoon. Leather covers, strong paper, black and red letters, and color pictures of Jesus and his Apostles. But he never told anybody about the moment in his office, the actual seed and fruition of his conversion. *At a dark moment, I feared for my soul. I prayed, and the Lord answered.* That was all anyone ever heard, but most of them understood. The details were irrelevant. All of them had had their own dark moments.

In his most private moments, Poynter could approach honesty. But that honesty was not shared in public. His public honesty was different: An honest Christian doing God's work. His reputation was enhanced early when he would condemn other Christian preachers, especially those on television, for their profligacy and hypocrisy. The Red Word Church was wealthy, with millions in the bank just waiting for a purpose, but Poynter was austere. He bought a new Ford in 1995 and was still driving it in 2007. His home on the St. Johns River had been purchased in 1985 and he still lived there. It had grown from a thousand square feet to three thousand square feet, but incrementally, and always out of his own salary. His wife worked in the Church office downstairs, but she was not paid. His sons had jobs outside the Church, but volunteered many hours of their free time. His clothes were 1950's Republican, blues and greys and whites, and seldom new. His public Christian life was a moral lesson, and his pastoring was an embrace for the neediest of lost sheep.

"The wealth of…," and he would often catch himself about to say "my church" but a rigid self-control always corrected him and he would say, "… our church is the wealth of the Lord." Much of that wealth was in the building itself. Each of the three thousand theatre seats cost hundreds of dollars each. All wood was mahogany. Carpets were thickly rich and crimson, and replaced every two years to compensate for the heavy foot traffic. The multi-media sound and video systems were state of the art, with dvds and cds of each service available within thirty minutes of their conclusion. Indeed, the Music Director of Red Word was paid more than Pastor Art, and as Pastor Rick joyfully admitted, "You get what you pay for."

If Poynter was guilty of any material indulgence, it was in his large private office overlooking the auditorium. Hand-crafted furniture, including a couch and original Morris chairs, a Persian rug covering the polished wood floor, a giant high definition television built into a maple cabinet, shelves full of purpose driven books and Apocalyptic novels. On the walls were matted and framed limited edition prints of Thomas Kincade cottages, as well as professional renderings of Biblical scenes. Prints of Dali paintings were next to black and white photos of calamus plants and other vegetation. On his desk was a collection of expensive figurines, glass peacocks, no bigger than a child's fist, but if seen from the right angle in the right light the reflection off the plumage was a colorful distraction.

In the corner of his office was his private Bible. Not his first Bible, his public Bible, but a limited edition oversized King James Edition that had cost a thousand dollars. It sat open on a pedestal, and Arthur Poynter would have to stand to read it. The very heft of the book had been its first attraction to him. Gutenberg originals might have weighed more, but they were certainly not more luxurious. The print was large, but the pages themselves were tissue thin and had to handled with great love. Poynter always made sure his hands were very dry before he would turn a page. He read it everyday, but he did not use it for his sermons. Red Word had gone with the liturgical flow years earlier and adopted the New Revised Standard Version. Poynter had helped steer them in that direction, but his motives were less than clear even to himself. All he knew, and which he never spoke aloud, was that he was pleased that he had kept the King James for his own reading. The over-sized limited edition had been bought before the Revised was adopted. No need to dispose of it. The Red Word congregation knew all about Poynter's office and its furnishings, even the thousand dollar Bible. He had always sought permission from the Church Board for any purchase, but everyone agreed: *In the big picture, these are small things, and Pastor Art has earned them.*

Poynter was not a warm man, his flock admitted, but he was charismatic in his own over-organized fashion. He had established the routine for his sermon preparation in his first years. Only the locations changed. He had the Gospel memorized for the most part and was always aware of any seasonal relevance, or perhaps an issue in the current news with Biblical parallels. The funnel of his mind opened itself to the outside world and then found an essence that was separated by the winnowing process of going through that funnel, down the narrow stem of his intellect, to be crystallized into a 2000 word sermon. He wrote notes from his random musings, then highlighted key words, then penciled an outline, then typed a rough draft of imprecise and sometimes repetitive arguments. It was polished by Saturday night, but Sunday mornings involved a final ritual. And that ritual required the absolute private sanctity of his office. He would stand and pace, sometimes unconsciously walking by the King James and letting his fingers pass over an open page. He gave his sermon to himself, silently, and then another time aloud, and then another, without his notes, but holding his old public Bible as a prop, itself a crumbling King James, while he quoted the Revised from memory. And, unknown to most, for the hour before his sermon, he would stand in front of the plate glass window in his office, the back of the one-way mirror, and look down on an empty auditorium come to life. And it was good. And he was pleased.

This morning in December, his congregation was expecting a sermon about the annual birth of Christ. On one side stage, the Red Word teens had constructed a manger scene. All was as it was supposed to be, but as Pastor Art walked to the center of the stage in the center of the auditorium, surrounded by the bodies and souls of Red Word, he kept hearing the voice he had heard in his office, the voice on the cd that had arrived unmarked in the mail the day before. As he stood silent in the center of the stage, longer than usual, silent so long that there was a stirring in the three thousand seats, and Pastor Rick was wondering if his friend might have become ill and would thus require him to come to his aid, Poynter forgot his carefully prepared sermon. Awakening as if from a trance, he looked around at the familiar faces, and he feared for them. Then, pulling up scripture he had not spoken in a long time, he preached.

"I want to talk to you, my brothers and sisters, I want to talk to you about false prophets. God has much to say about this subject, and much wisdom we should note. Listen first to Matthew, chapter seven, verse fifteen..."

The congregation had already had its Bibles open to the verses which had been listed in the program, so Poynter waited patiently as the auditorium was filled with the urgent whisper of pages being turned quickly.

"...so read with me and we will hear the word of the true Lord from Matthew 15-19: Beware of false prophets, which come to you in sheep's clothing, but inwardly they are ravening wolves. Ye shall know them by their fruits. Do men gather grapes of thorns, or figs of thistles? Even so every good tree bringeth forth good fruit; but a corrupt tree bringeth forth evil fruit. A good tree cannot bring forth evil fruit, neither can a corrupt tree bring forth good fruit. Every tree that bringeth not forth good fruit is hewn down, and cast into the fire. And more, brothers and sisters, as we turn to First John, chapter four: Beloved, believe not every spirit, but try the spirits whether they are of God: because many false prophets are gone out into the world, and then Matthew twenty-four, twenty-four: For there shall arise false Christs, and false prophets, and shall show great signs and wonders; insomuch that, if it were possible, they shall deceive the very elect."

Thirty minutes later, Poynter stopped, and his congregation exhaled. They had tried to keep up with him, but his spoken words did not match the written words in their Revised Bibles for the verses he quoted. Close enough, but different. He raised his hand as if to bless them, but he slowly lowered it before he had gotten too far. He looked at them, but he was now weak, suffering from another part of his sermon preparation ritual that was not known. He had not eaten in twenty four hours. He walked off stage, and the congregation waited for Pastor Rick to hurry forth and lead them in a closing hymn.

Back in his office, Poynter stood in the bathroom and began retching. *I am a fraud, a damnable fraud*, he told his reflection in the mirror. He unbuttoned his shirt sleeve and looked at the underside of his forearm. *I am a sinner and a fraud*, he whispered to his hand. Then he began raking his fingernails deep into the flesh of his exposed arm, leaving bloody lines to match the long scabs already there. Wrapping a cloth around his arm, he went to his window and looked down at his empty auditorium. Empty, until his eyes found a solitary figure standing against the wall under the choir loft. It was not that man's voice he had been hearing, he knew that. The man below was white, and gaunt, and trembling as if in a seizure. At that moment, Poynter felt closer to his god than he had in years. Of all the people who had been in the congregation this morning, the only person who understood him was the man down below. And that man was a sign to Poynter, as well as a gift.

February 23, 2008
Boiled Shrimp, Hush Puppies,
Cheese Grits, and Peppermint Chiffon Pie
Nora's Last Supper
Harry Spends the Night

The dinner was not a surprise. Dexter had told him about Nora's plans, but Harry was still surprised by the guest list. Prophet and "his Disciples" were expected because Nora had asked him to invite them, but why did she invite Jack Tunnel? And who was Jack's "special guest"? Harry understood the menu, surely it was Nora's private joke. But why even bother? She had made it clear to Harry that she thought the truth about Prophet was going to disappoint him when he found out. What that truth was, she did not know, but she was sure it was less than sacred.

He arrived early, wanting to make himself helpful, and hoping to be alone with Nora before anyone else arrived so that he could talk to her again about her past. But, as if anticipating him, she had made sure that Dexter was already there, as she explained later, "to light the goddam candles."

Harry stepped into the eighteenth century as soon as he entered the house on Water Street, a world without electric lights. Dexter met him at the door and led him through the hallways with candles lining the walls in brass holders, and into the kitchen, where Nora was cooking and drinking. Candlelight, dozens of flaming tapers, reflected off every stainless steel surface, modernity in the dark. A Poe story, or Hawthorne, or even Stephen

King? Harry wondered if Nora thought she was being funny, if all this was merely her passive aggressive comment on her impending guests, whose story she refused to read.

"Harry, Harry, come in and…oh, wait…you don't drink anymore. Well, come in anyway and have some sweet tea," she said, glass in one hand, spatula in the other. "And be damn sure you don't knock over any of the thousand points of light around here, or this place will go up in smoke in about ten seconds, you and me and The Travelers all raptured up…oh, wait…not me. I will simply be toast."

"Nora?" Harry let her name be the obvious question as he looked around.

She understood. "Relax, Harry. I'm just following orders. He wanted candles. I give him candles. He wanted fish. I give him shrimp. He wanted dinner. I'm feeding him and his hood. He called me after you talked to him. Everything is copasetic."

Harry nodded and asked, "Look, thanks for doing this. I know you haven't been feeling…"

"I'm fine, Harry. And I'm glad to do it for you."

He started to protest, "But I thought this was your idea. Dexter told me that."

"I just figured you would want this, Harry. It's for you, so it's your idea. *That* makes sense in my world. And, I'm glad to just see you. So, maybe as soon as we get the troops fed and out of here, Dexter too, you and me can talk, okay?"

"Yeh, yeh, send the children to bed so the adults can talk," Dexter laughed from the corner of the kitchen, where he was polishing wine glasses. "You two sound just like my parents."

Nora was quick to answer, "Except that you don't still live with *us*."

Harry looked at Dexter, who feigned a sulk by hunching his shoulders and grimacing, only to laugh again, "I promise, Aunt Nora, I'll move out when I win my first election."

"If you call me Aunt Nora again, I'll make sure you don't get elected dogcatcher, much less state rep."

Dexter took the tray of glasses to the dining room, and Nora spoke quickly to Harry, "You need to talk to him soon. It might save you some trouble before you meet his parents."

Harry said, "Will do as soon as I get his attention. He's spending so much time reading that I seldom see him. But now I have to ask you something about your guest list. Why is Jack coming? He wasn't on my list. Why did you invite him?"

"I didn't. It was Prophet. He asked me to call Jack and to invite Jack's friend. And you know how I do as I'm told by authoritative men," she said, handing him a pan of doughy unbaked rolls covered by a white towel. "Put this on the counter next to the oven and set the temperature for 400. We're getting close to show-time."

From the dining room, Dexter called to them, "Somebody's knocking. I'll get it. Ya'll stop making-out in there."

Harry almost blushed, but Nora ignored him. "You always wondered why Jack stuck around this town, why he never went national, right? You're about to meet the reason. It's been his secret for twenty years…"

"But you've known?"

"Well, duh, Harry, of course I've known. I know everything. I've known this ever since I had them over for dinner years ago. Jack's been in love for a long time and he won't ever leave this town unless the person he loves…"

"Harry Ducharme, I'd like you to meet a special friend of mine," Jack's voice was not the voice of the Jack Tunnel that Harry knew. He turned slowly, making eye contact with a grinning Nora James one last time, and confronted two penguins.

Tunnel and his date were both wearing tuxedoes, circa 1925, right out of a Gatsby party. Jack even looked slim and young. The older man next to him was taller and had eyes like Omar Shariff. They were holding hands. Tunnel was trembling, his eyes blinking, like he was a teenager about to introduce a prom date to his parents. The older man disengaged himself, stepped forward, and extended his hand, "I'm Paul Wharton. Jack has told me all about you, and, of course, I listen to your program, so I'm very pleased to meet you."

Harry was afraid that he looked very foolish at that moment, standing there speechless, shaking hands with the only person that Captain Jack Tunnel had ever loved in his life, knowing that Nora was behind him having a wonderful time reading his mind. In that first few seconds, all the clues became obvious. Ever since Harry had known him, in the right wing rantings of a thousand programs and hundreds of bar crawls all over St. Augustine, not once had Jack ever said anything hostile or condescending toward homosexuals. The conservative gay-bashing agenda was never part of his WWHD schtick. Jack Tunnel was a gay Republican, but he had never been a hypocrite about it. He did not live in a Log Cabin, but he did not lead a double-life. He had merely kept the truth to himself, and Nora's home was one of the few places that Tunnel and Wharton were together with anyone else, small parties that Harry had never heard about.

As Wharton stepped over to hug Nora, Harry and Jack exchanged looks. Harry's look said *You could have told me.* Jack's look said *I should have told you.* Harry turned back to Wharton and finally spoke, "I'm sorry. I was being rude."

Wharton was gracious, "No apology necessary. Jack had told me that you would be surprised, but the awkward introductions are out of the way, and I'm starved. I've been looking forward to this dinner for days. Perhaps we could have a glass of sherry before the other guests arrive?" He then turned to Tunnel, "Jack, come here and help us. And do tell Harry how we met. I love to hear you tell that story."

With Dexter in the mix, the four men stood in the kitchen as Nora finished getting ready for dinner. In thirty minutes, Harry got acquainted with Jack and Paul, two men who met in a boat yard. Wharton owned a yacht building company. His political hero was Barry Goldwater. He had been married and divorced, with children older than Dexter. The more the two men talked about themselves, the more that Tunnel relaxed. Harry had never seen him so calm.

Soon enough, Dexter was the center of attention, especially when he told Jack and Paul about his political ambitions. Nora muttered to Harry when the others were distracted, "Procrastination killed the cat, Harry. You should have talked to him before now, dammit. Thanks a lot."

Jack and Paul congratulated Dexter about his plans, and Wharton raised his glass for a toast, "To our future Republican rep." Harry wondered why he would have assumed Dexter was a Republican, other than the fact that the area voters were overwhelmingly Republican, so it made no sense to be a Democrat. You want to win office in north Florida, you run as a Republican. But, Harry's logic and Wharton's assumption were both wrong.

"I'm running as an Independent," Dexter said firmly, lifting his own glass of beer. "I've got plenty of time to get the signatures to get on the ballot, and since there is no incumbent it will be a three-way split. I am talking to a lot of people about helping me. I think it can be done."

Harry knew what Jack and Paul were thinking: *How very sweet, how very naïve, how utterly hopeless.* Harry broke the silence, "Dex, sometime soon, let's talk."

Nora had her elbows on the counter, her head resting on her hands, but Harry thought he understood what she was saying to him under her breath, *His parents are going to kill you.*

Jack and Paul were not as upset as Harry had expected. In fact, Wharton told Dex to send him a campaign contribution form as soon as they were printed. Jack volunteered his own money, and advice, "You'll need the money for sure, and you can list me as a supporter, but I gotta tell you…," with a wink at Harry, "…you keep listening to Harry Do-Charmin over there, and your chads will be left hanging for sure."

Harry had a response, but before he could speak he heard a knocking at the front door. He paused, waiting for Dexter to excuse himself and go let in the other guests, but everyone just kept talking politics. The knocking got louder. Harry looked over at Nora, who was opening another bottle of wine, oblivious to the men in the room, but also seeming unaware of the knocking. Dexter looked over and asked, "Harry, you okay?"

"I think somebody's at the door," he said tentatively.

The three other men looked at each other and then back at Harry. Dexter, with a knowing glance toward the other men, finally said, "Okay, I guess I should check," leaving the room just as Jack walked over and patted Harry on the shoulder, "I thought you had given up the sauce, my man."

From the hallway, Dexter called back, "They're here."

Harry's expectations about the evening were gone in the first few minutes. As soon as Dexter led Prophet and his followers into the kitchen, Nora strode over and hugged him as if he was a regular. She introduced Jack and Paul, and then, with a wave of her hand toward Prophet, asked him to introduce those with him. Half an hour later, they were all still in the kitchen, all of them drinking, except for Harry and Prophet, who sat quietly on the kitchen couch most of the time. Nora's cat Pitty Sing sat on the couch arm, tail swishing as it stared at the new guest.

Harry's most pleasant surprise was that everybody liked each other, or so it seemed at first. Jack and Paul liked to talk about themselves, and they never failed to entertain. When Dexter spoke, everyone stopped any other conversation and listened to him. The followers all told their stories about how they had come into contact with Prophet, all except the young girl named Charlotte Arnold and the stooping man named Lincoln Motes, whose furtive eyes and terse words seemed inconsistent with all the other followers. Harry found him fascinating, but not interesting. The two older men and the twin sisters seemed to be good people who had been moved to give up their old lives and dedicate themselves to Prophet. Lincoln and Charlotte made no public profession of their roles.

Soon enough, Harry could see the group dynamics sort themselves out. Peter Winston and Jack and Paul were instant friends. Charles Yates was obviously an organizer, the man who handled the small details of Prophet's appearances, and he was drawn to Dexter as soon as politics was mentioned. The Norville twins, Jane and Jean, were Nora's favorites, and the sisters were soon helping Nora cook and set the dining room table. When Jane told her story about seeing *the* Prophet on 9/11, with her sister nodding silently in agreement and memory, Harry was skittish for the first time. Nora had immediately known how he would feel, so she casually walked over and stood next to him, her shoulder touching his, pulling his weight toward her.

All in all, the biggest surprise and pleasure was that it was just another Nora dinner for the most part. It was not a tent meeting, a revival, or a Sunday service. Prophet's silence went un-noticed, and Harry drifted from one small group to another, observing and enjoying, seldom participating, but well aware that any time he got close to Charlotte she stopped talking.

Four of the six followers were, indeed, noticeably ordinary. Except for the tuxedoed duo, and Prophet in his usual black, everyone was dressed like middle-class citizens invited to a good restaurant. Indeed, the only person who looked like he did not belong at the gathering was Prophet himself. Lincoln Motes, extraordinary only in his obvious discomfort, lingered around Peter, Paul, and Jack most of the evening, but Harry also noticed how his eyes would often follow Dexter around the room, especially when Dexter happened to be talking to Peter Winston.

Charlotte had not told her story of meeting Prophet, and nobody asked. For the first few minutes in the kitchen, Harry avoided her. He was still processing the look she had given him at the Amphitheatre, at the same time remembering her voice as she sang. Nora saw him staring at the girl and made a special trip from behind the counter to whisper to him, "Jail bait, Harry, jail bait. Back away, grandpa."

Harry tried to poke her in the ribs as she passed, but Nora was too quick as she then announced, "Supper in five minutes. I'm about to drop the shrimp in the pot. Anybody who needs their drink topped off, tell me now. Water and wine glasses are already on the table."

Harry turned to Prophet, who was rising off the couch as if his back hurt, and asked, "You okay?"

Prophet shook his head, "Just getting old, Harry. I seem to be running out of steam." It was one of the last times Harry would see a fleeting vision of Bevel Summers.

With everyone headed for the dining room, Dexter lingered until he was alone with Harry in the kitchen. The change in him had been acceler-ating in the past few months. His voice was more assertive, and even his posture seemed straighter, and, as Nora had pointed out a week earlier while she and Harry dined alone, Dexter's wardrobe was finally beginning to confirm his adulthood. "You want some off the record news?" Dexter asked, facing Harry in the doorway, blocking him from catching up with the others. "Charlotte told me that the person that Prophet is talking about in his sermons, the Child to come, is here tonight."

Harry paused, noticing the absolute absence of irony in Dexter's voice. He was relaying this news as if it were…*gospel?* He was neither mocking nor skeptical. He simply said it as information that he wanted Harry to process with him, as they had processed fiction and fact many times in the past. Harry resisted his first temptation, to tell Dexter *You better not tell Nora about this, or she'll bite your head off for being so gullible.* Instead, he honored Dexter's seriousness with his own, "Did she say more? Or was she playing games with you? And why would *she* say this, and not the Prophet? I'm not questioning that she told you that, but I don't understand why this news comes to you and nobody else, and why from her and not Prophet. I mean, Dex, she *is* very young."

Nora called from the dining room, "Harry and Harry junior, supper is on the table. You're holding up grace, and we're hungry."

Dexter stepped aside to let Harry pass, but he then said, "Do you have any idea who she is?" He was obviously confused by his own realization that, except for Prophet and the other followers, he was the only other person who knew the truth. "Harry, she's the child Prophet saved from the water. She's the baby in the picture. And she is amazingly wise…and wonderful."

Harry led Dexter into the dining room, where all eyes turned toward them as they entered. He hoped that Nora was not reading his mind right then, because he was telling himself, *Oh my god, the boy's in love. And I still haven't had dinner with his parents.*

Most of the wood in Nora's dining room was older than the house itself. It had been salvaged from somewhere else and used to panel the walls. The floors were polished oak. The long planked table and sturdy cushioned chairs might have come from the court of King James. The room itself was much larger than the kitchen, with a wall of windows overlooking the side yard. The overhead crystal chandelier was unlit, keeping in the spirit of a no electricity dinner, so the twelve diners were ringed by tall candles on any available flat surface, and short candles on the table itself. With the glass windows and two large wall mirrors on opposite ends of the room, and the crystal above, light was bouncing all over the place. The only incongruous detail was a huge black and white photograph, matted and framed, centered on the wall facing Harry's seat. At first glance it seemed to be merely streaks and puffs of white lines and dots on a black background, but soon enough it was obvious that the picture was of a giant fireworks display, skyrocketing arcs and shimmering explosions in the sky, dominating a room of antiques.

Nora had assigned seats. Prophet had three followers on each side of him. Harry was to sit directly across from Prophet, with Jack and Paul to his left, Dexter to his immediate right, and Nora at the end closest to the kitchen, so she could slip back and forth as needed. It was a perfectly logical arrangement.

Harry wondered if there was any significance to the seating order, or was he simply assigning meaning to random atoms. Why was Charlotte to Prophet's immediate right, Charles Yates to his immediate left? The Norville sisters were to Yates' left, and Peter Winston sat next to Charlotte, with Lincoln Motes at the far end. But then he remembered. Nora had done the seating chart. It was her house. Everyone else was a guest. Sometimes a cigar was just a cigar.

As Harry sat across from Prophet, he soon had a new question, *Why are we here? Nothing is happening. Everybody is talking about the same things they talked about in the kitchen. There's no point to this gathering. That Lincoln guy at the end is still sulking. The twins still look like Mrs. Santa Claus. And why is that girl staring so much at Dexter? All we need is Jack to tell us that Jimmy Buffett is in the car, and can he bring his bird in to eat grits with us. And I know that Nora is going to just roll her eyes at me later and make fun of my thinking that this was a good idea.*

Charles Yates changed the direction of the meal when he asked everybody's permission to be quoted for the book he was writing, a history of the Prophet and the *New Child of God*. "I've got a ton of material, just needs a good editor and somebody who can turn a good phrase. Co-writer, ghost writer, somebody with a way with words." He also asked Harry if he could quote from old audiotapes of Harry's radio program, especially the first interview with Prophet. Tunnel good-naturedly objected, saying his feelings were hurt that *his* program wasn't being quoted, and then Nora piped in with her own request, wanting full credit for any recipes and "anything I say has to be printed in red ink." She and Jack were drunk, but Yates did not mind. He even joked, "I'll have my people contact your people." Wharton and Winston thought *that* was hilarious, but Harry kept his eyes on Prophet, who was looking down.

An hour passed, and some of the candles were beginning to flicker. Nora's food had met with universal approval, and her liquor cabinet had suffered a severe hit. The conversation had begun light, but as soon as Harry and Prophet began exchanging questions and answers, each with an equal supply of both, the tipsy others had fallen silent. Yates had assured everyone that his recorder had a two hour tape, but as soon as Nora announced, to Jack's approval, that it was "time for last call," Yates erupted with an unholy expletive, "Shit! This thing isn't working."

Harry looked across the table at Yates, whose eyes were welling into tears and his face was stricken with panic. He then looked at Prophet, but it was Charlotte's face which quickly caught his attention. She was staring back at Harry, a Cheshire smile on her face, her head tilted just a little toward Prophet. Keeping his eyes on Charlotte, Harry heard Yates plead, "I'm sorry, I'm sorry. I wanted to do this right, but..."

Prophet put his hand on Yates' hand on the table, leaned over and whispered something to him, calming him, and then announced to the entire table, "This is not a problem. You can each talk to Charles later. You can re-tell your stories. Tell what you remember. As I and Harry will do. Charles can re-construct this night with your help."

Nora tapped her water glass with a spoon, "You all have ten minutes to leave the building with Elvis, all of you except Harry." She leaned forward and turned in Harry's direction, "You, my darling, are helping me clean the kitchen."

Peter, Paul, and Jack offered to help, as did the Norville sisters, but Nora dismissed them all. Dexter then offered, but he was rebuffed too. "I'm drunk, I'm tired, and Harry owes me a favor. The rest of you...go away…go and sin no more, or something like that." Prophet stood, and his followers followed, and in rising, almost in unison, they thanked Nora for her hospitality. But, against her protests, they also picked up all their dishes on the table and took them to the kitchen. Jack and Paul did the same, at the same time inviting Dexter to go for a night cap drink, but the younger man declined graciously. Harry soon walked them all to the door, and then he was alone with Nora in a house of melting candles.

"Thank God this place doesn't have smoke detectors, or else we'd never get any peace and quiet," Nora said as she led Harry through the hallway, snuffing out candles, a process which created a puff of smoke for each one, until the house itself seemed almost foggy. "I'll turn on some window fans and suck this stuff out, Harry. Your job is to make sure I don't get lost in the dark."

From the dining room, through the long hallway, with side stops to extinguish a single wick in the seldom used parlor, Harry followed Nora into the kitchen. Entering where the evening had begun, her own first reaction made her almost laugh, "*What* a dump!" The kitchen was a mess.

Harry urged her to rest on the couch while he started scraping plates. He was mildly surprised when she agreed. Within a few minutes, everything was stacked, but nothing was clean. Nora sat with Pitty-Sing in her lap, her eyes closed, her head resting against the back of the couch, but she was awake, Harry could tell, because she was humming. Just as he started running some water to rinse the dishes, she sighed, "Harry, you're giving me a headache. Leave that stuff for tomorrow and come over here to sit with me. And bring one last glass of…something, anything…with you."

It was Saturday night, no show for him to do, and he could sleep late in the morning. No hurry. The kitchen still had a few candles burning, and the windows were open. The house was quiet. He sat with Nora and talked.

He wanted her impression of the night, especially her view of Prophet, but she disappointed him. "Oh, Harry, as soon as you and him started talking about how Christianity was broken, how all religions were failing, how the country was broken, how the damn world was broken, I stopped listening. And, you know, excuse me, but how can I really take seriously anybody who actually uses the name *Prophet?* It's always been my feeling that anybody who actually called himself a prophet never, never, was."

"But the others? Their stories? Well, those who would actually talk," he said, remembering how Charlotte and Lincoln were mute most of the night.

"Kool-aid, Harry. They drank the kool-aid. But, still in all, they seem like good people. Charles was very earnest, and I really liked the twins. I could have done without the creepy guy at the end, and Prophet was too Jim Jonesy for me, but they all seemed harmless enough."

Harry wanted to argue with her, to tell her how, at the end of the night, he had finally felt something profound happening. Not at the beginning, but more and more as he and Prophet talked and the others listened. But she was not interested. Then he realized that she had not commented on the girl. "How about Charlotte? If you thought the others were…"

"She was more so," Nora said, but her voice was weaker and her eyelids were drooping. "But you were so ga-ga over her that you probably didn't notice that she never said a word to you. Right? The Lincoln guy was in a funk to himself, but that girl was quite chatty with everyone but you, Harry. You got a reason for that?"

"I thought you weren't paying attention most of the night."

"I wasn't. I'm just taking Dexter's word for it. He leaned over to me at the table and told me that the girl had been told by Prophet to not talk to you, not a word to the co-host of this particular fete. The others gushed for you, but not her."

Harry did a split second processing of the night. Nora was right. Charlotte Arnold had never spoken to him, not even in greeting, not even as she left. The only time he had addressed her directly she had merely walked away. "Okay, okay, but did Dexter tell you who she was?"

"Harry, can we talk about you and Dexter and Prophet and the other merry pranksters saving the world some other time? I'm tired of this subject, I'm just tired. I want to go to bed."

He stood and offered his hand to help her up, saying, "Sure. I'm sorry. You do look beat. I'll see you tomorrow and ask you about…"

Nora looked up at him with sleepy eyes, and then she unveiled a new fork in the road for him, "Harry, I want you to spend the night with me."

"Nora?" But then he froze.

Still looking up at him, she said, "Oh, Harry, you are so sweet. But please don't get your hopes or anything else up, okay? I want you to stay with me tonight. I want you to go to bed with me. I am tired of sleeping alone, that's all. Tired of being alone every night. And if you don't snore, I might ask you to stay tomorrow night too. So, will you do that for me, Prince Harry Charming, will you sleep with me tonight? I even have some pajamas for you, if you don't mind a tiny bit of mothball odor for the first few minutes."

He looked around the dim kitchen, and down at Nora, breathing deeply as he said, "I'd be honored."

"Will you respect me in the morning?" she tried to smile as she extended her hand for a lift up, but Harry saw her wince as soon as he began to help her rise.

"Nora?"

"Harry, if you ask me one more time if I'm okay, I'll rescind my offer. You can sleep in that wonderful Buick of yours again."

The trip from kitchen to sleep took him from the ground floor to her third floor bedroom, with her leading, candle in hand, and him following like they were on a ghost tour. He tried to talk to her as they walked, but she shushed him every-time, as if she were afraid of waking the original owners of that old house. He suggested that they turn on a light, but she accused him of being a sissy. Finally in her bedroom, filled with an ancient *armoire*, antique chairs, small tables and stands, a large writing table near the window, and a huge four-poster canopy bed, Harry soon focused on the single source of electrical illumination. As Nora went to the closet to change into her sleeping gown, Harry walked softly to the far end of the room and stooped down, almost to the floor, where he could recognize and consider a Virgin Mary, child in arms, night-lite.

"And that," Nora said, having come silently up behind him, "...is Abe's idea of a joke." She handed Harry some pajamas. "You can change in the bathroom down the hall. Don't trip in the dark."

"And these?" he said, taking the pajamas. "Are they his too?"

"Not unless he used to be four inches taller and two sizes bigger. No, Harry, not Abe's. And if you keep asking silly questions, you'll make yourself crazy. Relax. We're having a sleepover. Put it in your diary tomorrow. Now, put these on and come back. I'll be in bed waiting for you."

As soon as he slid under the covers she rolled over on to her left side and scooted her bottom toward him, telling him quietly, "Night, night, Harry. Don't let the bed bugs bite."

"Do I get one more question, and, I promise, nothing about you or me or the Prophet. Okay?" He was fading fast himself, but he wanted to know if she had seen the same thing he had seen that night. She muttered some version of *sure, but keep it short*. As he reached his arm across her, his face resting near the back of her neck, he asked, "Did you notice the look on Jack's face tonight? How happy he looked, especially when he was looking at Paul, even when Paul was looking somewhere else. I thought to myself, I mean..."

She nudged backwards with her bottom, talking into her pillow, "Harry, get to the point."

"No point, I was just noticing that Jack seemed very happy tonight. And I wondered if..."

She nudged him again, "He's in love, Harry. People look like that when they're in love. And if you think Jack looked so happy tonight, how come you didn't notice the look on Dexter's face."

Harry stopped talking. She had answered a question he was going to ask her tomorrow, how she felt that Charlotte and Dexter had acted at dinner earlier that night. But it was not the question he had been trying to articulate without being too obvious. He knew that his real question should be one to begin a conversation, not one to end an evening, but he blurted it out anyway. "So, tell me, Nora, has anybody ever looked at you that way?"

She lay there without speaking, her breathing slower and deeper, and Harry thought she was simply going to ignore him and go to sleep. The wind rattled the branches outside, and he could hear the distant clicking of cicadas in the marsh a hundred yards away. He lay there in that few seconds, knowing that if the wind died down, and the cicadas fell silent, then he might, just might, hear the ocean.

Nora squeezed his hand and held it briefly against her chest, "Harry, I'm thinking that the real question you want to ask me is different. I'm thinking that you *really* want to ask me if *I* have ever looked at somebody else that way. But we can tell love stories tomorrow, okay? I'll give you all the dirt. But for now, I'm going to sleep. I'll see you in the morning. And, by the way," squeezing his hand again, "thanks for staying with me tonight."

She went to sleep, her back spooned up against his stomach and chest, her breathing almost a purr. He lay there, his right arm across her waist, his hand held by her hand, wondering how he had gotten from Iowa to Florida, from the Cedar River to the Atlantic Ocean, from poor parents to wearing another man's pajamas.

Dexter Knows His Future
Harry Knows Nothing

Harry kept talking late at night on WWHD, but less frenetic, less intense. In his own words, he "stopped preaching." During the day, he would spend more and more time with Dexter, marveling at the audacity of his hopes and plans. Dexter was convinced that he was going to win the election in 2008, and then another, and then a higher office, and higher. Harry had no defense for Dexter's optimistic idealism. The young man had seemed to grow taller in the past year, and he certainly put on more weight, but the effect was to make him look even more handsome. His voice seemed to have gone from tenor to baritone, as if puberty had been delayed twenty years and was catching up in a hurry.

At first, Harry had avoided asking Dexter about his personal plans, especially his feelings toward Charlotte Arnold. Since the dinner at Nora's, Harry had not seen Dexter and Charlotte together, nor had Dexter spoken of her, but Harry knew something was happening. All he needed was the right opening. When it came, he was still not prepared.

"Have you seen that girl lately?" he had asked as they sat in Nora's kitchen the first Sunday morning in March. Nora was asleep on the couch, and the two men were whispering.

"Almost everyday," Dexter said. "She's working on my campaign."

Harry had always thought that Dexter's use of the word "campaign" was amusing. So far, that campaign, for an election a year away, had been mostly idle, albeit constant, conversation between them.

"She your campaign manager?" Harry had winked when he said it, not wanting Dexter to take him too seriously.

Dexter smiled back, "No, Harry, *you* are going to be my campaign manager, with the help of Charlie Yates. We'll discuss that in a few months." Harry stared at him, realizing that he and Dexter were about to have an adult conversation, and that he was no longer *Uncle Harry*.

In fact, Harry felt like a man whose secret life had never really been secret, that others around him had merely played along, waiting for the right moment to expose him, to tell him to quit playing games. It was time to get seriously honest. Irony was no longer a defense.

"Charlotte is working on a volunteer list. She thinks she'll have a few hundred people committed by the middle of summer," Dexter said, looking over at Nora to make sure he was not disturbing her sleep, then back to Harry with the look of a man who was plotting a palace coup.

When did he change? Has it been too subtle for me, or too quick? Harry stared hard, and tried one last stab at humor, "But she's so young," knowing that he was not thinking about her age in relation to politics, but her age in relation to Dexter himself.

Dexter answered the real question, "You know that's not true, Harry. You, of all people, know how so *not* young she is."

Harry rose to Dexter's level. "All I know, Dex, is that you're dealing with people who might be more, or less, than they seem. As long as I have known Prophet and his people, I still don't quite get…get *it*. Know what I mean?"

Dexter did not speak for a moment, simply looking hard at Harry, as if he was a painting on the wall. "Charlotte tells me that you'll understand eventually, that you actually know more than you realize, and that…"

Harry almost raised his voice, "So why is it that she'll talk to you but not to me? She'll tell you all about me, but she won't speak to me. Isn't that what you told Nora? So, why am I kept in the goddam dark?"

Dexter took a deep breath and let it out slow, slowly shaking his head as he spoke, "Hell, Harry, I wish I knew. I've even asked her. I've told her that you're essential to my plans, and that you're one of my best friends.

But all she tells me is that what she has to say to you has to wait. For what, who knows?"

"Dex, do you really trust her and the rest of them?" Harry could see how troubled the young man was.

"I more than trust her, Harry. You know that. You and Nora both know that."

Harry knew that he had to tread softly, but he was beginning to feel that Prophet and his people were starting to use Dexter for their own purposes, whatever they were. That was a feeling, and feelings might be wrong. But Harry *knew* that Dexter was more important to him, even after only a few years, than his own son had been before. He had to protect him, but he knew that if he criticized the girl too directly it would merely make her more appealing. Dexter might be a grown man, but Nora had made it clear to Harry: Dexter had never been in love before. This was all new to him, and he was as defenseless as a teenager.

Harry wanted to change the subject, back to ideas about a campaign, but the rock in the middle of the road could not be gone around. "Dex, do you even know where she lives? Do you have a phone number for her? If you had to talk to her or the Prophet at this exact moment, as if your very life depended on it, could you get in touch with them?"

Harry knew the answer. Nobody knew where Prophet or his people lived. Nobody could contact them. They appeared, and they disappeared. A *St. Augustine Record* reporter had followed what he thought was their van after the meeting at the Amphitheatre, but it had been dark and the van was dark and it crossed the Bridge of Lions right before the draw was lifted. The reporter could not catch up, and by the time he got to the other side the van was nowhere to be seen. And, except for Harry's radio program, Prophet had never done an interview. Harry wanted Dexter to consider the significance of *that* fact.

In response, Dexter reached into his pocket, pulled out his cell phone, hit two numbers, and handed the phone to Harry, "She'll answer, but she won't talk to you. Ask for Prophet if you want to. And, relax Harry, I'll be okay."

March 25, 2008
Torches on the Beach

Harry had begun re-reading everything he had read in the past, convinced that he had missed something the first time. He had been too young, he told himself, and, like love, art was wasted on the young. The meaning had always been there, hidden in plain sight like a purloined letter. He was convinced that some writer, somehow, had already written about him, Harry Ducharme himself. He wasn't in the Bible, he knew that, but he was in fiction or poetry. Somewhere, a *single* line explained him. The words had not changed, just the context. He *must* be part of some design, but he could not see it.

He had told Bevel Summers, on a rare occasion when Prophet disappeared, about his re-reading agenda, but Bevel only nodded, as if agreeing but not understanding. Harry's view of Bevel had evolved as well. He was more human than Harry had first thought. In rare moments, sitting in Harry's Buick as they drove around St. Augustine, just the two of them, Bevel almost seemed afraid. He still preached in the dark, still referred to himself as a Prophet, he still spoke in low tones of a Child being born who was already alive. But, in Harry's Buick, he would admit that he was not sure that the Child would understand why it had to die soon after he himself did. His own death did not bother him, and there were moments when that death seemed a relief to him. The Child would die, that was certain, but for the plan to unfold as Prophet foretold, the Child had to choose death. For the future to happen, the Child had to die of its own free will. The fact that he constantly prophesized his own death did not seem to bother Bevel. He merely referred to it as his "role."

Harry wanted to ask about what Charlotte had told Dexter at Nora's dinner, that the Child was at that meal, but he knew that Bevel would not explain any further. Harry had to figure it out all by himself. The only person he thought might be able to help him, however, was the person who least believed in the Prophet.

Sitting in Nora's kitchen the Monday morning after Easter Sunday, as she peeled apples for three pies she was making on-air, he asked her if she would talk about Prophet after her show, only to be stunned when she repeated his question to her listeners, "Folks, my dear lost soul Harry Ducharme, here for a free meal, just asked me to talk about his snake-oil salesman friend, Moses Q. Prophet."

Harry sat on her couch and stared, thinking, *Why is she so angry about this? Why so contemptuous?*

Nora kept talking, the peeler in her hand no longer satisfied with the apple skins. She stabbed one apple with it, tossed it aside, and reached for another. "Harry wants me to explain the…fu…frigging…mystery of life to him. Is that right, Harry?" He could not look at her.

Her WWHD phone started ringing, but she ignored it. "No calls, folks, I can handle this one on my own."

Harry looked around, anywhere that was not Nora's face, wishing he had not asked her, wondering if she wanted to see him later that night after his show was over, for him to return to Water Street and sleep with her. At that moment, smelling apples and fresh baked bread, he was afraid of sleeping alone again, of being cast out of Nora's home.

"Harry?"

He had stood and was heading for the door, unable to say goodbye, but Nora whispered to him, her hand over her microphone, "Harry, please stay a second." She wiped her hands with a dish towel and reached for a PSA tape to play, then looked back at him with a smile. Harry noticed again how tired she looked. "I'm sorry. You're not fair game. But I'm worried about you. You want him to be real, but what if he's not? What if he's conning you and everybody else? What if he's crazy dangerous, and his people do something crazy too. His crowds get bigger and bigger, and you help make that happen, and someday somebody is going to get hurt, Harry, and I worry that it's going to be you."

"Nora…," he started to say, but the 30 second PSA was almost over, so she waved him off, whispering, "Talk to me later tonight when you come back, okay? I'll be nice, I promise."

Harry went back to his apartment and slept until it was almost time for his show. He woke up hungry, his stomach reminding him that he had missed his meal at Nora's that afternoon. He went through his refrigerator and scavenged some leftovers from his last meal, fixed himself some coffee, and walked to WWHD. In that three minutes, he looked up at a black-clouded sky, disappointed that he could not see the moon, and realized that he had no idea what he was going to talk about that night.

He opened with a different Harry Chapin song. "W.O.L.D." had been replaced with "Dance Band on the Titanic." No particular reason, he just wanted a change, and he always liked "Dance Band." But as soon as Chapin hit the line, "The iceberg's on the starboard bow, won't you dance with me," Harry started singing along, out loud, loud enough to wake Jimmy Buffet and send him into a spasm of squawks, and Harry sang and laughed along with Chapin. At that moment, "Dance Band" was the funniest happiest song Harry had ever heard. He started tapping his fingers on the table in front of him, then grabbed two ball point pens and used them as drum sticks. Harry and Harry both sang, "There's no way that this could happen, I could hear the old captain curse. He ordered lifeboats away, and that's when I heard the chaplain say, Women and children and chaplains first."

The phone light started blinking. Harry played the song again, telling his listeners to "listen this time, because this is the funniest song ever written." And he sang along again, realizing that he could remember lots of songs from his past. Both station lines were blinking. Harry ignored them. Any other night he would be thrilled to get a call, just as proof that somebody was paying attention. Tonight, he wanted to sing. His cell phone rang. It was Jack Tunnel, laughing, "You're a damn nut-case, Harry, you need prooooooo-fessional help," and then he hung up. Harry called him back, not bothering to say hello, just launching into, "I left my chevy on the levee…," and Jack instantly chimed in, "…but the levee was dry. And those good old boys were drinking whiskey and rye. So it's bye-bye, Miss American Pie…" Harry hooked his cell phone into the control panel and the two men serenaded St. Augustine with their spontaneous anthem to the death of great American music. The phone lines kept blinking. Harry became more manic, mixing lyrics from different songs. Knights in white satin were soon flying in their taxis, getting stoned, while white rabbits were floating on a moon river.

Two hours into his show, Harry finally sat down. His shirt was soaked in sweat, and his voice was hoarse. *Where did all this come from*, he wondered. *No matter, it just is. Maybe I've been looking in the wrong places. Maybe the answer's not in the books or the poems. Maybe it's in the music. Or, not. Who knows anything anymore?*

He spent the last two hours of his show talking about his childhood in Iowa, explaining the art of corn de-tassling and revealing other agricultural do's and don'ts. When he got to the story about the cemetery near his house in Springville, he found himself talking about John Brown, and that led to his talking about Henry Thoreau's essay about John Brown, a seamless discussion from corn to literary explication and American history. No good reason, he knew that, just bouncing from topic to topic, one idea connected to a bigger idea, and the phone lines stopped blinking. A few minutes before 2:00 A.M., when he knew for sure that nobody was listening, he announced, "Okay, St. Augustine, another night, another half dollar. I am just about out of here. Carlos Friedmann is outside waiting to get this microphone. His special guest tonight is a Gloria Estafan impersonator. Stick around, the night is young. "As for me…," and he paused, realizing that his usual sign-off … *the night is young, but I am not*… did not fit this night. He did not feel old. He felt young, and he wanted to go to the beach, and so he closed with, "The night is young, and I'm wide awake. I'm taking my big flashlight and headed for Vilano Beach to hunt snarks and sharks. Come on down if you're still up. Talk to you tomorrow."

As he left WWHD, Harry lifted the cover off Jimmy Buffett's cage. The parrot was pacing his perch. Instead of a squawk, the only sound out of his beak seemed like a growl. Carlos had told him, "You're gonna give that *loro un acceso de carazo uno* of these days, and I'm gonna help you."

There might have been a moon and stars in the sky, but the black clouds hid them. A storm was coming, and the beach was dark. Harry had done it hundreds of times in the past seven years, walked alone, his four-celled flashlight brought along but seldom used. When Nora walked with him, they would take their time, listening to the waves. Sometimes they caught lovers who had brought their blankets and assumed they had privacy. Still, even with that privacy breached, the lovers would pause but not stop. Harry and Nora would walk past, whispering to themselves, as if the bodies on the beach were merely sleeping. Once, under a full moon a year earlier, they had seen lovers far in the distance, walking out of the Atlantic. At first glance, it was not obvious that the two young people were naked, but, as soon as Nora realized they were, she made Harry stop. The young couple seemed oblivious to the adults a hundred feet away. The girl had laughed at something the boy said, and then she had run away from him. He did not follow, seeming to know that she would return. Further away, Harry and Nora watched her turn and look at the boy, whose vision of her, because closer, was surely more clear as she slowly walked back to him, shaking water from her long wet hair, her firm and soft body shimmering in the moonlight as the tide rolled in to almost touch her feet. "Surely," Nora had whispered to Harry, her arm entwined in his, "surely she must see us. If we can see her so clearly, she must see us too." But the girl ignored the older couple, if, indeed, she had seen them. She stood next to the boy and let him put her arm around her waist, and they began walking away. Harry turned and wanted to walk in the opposite direction, leaving them alone, but Nora wanted to follow them at a discreet distance. Harry insisted that the young people should be given their own space and privacy, and Nora reluctantly agreed, with a sigh and a soft squeeze of his arm, "Oh, Harry, you've never had sex on the beach, have you? And you probably haven't even ever gone skinny-dipping, right?" She had then laughed, after looking back over her shoulder one last time at the receding lovers, "But, as I recall, you can't even swim, can you?"

Two-thirty this morning, Harry remembered that other morning. The motion of the moon-basked girl as she walked toward her lover, the sway of naked breasts and hips, but most of all he remembered Nora's whisper about sex on the beach. She had been right.

With no moonlight to guide him this morning, he switched on his flashlight and shot beams all over the beach and then into the sky. Except for some scurrying sand crabs, he was still alone. The air was warm and humid, and even the strong wind was not enough to offer relief. He took off his shoes and socks, rolled up his pants legs, and walked along the creeping edge of the incoming water, the wet sand spongy beneath his feet. He was not tired, and he still wanted to sing, but the surf would not cooperate. The tempo was too slow, but it was so loud that he could almost not hear himself speak as it crashed. He looked for shrimp boat lights out on the ocean. Seeing none, and starting to tire, he decided to leave and go to Nora's house. But as soon as he got to the top of the first dune ridge he stopped and sat down, his bottom on dry sand, his chin propped on his hands, his elbows propped on his knees. He closed his eyes, and, having no control over the music of the ocean in front of him, he simply listened to the crash and retreat of the tide.

"Harry, where are you?"

Dexter was calling him. Harry opened his eyes, blinking, shaking his head. He was still on the dune. But he was somewhere else. Some other time. That was his first impression. The weather had changed. The clouds were white, not black, and the moon was glowing through them. The wind was much calmer. The ocean was placid, and the horizon was lined in golden-orange. There was no surf. The Atlantic was an expanse of soft waves, like a backyard pool, and the clearest sound was Dexter's voice, and then more muffled voices in the distance. The beach was teeming with beams of light shooting and crisscrossing each other. Hundreds of beams.

"Harry Ducharme, where are you?"

"Here, I'm over here," Harry shouted as he stood up. A beam of light hit him in the face, and then, as if by order, those other beams all pointed in his direction, a phalanx of light, blinding him. He waved his hands in front of his face, and the beams seemed to shoot straight up into the air, like spotlights at a premiere.

"Dammit, Harry," Dexter laughed as he reached him, "You invite people for a walk on the beach and then you disappear? Not very gracious, if you ask me."

The crowd was coming closer, and Harry thought that he could see people he knew. "You were listening?" he asked.

"Well. not really. But Nora was, and she called, woke me up, and asked me to bring her down here to meet you. These other people...," he said, sweeping his hand around him, "...I take no responsibility for. They are on your tab."

"Nora's here?"

A voice in the crowd, "He's up there!"

Dexter took Harry's arm and pointed him north. "You go that way. She's about a hundred yards up the beach. Too tired to walk anymore, so I told her that I'd find you. So, go. Me, I'm going to sacrifice myself so you can make your getaway, but you gotta promise to come back soon. This is your audience, your fans, not mine, but I think I can line up some votes here anyway. I brought a few hundred cards to hand out. Three months until the filing deadline." Reading Harry's mind, he then added, "And, yes, Harry, me and Charlotte and Charlie Yates will make sure there's no litter left."

From a distance, Harry and Nora watched the crowd. They were sitting side by side, her arm entwined with his, waiting for the morning sun to rise. Harry was a happy man.

"You going to come see me when I'm dead?" She asked after a long silence.

"Where should I look, since you don't believe in heaven or hell?

"The time comes, you'll figure it out."

He nudged her with his shoulder, "And, besides, best I can figure, you'll outlive me by years."

She sighed, "Sure, I'll live forever. I'll cater your funeral. I'll scatter your ashes at The Tavern. I'll...," but she stopped. The crowd seemed to be moving toward them. "Harry, I need to go home. I still have a show to do in a few hours. Polly's down there somewhere, probably trying to get people to get naked and go swimming. Go find her and ask her to take me back. You and Dexter can feed the masses and round up voters at the same time. Me, I've got biscuits rising in my kitchen. And Pitty-Sing needs to be fed too."

Helping her stand up, Harry protested, "But you'll miss the sun coming up. Won't you stay to see that?"

She brushed sand off her skirt and then put her arms around him, her face pressed against his chest, "Harry, it happens everyday."

August 3, 2008
First the Chill
Then the Stupor
Then the Letting Go

Nora never told him any more love stories. He might hint, he might ask directly, but the mood was never right. Still, Harry kept going back to sleep with her every night. She gave him a key so that he could let himself in after his show during the week. On the weekends, he would go early, sometimes take a video for them to watch, or sometimes they would just sit and read, ignoring each other, as if they had been married fifty years and knew each other's rhythms without having to speak. Harry assumed that their arrangement would last a long time, but it ended August 3.

In the beginning, sleeping together was their secret, but such a secret was impossible to keep in Nora's small world. As soon as Polly figured it out, she called Harry and teased him about sleeping with a ghost in a haunted house. Of course, Dexter soon knew and the young man began calling him *Harry James*. When Jack Tunnel asked him about it, Harry prepared for more ribbing, but Jack's only comment was, "You're a lucky man, and I'm glad for you." He was absolutely un-ironic, and he did not ask for a single detail. Down at The Tavern, Michelle had leaned across the counter and simply asked, "Is it true, what I've been hearing?" Harry had nodded, and Michelle's only other comment was, "You've come a long way, Harry. Too bad you're on the wagon, or else I'd buy you a drink."

"Take me to church, Harry. Let's see if this god guy is paying attention," she told him the morning of the third. Nora was in a good mood, full of more energy than usual, and her morning show had gotten a lot of calls asking her opinion of a new restaurant opening in St. Augustine. She promised to get back to her listeners as soon as she had actually eaten at the new place, but she warned everyone, "I've seen the menu. Same old, same old. Unless they have a magic chef, I'm not expecting much." Harry was sitting on a stool next to the counter as she swirled around her kitchen, his coffee just starting to make the world a manageable place. Pitty Sing was brushing up against his leg, and he took that atypical affection as another good sign.

"I feel like getting out today, Harry. Take a stroll downtown, pop into the Cathedral and see if we can buy some old bones of Jesus. You got plans?"

He shook his head, enjoying a happy Nora. If she stayed talkative, he knew he would ask more about her past. "You want to see anybody else down there? Jack or Paul or Michelle, anybody?" he asked, hoping the answer was no.

"Nope, just me and you on a road trip, Harry. And I'm serious about going to church." She smiled at him, not the look he wished he would see in her face as she looked at him, but it was enough for the moment.

Show done, kitchen cleaned more thoroughly than usual, furniture dusted, Pitty-Sing fed, Nora went upstairs and came down in a summer dress with spaghetti-thin shoulder straps, sunglasses propped on her forehead, and a giant straw hat. The dress was too big for her.

"I'm ready for my close-up, Mr. Ducharme."

An hour later, after getting some ice cream at a shop on St. George Street, they walked around the corner to church. Harry had been there a few times in the past, but never for a service. Nora knew all the history and gave him the highlights: New World settlers built a church that sometimes got burned down by pirates, a coquina stone building in 1797, eventually enhanced by Robber Baron money in the form of a steeple funded by Henry Flagler. The final Spanish Colonial Renaissance style structure, the one in which they sat, was built in 1797 and reconstructed in the late 1880's. It was in all the tourist guide books, but Nora assumed Harry's ignorance.

His response to her history lesson was his own flashback, "You know, the church I went to every Sunday when I was a kid…it didn't even have a cross in it. All I remember is a lot of old people being very quiet. But it was okay, I think it was okay."

They were sitting in a pew near the altar, surrounded by icons, idols, and craven images. Except for a few elderly and solitary women in distant pews, they were alone. Nora pursed her lips and blew out her breath, saying, "Not us, we go for the full monty hats and horns."

He turned to her slowly and asked about her pronoun choice, "We?"

She did not look at him, but sat there looking straight ahead, then she looked around, then straight up, holding that pose long enough for Harry to wonder what she was looking at, so he looked around and then up too. He had not paid attention to the ceiling and walls at first, but there was color everywhere, gold and blue and silver and red, brighter than he had ever seen, erupting colors that had been frozen in place, so that somebody, if they looked close enough, could see where all the lines went and the colors interconnected. It was like being inside a Fourth of July skyrocket as it exploded, surrounded by swirls of light and energy, but stilled in a photograph.

He was still looking up when she asked him, "See anything?"

Harry could not take his eyes away from the ceiling. There was *something* up there in that color. He answered without looking away, "I'm not sure, but I think…almost like a face?…or some sort of design…or…," and then he felt self-conscious and stopped himself, shifting the burden back to her, "So, what am I supposed to see? What do you see?"

Nora looked back up, as if to confirm an earlier opinion, and said with a shrug, "Nothing. Not anything. I sat here forty years ago and looked at other people looking up, who saw something, and I looked up too, but it was the same then as it is now. Nothing. Just some paint on the wall."

Harry looked again. She was wrong.

The Plaza across from the Cathedral was shaded but not cool this August afternoon, and Nora was tired again. When Harry saw her shiver, he took off his jacket and wrapped it around her bare shoulders, suggesting that he take her back home, but she asked him to stay with her a few more minutes. "I always loved this spot, even as a kid." Seeing him stare at her, waiting for more, she relented. "Surprise, surprise, Harry. I grew up in this town. Went to the cathedral school a few blocks away, walked to Mass right here every Wednesday morning led by the nuns, wore a uniform in high school. I was christened over there, and I thought I would get married there, back when I was a marrying kind of girl."

Harry knew that this was the opening he wanted, but he also knew that Nora would not answer anything he asked. He would have to settle for whatever she gave him.

Straw hat on head, her eyes hidden behind sunglasses, she looked away from Harry as she rambled, "Bus station used to be west of here a few blocks. That art store at the corner used to be a bookstore I worked at. Even had a Woolworth's behind us. Greek restaurant, there, is the same. The Tavern and the Tradewinds are equal distance from this exact spot in different directions. I walked it off when I was in high school, counted the steps, the same, or about the same, close enough." She stopped, and it was obvious to Harry that she was processing something in her mind. "You know what the nuns used to say to me? They'd sit me down and pop the tops of my hands with a damn wooden ruler, and they'd spit out, *Little Missy, do you think that the rules do not apply to you?* I'd keep my mouth shut, but I always wanted to say, *You're goddam right. The rules don't apply to me.*"

"Now, there's a girl after my own heart," Harry said kindly, wanting her to keep talking.

"Not really. If I know anything about you, it's that you're a rule kind of guy. You might want to change some of them, but you believe in them. You just want to understand them. Trust me, you wouldn't have liked me back then."

"Nora, I didn't even like myself back then, whenever that was, so we're even, okay?"

"Well, the thing is, I do understand the rules now. Everything has rules, even adultery and love, and I finally know all this too late. Harry, I'm not making much progress with my life. I grew up in this town. Then I went away. And I came back, but as somebody else, thinking I was different, but here I am sitting where I sat forty years ago, my butt and this bench old friends. That's it, Harry, the sum total of my wisdom: The rules matter, and my butt hurts."

The Cathedral bells started ringing. Harry looked at Nora, and they could read each other's minds for that one brief moment, *How perfect*, and then Nora laughed out loud, a from-the-bottom-of-the-gut laugh that Harry had never heard from her before, a laugh at herself, a laugh too happy not to catch, and Harry started laughing too, almost choking as he tried to talk, "And you wondered if God was paying attention when we went to church?"

Nora took a deep breath, still giddy, and sighed, "Those bells are on a timer, but I'll take any small sign I can." She then stood up and nodded toward Harry's Buick parked on the street on the other side of the Plaza, "Take me home. You told me that you were doing a live show tonight for some reason, I forget. Something about making up some hours from earlier in the week. Me, I need to rest. Take me home and tell me all about Dex's plans on the way. And then come to my place tonight. I'll wait up for you."

Harry did all the talking on the short drive back, condensing a lot of information about Dexter and Charlotte and Prophet into ten minutes, promising that he would give her more details later that night. He kept one thing to himself, his premonition that Dexter was headed for some sort of trouble, that too much about Prophet and his people still did not make sense. But there would be time for that discussion later. The last thing that Nora said before he left her that afternoon was, "Dex has always had this cocoon around him, of good luck and happiness. He's not like his father at all, all gloom and doom Abe. People are drawn to Dex in odd ways, Harry. The more I think about it, the more I think he might do okay in politics. But I don't think *that* much about it. I'll leave that to you and his parents. He's coming over for a late dinner tonight. I'll see if he opens up about the girl, and then you and I can compare notes."

He helped her to her front door, holding her arm as he helped her into the house and made sure she was comfortable on the couch. Then he went back to his apartment to do some final prep for his show. He wanted to talk about the court case that had gone against the Fred Phelps church a few months earlier. The *God Hates Fags* sect had finally angered the wrong parents when it protested at the funeral of a soldier killed in Iraq. Harry had a special animus toward the Phelps crusade, but he was actually ambivalent about this particular judgment. It was the issue that he wanted to discuss this night: How much freedom to be hateful should anybody be allowed?

It was going to be a hot night in St. Augustine, and the WWHD building did not have a good air conditioning system. The studio equipment generated more heat, but an hour into his program Harry was being kept cool mainly by the iced coffee in his thermos. He was full of caffeine, as he had been in the morning, looking forward to the end of the show, when his cell phone rang near midnight.

"Harry, this is Dexter. Can you please come to Nora's house as soon as possible? I need you."

At 9:00 AM the next morning, Captain Jack Tunnel surprised his listeners with an announcement, "Folks, an hour from now I would always turn you over to Nora James, but I need to let you know that Nora is going off the air for awhile. She's feeling poorly, so her time slot will be...," and he paused, "...will be filled with some tapes from her old shows. Stay tuned for more news about her later." Jack sat there and looked at the clock in the studio. An hour to go in his own show. Jimmy Buffett had been kept out of the studio this morning, and Jack's delivery had been more low-key than usual, accounted for by him saying that he had had a "late night." An hour to go, he reached for a tape. "You know, folks, I'm not feeling too good myself. I'm going to cut this short this morning and take a few days off, but I guarantee that I'll be back on Monday. Just like...MacArthur?...I shall return." With that, Tunnel flipped a switch, but he did not move. He sat in the studio for an hour and did not say another word. Sometime in that hour, he wished he was Harry Ducharme, because *If I was Harry, I'd know a poem that fit this moment. He's good at that. Knowing what somebody else has already said. But I'm just me. I'm just Captain Jack Tunnel, and nothing I say will match how I feel. One line from college, all I remember of Shakespeare. I think it was Shakespeare. Something about sound and goddam fury, signifying nothing. That's me. That's all I am. Nothing.*

When Harry got to Nora's house, she was gone. He did not know it then, but he would never see her again. He could not park close to her house because there were two black Cadillacs taking all the available spaces in front. No ambulance, no hearse, just two black *Coupe de Villes*. Dexter was waiting at the front door, but so were two other men that looked like him.

"Harry, these are my brothers," Dexter said, introducing the older men. Harry shook their hands, but he never remembered their names. "They're here to…," and then Dexter began crying. Harry stepped up and put his arms around the young man and held him close as his chest heaved in sobs. The two brothers each put a hand on Dexter's back, and Harry did not let go for a long time.

Nora James was gone. Nobody used the word *dead*. She was merely gone. Harry followed the three brothers into the house, assuming that he was there to help Dexter, time later for himself, but for now the youngest was the most needy and had to be served first.

They went to the kitchen, where Dexter told his story. He had come for dinner, and he thought she was asleep on the couch, but she would not wake. Except for calling his parents, everything after that was a haze for him. He did not even remember calling Harry.

"My mother called us," one of the brothers said, the other nodding. "We came as soon as we could."

Harry felt something rubbing against his leg. He looked down as Pitty-Sing looked up, and then he realized what was missing. "Where is she?" he asked. "I mean…I don't know what I mean." But he did know what he meant. He wanted to see her, to tell her good-by, but the three men with him did not answer. One of the brothers excused himself and left the kitchen. Dexter and his other brother did not speak, did not look in his direction. Harry was about to ask again when he heard his name.

"You must be Harry Ducharme."

Two tall men stood in the kitchen, Dexter's brother behind them. These two new men had a trace of Dexter in their faces, but they were even older than Harry, and their dark suits and dark ties seemed out of place in the scene in which Harry imagined himself. There had never been anything *that* formal about Nora's kitchen.

The older of the two men extended his hand as Harry rose, "My name is Turner West, and this is my brother Dylan. We're from Jacksonville, here to handle the arrangements."

Turner West? Harry struggled with his memory, knowing he had heard this name before, and he held on to the man's hand until he felt himself almost shudder with the recollection of why he knew that name. Turner West was dead, his name on a tombstone in a cemetery that Nora had shown him. Turner West was dead and buried near Dexter's grandparents. *Perhaps Polly's right,* Harry thought, *perhaps I have been sleeping with ghosts.*

"Mr. Ducharme?" Turner West's eyes were locked on Harry.

Harry looked back at Dexter for help, but he was still looking at the floor. Finally, Harry plunged ahead, "You have the same name as a dead man whose grave I saw awhile back. Probably just a coincidence?"

"That was my father. I'm his oldest son. Dylan is next. We took over the funeral service from our father. Dexter's mother is our little sister."

West almost smiled when he said "little sister," but he stopped himself and waited for Harry to catch up. But all Harry could do was sit back down next to Dexter. West turned back to his brother and nodded toward a small black bag on the counter. Then he turned back to Harry, "You'll be notified about a memorial service. There was a request made that only a few friends be invited, and the interment itself will be closed to the public. It will be for family only."

Harry had gone back to Iowa for a moment in his mind, but he returned to Nora's kitchen in time to ask, "She had a family?"

West looked at the other men in the room before he answered, "I meant to say, the Lee and West families, as well as two other close friends."

Harry knew that he meant Polly Jackson and himself. There was no one else as close to Nora as they had been. Still, he felt sorry for those such as Jack and Michelle and Paul, whose feelings would be hurt by their exclusion.

Dylan West left the room with the black bag in hand. Turner West saw the question on Harry's face. "Dexter's father has instructed us to change the locks on the doors and to close down the house as soon as possible. It's my understanding that you have a key. Is that correct? Would it be possible to get that back, if you don't mind."

Harry felt sand shifting under his feet, as he had felt the first morning he stood on the St. Augustine beach. But all he could mumble was, "You change locks too?"

"We handle all the family's business," was West's only response.

Harry lied to him, almost angry, "I left it back at my apartment. Truth is, I lost it. Never needed it lately. Nora was always here. But if you change the locks, it's all a moot point anyway, right?"

"Please don't misunderstand, Mr. Ducharme. This isn't a reflection on you. I'm simply acting on a request of Mr. Lee. This is his house. It was his key. He wants it back. Please look for it and return it to Dexter or his father as soon as convenient."

With that, and with the return of his brother to the kitchen, Turner West said, "Gentlemen, we've done all we can do here. I'd suggest that we go home."

Four hours later, as the sun rose, with a glass of water in his hand, sitting in an apartment that was the only home he had left, and after calling Jack Tunnel with the news, Harry had reduced the meaning of life itself to a single unresolved question: *Who's going to take care of the cat?* He thought that Nora would understand why he asked.

"Harry, you going to come see me when I'm dead?"

"Where should I look, since you don't believe in heaven or hell?"

"The time comes, you'll figure it out."

❦

Nora James was gone. She was not dead. That was the official story from WWHD. She might return, she might not. The station would alert its listeners when it knew more. Dexter had called Harry, who called Jack, who told Paul, who told nobody. Dexter's father had called Polly Jackson, who told nobody. There was no agreement, no conspiracy, at first. They simply did not talk about it except among themselves. The memorial service was on Jack's boat, and nobody cried in front of the others, except Polly. Then, as weeks passed, their secret became valuable in itself. Her departure was their bond, not to be shared. There was no funeral, no visitation, Nora was gone. She was not dead. Her name and picture were not in the *St. Augustine Record* obit section. There was no death certificate at the county courthouse. She was not dead. St. Augustine waited for her return, but Harry knew that towns were like people. After awhile, they get tired of waiting. Life goes on. It might take a few months for most, years for a few, but even people like Michelle at The Tavern would stop waiting for Nora. Life goes on.

Harry had asked Dexter what plans had been made about Nora's body. Dexter was evasive, saying that he would let him know as soon as his father had decided. Harry called Polly and asked her. More evasion. Three days passed, the small memorial service came and went, and Harry could not get an answer from anybody about where or when Nora was going to be buried. As a last resort, he called the West Funeral Home in Jacksonville, hoping that he would not have to actually talk to Turner West. The woman on the phone was obliviously helpful: "Mr. West and his brothers are attending a private funeral this afternoon at the family cemetery."

The time comes, you'll figure it out.

Harry put on his only suit and went looking for that giant curve on A1A. As he got closer, a perplexing thought occurred to him, almost a wish, *I hope Prophet and his people aren't there. I hope Dexter didn't invite that girl. Nora wouldn't want that.*

It was a cloudless bright blue day, but cooler than usual, especially for August. Harry could see the black Cadillacs and a single black hearse lined up against the stone fence of the cemetery.

Why wasn't I told? I had to be one of the two friends. I had to be.

The entrance to the cemetery was an iron double-gate, and Harry remembered how hard it had been to swing it open when he and Nora had gone there earlier. As he got closer to the gate, he could see through the bars. He quickly counted the black-clad figures, their backs to him, all of them sharing the shade of a half dozen large black umbrellas. Twelve people. He counted down: Dexter, his parents, and his brothers were five; and he knew that Turner West had five brothers, all accounted for. That made eleven. Another female, blond, that had to be Polly. Twelve. But, family and *two* friends? There should be thirteen. Then, as two of the men parted slightly, Harry saw another woman, much shorter than Polly or Dexter's mother. The other friend? But someone he had never met. It was not Charlotte Arnold. But who?

He put his hand on the gate, but before he could pull it open a tiny man seemed to appear out of nowhere and block his way. He was the starkest of black and white. An old black man in a black suit with white shirt and black tie, his black head framed by solid white hair on the sides.

"I'm sorry, Mr. Ducharme, but this is a private service. You're certainly welcome to visit later, but the families would like to have this occasion to themselves. I'm sure you understand."

Harry did not understand. "Pete? From the Goose?" He kept his hand on the gate.

"Yessir," the old black man said, but he did not step out of the way.

Harry looked past him and counted the mourners again. Thirteen. Where did Pete fit in?

"But I should be here. I promised Nora. I mean, you can ask Polly or Dexter or one of the others. They know me. *You* know me, for chrissakes. Just ask somebody."

Pete did not move. "You must have come to the wrong place, Mr. Ducharme. I don't know anything about a Nora woman. This here today is for Miss Alice. You're not part of her story, so I guess that's why there's some confusion. Still in all, I have to go pay my respects now. Mr. Lee will want a few words from me, and I've been choosing them for a long time. I'm the last to speak. So, you'll have to excuse me."

As Pete was about to turn, Harry blurted out one more question, "The short woman, who is she? Is she from here?"

Pete's face instantly went from sorrow to a smile, "Oh, Lord joy, that is Miss Louise, Mr. Abe's sister. Young Dexter's aunt. We haven't seen her for a long long time. She's come home for Alice. But she'll be gone tomorrow, probably not coming back until it's my time. I made her promise."

With that, he turned and his tiny black shape limped over to the other mourners. Harry realized that Pete, as he blended into the family, was the second friend, the last mourner.

He walked to his Buick, which was parked across the street. He would come back another time, alone. At that moment, however, he stood and looked out over a huge empty lot between him and the ocean. He could see where the sand was still sculpted by a hidden concrete foundation. Off to a far side was Pete's caboose. On the distant ocean, a blue-hulled sailboat was headed south to St. Augustine.

Harry knew all about the stages of grief. He had read those books too. In his successful past he had interviewed well known psychologists as well as quack healers. The collective program was simple: Time cures all wounds. Support groups weren't a bad idea for some people either, but not for Harry. With his son's death, he had simply drunk himself into a stupor and tried to shorten the process, or at least remain numb for the duration, but all he did was extend his grief and compound his guilt. Nora was different. Nora was grief without guilt. There was still no book for him to read. But there was a story.

"Harry, I promised her that I'd go for a walk on the beach with you. You doing anything tonight?"

"Polly?" Harry was cleaning his apartment. It was not dirty, nor was it messy. If anything, his apartment was carefully arranged. Clothes were never strewn around, dishes were never left in the sink, even the magazines were stacked neatly, but a long time ago Nora had seen his apartment and laughed at him. "You ever heard of a dust cloth, Harry? Why is it that men know how to vacuum, but they refuse to dust?" When Polly called, he had been wiping down every surface in his apartment.

"Nora asked a favor from you…about me?" Harry hesitated. What he really wanted from Polly was an explanation about what had happened that afternoon, why was he excluded from Nora's burial? Everybody else seemed to have a role, but not him. "Tonight? You sure? Why so soon?"

The *Why so soon* was Harry's opening for Polly to discuss the funeral. *Let her open the door,* he told himself. But Polly ignored him. "She told me a long time ago, back in March, I think. Told me to take you for a walk on the beach and drag your sorry ass into the water if the mood hit me. You up for that, Harry? That is, after I tell you something about her that she said you needed to know, and you *alone.*"

"I don't swim," Harry said softly, dropping his dust rag on the kitchen counter.

"Yeh, yeh, she told me that too. You're such a broken record, Harry, or maybe just all scratched up, and sorta pathetic." She said it with a laugh, and he almost laughed himself. *A broken record, all scratched up…*from whomever the comparison came, Nora or Polly, it was true.

It was almost ten o'clock before she showed up at his apartment. She had insisted that he not come get her. "Getting a make-over before my hot date," she had said. The truth was less glamorous. Polly was drunk, but she also looked like she was sixteen again. That was Harry's first thought, sixteen again. And she smelled like a bordello.

"Take me to a movie," she purred as soon as she got into Harry's Buick. "And feel free to call me Miss Daisy."

"There are no movies this late," he started to protest, but she cut him off.

"She said you'd figure that one out. Said you'd know what to do. Please, Harry, don't disappoint her, or me. Take me to a goddam movie."

They had been driving over the Usina Bridge, heading for Vilano Beach, where he and Nora had usually walked, but as he reached the bottom of the bridge where it t-boned with A1A, where he would usually go south, he turned north, suddenly knowing what Polly had meant. As soon as he turned to head toward Jacksonville, she scooted over to the middle of the front seat and sat next to him, nudging him with her shoulder, saying, "Put your arm around me, Harry. This is a date. Treat me like a white girl." That demand satisfied, she had another, "Open the windows and let the air in, noise be damned. My hair is still wet."

Harry ignored her. Instead, he opened the sun roof. She didn't protest. She merely laid her head back and looked up at the moon overhead. "I love this car, Harry. It's like riding in a cloud. But I guess all the girls tell you that, eh?"

He drove without responding, not bothered by his sense that she was talking to herself as much to him, that the booze had been like medicine to her, and she was numb to some pain that had earlier almost paralyzed her. Still, he kept trying to connect this moment back to Nora's funeral only a few hours earlier. *Life goes on, with or without us*, he told himself. Not an original insight, he knew that, but Polly was right about one thing. Driving his Buick *was* like driving a cloud.

Fifteen minutes later, they were walking on the beach, across A1A from the West Cemetery. A darkened caboose, its exterior lit by a kerosene lantern hanging off the back railing, guarded the north boundary. Harry and Polly went south.

She was barefoot, her short thin dress billowing in the wind, swirling up and around her in gusts, and Harry did not resist when she entwined her arm in his and leaned on him for support as they walked. It was a different feeling than the times Nora had done the same. Some portion of him, totally un-related to his heart, was aroused.

He was sweating. A hot humid night, with Polly rubbing against him, Harry's mind was having a hard time controlling his body. He wanted Polly to talk about Nora. And he wanted Polly to not let go of him. She solved his dilemma by speaking first.

"We went swimming on this beach all the time, late at night. Well, me and Abe's sister and the Flagler boys would go swimming. She always said she was saving her virgin naked body for some lucky husband, that *we* weren't privileged."

"You mean Nora?" He knew the answer, but he wanted Polly to keep talking.

"Oh, yeh, the Nora," she said, slowing down and then separating herself from Harry to walk toward the edge of the water. The moon was low on the horizon, and the light shone through the sheer dress she was wearing, outlining her hips. "You know, Harry, I'm not as dumb as people think. She knew it, and I loved her for that. But she never liked it when I told her that it took more than a name change to change who you are. On that one single point, I was smarter than her, and even though she always let me be smart, I was *never* supposed to be smarter than her."

He started walking toward her, but she waved him back. "My dime, Harry. This is my damn dime and I get to do all the talking."

He flashed back to that afternoon, to seeing Polly in black, standing next to Dexter's father and mother, part of their family. He looked back toward the caboose in the distance, the single lantern still swaying.

"It's all gone," she said with a sniffle, and then another, and then tears. "It was the best summer of my life, and she took care of me. She made them take me into their home. I lived with them. Just like her. Right here on the beach, in the world's biggest movie screen, inside of it, and the old man was crazy but she knew how to handle him. And Abe was so sweet. Oh, Jesus Harry, she was my first real friend. She was my mother, I wished she was, at least. My own mother was a piece of shit, but Alice was like my real mother. And she's gone, Harry. It's all gone. And when Pete dies, all that'll be left is an empty beach."

She stopped talking and started walking into the water. The ocean was up to her knees before he could shout. "Polly, don't go any further," but his feet were frozen. He had never learned to swim. He could never save her if she went too far. But he went into the water anyway, sloshing toward her, grabbing her hand and turning her around, then pulling her back to shore. His reward was her crying laughter.

"Oh, Harry, you are so incredibly sweet and brave, but, honey, I swim like a fish. I wasn't going to hurt myself. I promised her that a long time ago.

I just wanted to get in the water. It's a hot night. The water is cooler than the air. I'm going swimming."

With that, she stepped back and began unbuttoning her blouse. Harry was paralyzed, but he forced himself to ask her, "You've got to help me, Polly. You're the only person who knows everything about the past. All I get are bits and pieces of her history, but nobody will tell me the whole story. This beach, the theatre that doesn't exist anymore, the Lee family and the West family. I don't even understand the present, all this stuff about Prophet and his people, and all I want is somebody to explain it to me, the past and the present. The big picture. The design. The future will take care of itself. You have to help me understand Nora. Anything, just help me."

Her blouse was completely unbuttoned, but she paused as she was about to slide it off her shoulders. "Here's the only story about her you need to know, Harry. And she'd kill me if I forgot to tell you," making herself laugh at the idea of her friend coming back to haunt her. "She went away as Alice, and she came back as Nora. But I know that it's Alice that you really want to understand, right? So here's the short version. Alice fell in love with an older man a few years after she left here the second time. No, not what you're thinking, not anybody around here. Not anybody we ever saw. She never even told me his name. Nobody you'll bump into. But he was the only man she ever truly loved."

He looked away, anywhere but at Polly, but she would not let him escape the moment. Still, her voice was not unkind, "Harry, she was never going to fall in love with you, not with you or any of the others."

"This is not fair," he said, his throat almost choking. And then, almost angry, "Is this the favor she asked of you?"

Which made Polly angry, "Are you listening to me? Did you hear me when I said she'd kill me if she thought I *didn't* tell you?"

"But why are you telling me? Why didn't she tell me herself?"

"She never wanted to see your face, Harry, hurt like I'm seeing it now, even if this is only moonlight. And me, as messenger? Because I like you, Harry. Is that so goddam difficult to understand? I like you enough to be honest with you, which is more than she ever was. You always want the answers to everything. All you do on your program is ask questions. And all you do around me…thank you very damn much…is ask me about her. I'm not doing this to hurt you. And I'd bet that she didn't tell you when she was alive because she didn't want to hurt you either. So she's letting me do it."

She started to re-button her blouse, looked at him, and then unbuttoned it again.

"Is that it?" he asked, surrendering his eyes. "She loved somebody else, so she couldn't love me?"

She took off her blouse, but the moon was behind her, so her bare chest was in shadows. As she tossed the blouse at him, she added, "Harry, this is not about you. It's about her. About how she became Nora. And you'll be a lot happier when you figure out that you don't love *her*. You love the *idea* of her." She reached for the buttons at the side of her skirt. With one motion, the skirt was off and then held up against her, hiding her naked body. "She fell in love with an older…married…man, somewhere a thousand miles away, and then she did something that broke his heart, just like she would have done to you if she lived longer, and he killed himself. He wasn't the villain. It was her, she told me over and over, it was her, and nobody would ever know, except herself, how much of a mistake she had made by just being herself. Married or not, he was the only man she ever loved, the only man who made her feel, in her words…*uncommon*. And the only thing she ever tried to explain to me was that when that man died, so did Alice. I don't know the whole story. But Alice died and Nora came back to St. Augustine, and Abe bought that house for her, and Grace forgave her, and until you came along she seldom ever left that house. You get credit for that, Harry, getting her out of the house, but if you want to really understand her you'll have to get something else from somebody else, because that's all I know. Except for this, you're lucky she died. Sooner or later, she would have broken your heart too."

"That's not enough," he protested. "There's got to be more to her story. She must have told you more."

"Harry, even when I knew Alice, forty years ago this summer, I never knew it all. Fair or not, you never get to know the answers to all the questions. Alice told me that bit of warmed over wisdom the morning she left town a few days after Abe's mother died, and then she went to see Abe to tell him something. I suspect he could tell you more, but he won't. Of all people, her secrets are the safest with him."

Clouds had appeared. The moon was almost hidden. The ocean was quiet. Harry looked at Polly, who dropped the skirt she had been holding in front of her. "And now, Harry, we need to talk about the other favor she asked of me. The promise she made me make. And it's okay. She told me that you'd be thinking of her, not me. But I owe her. So, *you*, Harry Ducharme, are about to do something you've never done before. She told me all about you. All about you and the beach. And she told me to tell you that it might be your last time, so enjoy yourself, and never forget her."

September–2008
Poynter Asks the Question
Sunday in Jacksonville

Arthur Poynter closed his Bible and prayed. At least, that was his intent. But the *Times-Union* headline stood between him and God. More than stood, the headline was a hand on his throat. The headline mocked him, choked him, him and his church.

Mystery Preacher Coming
Soon to Alltel Stadium

He was an hour away from his Sunday service, and much thought had gone into his preparation, but the spirit was now gone. A new year, and he was being mocked. The words so carefully chosen and honed were now empty. He had called his colleagues on the Duval Council of Christian Churches, and they agreed, but they were as weak as he to stand against this black tide coming. All the stories had been told in private, all the fear and resentment of this Satan changeling who lured the weak, those who needed the protection and guidance of men like Arthur Poynter and his brother pastors. They had preached the Word of God, and this black man taunts them with his promise of a new Child of God. And the fools believe?

Alltel could hold 76,000 souls. Would he fill it? Poynter was not as confident as his colleagues, who were assured by Alltel officials that the stadium had not been contacted by anybody from Prophet's group. And if contacted, Alltel would not make itself available. Indeed, the *Times-Union* story had indicated that it was merely a plan, some nebulous time in the future. Any use of Alltel would be illegal. Security would prevent them from entering. Poynter reminded them of what had happened in St. Augustine, but they responded, "That was a fluke. The Amphitheatre had no advance notice. And, of course, St. Augustine is hardly comparable to Jacksonville." The 76,000 seats were to be denied Peter Prophet. Poynter reminded them that Prophet's visit in St. Augustine *had* been announced over and over, late at night on the radio, when most true souls were asleep. Word *had* been spread. The mistake made was in *not* taking the news seriously.

Poynter marveled at the foolhardy smugness of his fatted colleagues. Billy Graham had been to Alltel. The Promise Keepers had been to Alltel. Even they, he was assured, had had to follow the rules, book in advance, seek permission.

He railed against them, those who were warned but did not heed. *Do you not see that this man honors no rules. Do you not see that this man is a seducer. Do you not see that this man is the beginning of the end?*

The eve of the ninth Sunday of the year, he had seen the two false apostles speak in Treaty Oak Park. He had been there many times before, reading his old King James, sitting near the massive live oak at the center, two centuries old, a trunk over 25 feet in circumference and over 70 feet tall, *God's Shade* he had called it, and he would meditate as he took the five minute walk to the St. Johns River nearby. Over time he had appropriated the park as his own refuge, but it had been violated that night by heresy. Nobody had told him it was to happen, but he was drawn anyway.

He had stood at the edge of the crowd, looking for Prophet but having to settle for an up-close vision of Prophet's first followers. Three were there, but only two ministered. The man Yates spoke of his conversion at the edge of raging waters, his picture of Prophet's hands and the baby saved, and numbers of the crowd held their own copies aloft, as if beseeching Prophet to appear from the sky. With the final word of Yates came the siren's song, the young woman whose voice was both fire and ice, whose silver hair floated as she sang, whose blue eyes were a flame. Poynter turned away, unable to listen and see her at the same time. In that moment of aversion, he thought he saw members of his own congregation in the crowd. But he would not believe that. Men and women he had baptized, it was not possible. He turned further away. He looked toward the darkening street, but the faces coming toward him into the light of the park reminded him of the faces he would see the next morning. He resolved to leave the park. He had seen enough, and his wife would be expecting him soon. But then the second speaker announced himself. The man Winston asked everyone to come closer to the Oak itself, to gather round, and Poynter was sure he heard the words but later told himself that he had misunderstood. Winston had not really, surely not, called everyone to stand near the *Tree of Life*. Poynter himself must have been thinking about his sermon for the next morning, and his mind and Winston's words had become blended into a misunderstanding. Still, he had turned and returned to the edge of the crowd, to hear the man Winston describe a time when a stone wall which had surrounded his heart had been torn down by Prophet, how he had waited almost forty years to be called to serve him, but the time was now. A New Child of God was coming.

Winston was a sodomite without guilt. He was not converted by Prophet. He had simply been accepted. This New Child to come would personify and manifest that acceptance. Winston talked of how the mind of God had been mis-interpreted by men whose fear had been codified as truth. Winston pulled men and women from the crowd and told them that their sin was not sin, that their depravity was natural. Poynter heard all that, he was sure. Even if the words of Winston were not that precise, Poynter knew their meaning. He had felt them all these years, having told himself the same words in his darkest most private moments, but he had resisted their temptation. He had scourged the words out of his mind and body. He had rejected them at a great cost, but he had won his soul. His reward, surely, would come later.

He looked at the words he had written the day before he went to the park. He knew they were irrelevant this morning. He would speak from the heart.

Poynter went in front of his congregation and looked for faces he had seen the night before, but these people, his flock, were spotless. In the Sunday morning light, they were surely of the Elect and the Sainted. He wanted a balcony, but he settled for center stage. Sin must be announced and purged. The connection between thought and act must be made clear. Consequences must be acknowledged.

He began, "We cannot avoid this truth. God watches us. At every moment. But we must watch ourselves. We must see more than ourselves. We must see that AIDS is not just God's punishment for homosexuals; it is God's punishment for the society that tolerates homosexuals. Even the cataclysm of September 11 has meaning. The abortionists have got to bear some burden for it because God will not be mocked. And when we destroy 40 million little innocent babies, we make God mad. I really believe that the pagans, and the abortionists, and the feminists, and the gays and the lesbians who are actively trying to make that an alternative lifestyle, the ACLU, People for the American Way—all of them who have tried to secularize America—I point the finger in their face and say, *You helped this happen.*"

His congregation closed their Bibles and listened as he told them, "If you're not a born-again Christian, you're a failure as a human being. And you are lost. Your choices will save you or damn you. I truly cannot imagine men with men, women with women, doing what they were not physically created to do, without abnormal stress and mis-behavior. Someone must not be afraid to say, moral perversion is wrong. I say it now. You must say it despite the ridicule of the base society around you. If we do not act now, homosexuals will 'own' America! If you and I do not speak up now, this homosexual steamroller will literally crush all decent men, women, and children who get in its way...and our nation will pay a terrible price!"

He no longer looked at his congregation; instead, his eyes searched the ceiling of his church, as if his true audience was above him.

"Mark my words, and the Word of God. I have told you about false prophets. I have told you about the price of mocking God. Such a prophet is out there, as a beast in the jungle, a priest of the anti-Christ, and he stalks us. He preys on us. And God has just one question for you and me, you and me, every single person in this hall today. Will you be tempted? Or will you cast out the priest of the Devil? God's question to you, his charge to you, is clear: *Who will rid me of this meddlesome and turbulent prophet?*"

Poynter lowered his eyes and searched for his answer. At the back of the room was the gaunt man from before, the same gaunt man he had touched in the park the night before.

September 26, 2008
The First of Forty Days

Fred Tymeson had served two tours in Vietnam as a combat medic. Like most vets, he did not talk much about his experiences. *How do you explain it? Even describe it? The things I did or saw?* He had spent many mornings or afternoons trying to save a wounded man's life, dodging bullets at the same time. Medics were a favorite target of the Viet Cong. But he still served two tours. Back home, he became a fireman, telling his friends that *walking into a burning building was not a rational response to danger, which ought to say something about me.* Over time, the fire department became part of the First Responder unit, often getting to a car wreck or heart attack before the police or an ambulance arrived. Over forty years on the job, long due for retirement, he had seen hundreds of charred or bloody bodies, and convinced himself that he had grown immune to shock or surprise, or even disgust.

911 had gotten the call at four in the afternoon. A woman's voice, surprisingly calm, asked for help as other female voices in the background seemed to be wailing. A man was dead. The dispatcher asked if the woman were sure, was the man dead for sure? The woman was sure.

Tymeson's station was only a mile away from the scene, so he was not surprised to be there first. The old van was parked under a massive tree at the far end of a street that led to some private docks on an inlet. Although under the tree, it should have still been clearly visible to the surrounding houses. The police could sort that out later. His first job was to determine if there was any need for medical help to hurry, then to supply temporary aid if beneficial, and then to secure the scene. As soon as he saw the body, Tymeson slowed down. Time was irrelevant.

The van was pointed away from the water, but he could see that the back hatch had been lifted. Two older women were standing in front, their grief visible from a distance. Tymeson walked past them, remembering them from the Amphitheatre months earlier, and then came upon the young woman, her back to him, her body blocking his first view. He could hear sirens far away, but getting stronger. It was when the woman stepped to the side, without turning around, that he saw the old black man's gutted body, his legs bent at the knee and hanging out of the van, the rest of him laying inside. He asked the young woman if she was okay, but she did not respond. She kept looking at the body, her own hands and her blue cape covered in blood. Tymeson reached over and put his hand on her shoulder, slowly turning her away, suddenly remembering her face, those eyes and hair, and her voice as she had sung in the amphitheatre. He remembered that voice, but this girl, not much more than a child, was silent. And why, he wondered, would she be wearing a cape on such a hot day?

Minutes later, all three of the women were lined up in front of the van being questioned by the police. When asked if they had any idea who might have done this, the two older women shook their heads vigorously. The young woman did not respond. Neither yes nor no, she closed her eyes. Overhearing that question, seeing her face, Tymeson knew whom he had to call.

The invitation had come by mail, much more formal than Harry had expected. A hand-written card, with lettering so graceful that he knew it had to be a woman's hand. Only a few lines, but he read them over and over. *We would be very pleased if you would join us for a conversation on the twenty-sixth. Dexter can tell you how to find our home. We have heard much about you, so it would be our honor to finally meet you. (signed) Abraham and Grace Lee.*

A conversation? If anyone was more nervous than Harry about the prospect of meeting Dexter Lee's parents, it was Dexter himself. He had told Harry many times that his parents were unhappy with his decision to run for office, and that, in their minds, that decision had been encouraged by Harry. More than encouraged, the idea had been planted by him. "Harry, right or wrong, they think I wouldn't be doing this if it weren't for you."

Harry began discreetly asking around about the parents, wanting to understand them before he met them, but his sources were limited, especially about the father. The only person who had any long-term knowledge about him was Polly, and she had been as adamantly protective as Nora when it came to Abraham Lee, "You treat him right, Harry. He's very special to me. Grace is a tough lady, but Izzy's a wounded soldier, sort of. And remember, Dexter is his favorite. Even his brothers accept that." Harry did not broach the subject of sex on the beach, but Polly gave him some preemptive advice anyway, "And do yourself a favor. Do *not* mention around Grace that you know me."

"Okay, I'm the soul of discretion, but surely there's more you can tell me about them," he pressed.

"Sure, but I won't explain it. All I'll tell you now is that you had better like children," Polly said, almost laughing.

"You talking about her church work?" Harry knew that Grace Lee was almost a mythic figure for many people. Dexter had told him all about her work in the pro-life movement, and Harry had been intrigued by his obvious pride in his mother's efforts, even though he disagreed with her. Of the many issues that he and Dexter had discussed, abortion pros and cons were always heated, but the two men held similar views about women being able to choose to end their pregnancies within reasonable limits. It was during one of those discussions that Dexter had told Harry about his mother. Grace Lee never made a public statement on the issue, never wrote a letter, and would certainly never join a picket line in front of an abortion clinic. She was known, and worshipped, for one thing: If she ever talked to a pregnant woman, face to face, quietly and privately, that woman never had an abortion. In the minds of Catholic women who knew her, Grace Lee had saved hundreds of lives. Those hundreds would eventually, everyone knew, lead to thousands of future children. Grace did not travel, did not speak in public, but she was known.

As much as Grace Lee was known, Abraham was not. His wealth had brought him comfort and solitude. Grace would be seen around St. Augustine, but Abraham was known only because of his photographs. Harry knew the sketchy history of him and his sister growing up in a theatre on the beach, about the Alice who became Nora, and Polly working there, and Blue Goose Pete too. But that was forty years earlier, and memories fade. The full story of that past would always be hidden from him. He was merely going to meet the symbols of it.

At the edge of Lincolnville, near Lake Maria Sanchez, the Lee estate, all ten acres of it, was surrounded by an eight foot high wrought-iron fence, and the outer side of that fence was completely hidden by years of unkempt growth. Sawgrass, bamboo, marsh reeds, fir shrubs, a motley creep of vegetation telling the world to go away. As soon as Dexter told him where his parents lived, Harry had driven slowly by the grounds one night, wondering why so much light seemed to be flooding up from the other side of the fence. He asked Polly about that light, and she had shrugged, "You're asking me? Hell, Harry, I've never seen the place, just heard about it. Not many people have seen it, probably not even Alice...or Nora...so I'm expecting *you* to tell me all about it."

Harry stood at the only entrance gate, solid wood double-doors, and pushed a button to be admitted, as Dexter had instructed him to do. A woman's voice came though the speaker next to the button, "Mr. Ducharme?" Harry said, "Yes, I hope I'm not too early..." and the doors slowly opened as the woman said, "Not at all. Please come in and walk to the grounds around at the back of the house. Abe and I are expecting you."

He walked through the entrance and stopped almost immediately. The gate closed behind him. He did not move. He had stepped into a world that surely did not exist, at least not in this century or this country. The red brick path under his feet led directly to an enormous mansion that was on fire with light. Every room on each of the three floors was illuminated. The house was partly Moorish, partly Gothic, and had stone turrets at each corner. Seven arched entranceways stretched across the width of the ground level, opening into the covered veranda, from whose ceiling hung barely swaying chandeliers. Through the center arch, Harry could see the front door of the house itself, giant double-doors wide open so that he could see the entrance hall, which was crowned by another enormous chandelier. The house was a sun of light.

He still did not move. He stood and stared, whispering to himself, *So this is where Dexter grew up?* And he tried to joke to himself, something about the sight in front of him being *Al Gore's worst nightmare, an enormous carbon foot print of indulgence.* But he stopped himself. He remembered

Nora's admonition about respecting Abraham Isaac Lee. He almost heard her whisper to him, *You will not mock this man, Harry Ducharme. You will not ever…ever disrespect this man.*

Eventually, he stopped looking at the house and scanned the rest of the grounds. Scattered all over were dozens of what seemed to be street lamps from the nineteenth century, gas-wicked flames, all adding to the effect of it being day at night. There was no pattern, no reason for any particular lamp location. For any intruder who might have jumped the fence, there was not a dark place to hide. The scattered trees on the grounds, although substantial, did not cast a shadow at night because of the surrounding lamp light. Harry imagined that the only time there was darkness here was in the daytime, unless, of course, the lamps were never dimmed. Halfway to the house, the brick path split, with forks that went to each side and toward the back. He took the path to the right. As he turned the corner of the house he saw another smaller house at the far edge of the grounds, itself completely illuminated, and then another even smaller house at a distant corner, and children.

Children, mostly very young, toddlers; and young women, many of whom were teenagers, holding babies or watching them crawl on the ground. Some mothers who were barely teens, some mothers who were old, but more children than mothers.

Harry had gone from manicured park in the front of the house to a playground behind it. Swings and teeter-totters and merry-go-rounds and slides, picnic tables and benches, even a small carousel of sea horses and winged elephants, ridden by laughing children. No other sound, not even piped music from the carousel, just the sound of laughing children.

Harry looked for his hosts, but all that seemed to be in front of him were mothers and children. Then one of the young mothers started walking toward him, aging as she approached. He soon recognized half of Dexter.

Hand extended, Grace Lee welcomed him, "Mr. Ducharme, it is so good to finally meet you. Your fame precedes you, of course."

Was she being ironic? Harry was confused. The woman in front of him, whose soft hand would not release his, was beautiful in the way that some special women become beautiful as they get older. Their eyes, especially, look brighter, their bodies more slim, their skin paler, their smile more sincere. Grace Lee, mother of three, was pushing sixty, but she looked forty. Only her hands betrayed her age. The flesh was tissue thin and faint spots were beginning to appear. Harry had always wanted to meet Audrey Hepburn. Grace was as close as he would ever get.

"I'm pleased to finally meet you," he said, and then it hit him, where he had seen her face before. She had been in one of the pictures back at Nora's house on Water Street, her and her father, her as a teenager. And another, her and a young Korean boy holding boxes of popcorn, the picture snapped just as the boy was sneaking a glance at her, obviously in love.

"You'll have to excuse Abe for the moment. He's in his studio right now, preparing a gift for you. A secret…," she arched her eyebrow, "…something about something between you and him. A connection. I apologize for his absence. And, if Dexter has not told you yet, his father tends to be a bit melodramatic. I blame that particular trait on Abe's own father."

For the next hour, Grace walked Harry around the grounds of the Lee home, explaining how the women and children were temporary guests in the two smaller houses, and then talking about her other two sons and the work they did. She asked Harry to talk about Dexter's plans. He thought that was odd, it being a topic he assumed that both his parents would want to discuss with him, not just his mother. She asked for specifics, surprising Harry with her own knowledge of how political campaigns could win or lose. She even asked him about Prophet and his followers, but she did not ask about Charlotte Arnold in particular. As the hour ended, Harry had come to a conclusion about Dexter's mother. She was not a woman to be under-estimated.

Their walking tour had taken them to every corner of the ten acres, and it ended at the front door of the house. Harry considered the contrast between the barrier and seclusion provided by the overgrown, wrought iron fence around the grounds, as opposed to the openness of the house itself. As best he could tell as he and Grace had walked around, all the doors and windows of the house were open. If a person were anywhere on the grounds, he could simply walk right in.

"You must excuse me for a moment, Mr. Ducharme. And I apologize again for Abe's absence. He sometimes becomes absorbed in his work, so I'll have to go get him and remind him of his manners."

With that, Grace turned and walked up the wide staircase, pausing halfway up to turn back and speak one more time, "I've enjoyed meeting you, Mr. Ducharme. If I don't see you again tonight, please remember that you are always welcome here."

At the foot of the stairs, his hand on the edge of the railing, Harry nodded a thank-you as he watched her ascend to the landing at the top and then disappear.

He waited. And waited. Except for the laughter of a child outside and the distant bark of a dog, the house was silent. Awkward minutes passed, and then, just as he was about to look for the kitchen and a drink of water, he thought he heard Dexter.

"Harry, I have a gift for you..."

He looked toward the top of the stairs, but the voice was behind him.

"...and I hope you will accept it with my gratitude."

He turned around slowly, expecting to see Dexter, but came face to face with another half version of the young man.

"I'm Dexter's father."

Abraham Isaac Lee was a full-blooded Korean, black hair streaked with grey, dark eyes, broad nose, skin a blend of yellow and brown, wearing black slacks and a white dress-shirt with its sleeves rolled up past his wrists. Harry grasped for the right single word to describe the man in front of him. He was handsome in a mature model sort of way, distinguished to the point of being unique, but *handsome* and *distinguished* were imprecise and inadequate.

"I've seen your pictures," were Harry's first words, and he instantly realized that it was not what he meant to say, especially since Nora had told him to not tell anyone about getting access to the gallery in her house. "I mean, hello," he began again, extending his hand.

"Yes, she told me about that. That room is usually locked, but I suppose there was no harm done. My pictures are in galleries all over the country. You would have seen them anyway," Abraham said with a shrug.

Harry was about to correct his host, but he stopped himself in time. When he had said that he had seen the pictures of Abraham Lee, he did not mean the pictures taken *by* him, which were on public display. He meant the pictures *of* Abraham Lee, the pictures of him as a child and teenager, him and his family from back in the Sixties, of him and a young Grace, of him and the younger version of Nora. Those private pictures from the past which were never intended to be seen by outsiders like Harry Ducharme.

He kept struggling for the word that connected the man in front of him with the face of a young boy forty years earlier. The quality.

Nora's description came back to him, her explanation of Dexter's parents. *Harry, when you meet Grace you'll find a really smart woman. A strong woman. Abe is different. He's more than smart. Abe is wise, the wisest man I've ever met, and I finally realized that he was wise even when I first met him, when he was fifteen. He was just like his mother.*

"You look as if you're about to ask a question," Abraham said. "Perhaps you'd like a glass of wine while we sit in the study?"

Harry shook his head quickly, "No, no, thank you. But I really would like a glass of water."

Abraham seemed to wince, "Of course, an awkward offer. I apologize. She told me you had quit drinking."

"Nora?" Harry asked, knowing the answer, but wanting to see how Abraham would respond.

Abraham tilted his head slightly, as if studying his guest, before speaking slowly, "Yes…Nora."

Harry was disappointed, and he knew that his reaction was obvious, but Abraham did not elaborate. The woman named Alice was to remain in a story that Harry would never be allowed to read.

The two men were in a standoff, each waiting for the other to speak. It was Harry who blinked first, finally saying, "I went to the funeral." The other man merely nodded. "Pete wouldn't let me in," he continued, earning another nod. "She was my friend too," he finally said, feeling foolish.

"And this gift was her idea," Abraham relented. "She specifically picked this picture for you. As much as she told me about you, I would have chosen something else, but she insisted that this was the one for you." He had been gripping a large flat package, wrapped in brown paper, and he handed it to Harry, saying, "It's an important picture for me, but she assured me that you would appreciate it as well. I should tell you, however. This is merely a copy of my original."

Harry flashed back through the private gallery on Water Street, wondering which of the pictures of the girl who was Alice would be the picture that Nora had suggested to Abraham, because, surely, she knew how much he had been mesmerized by the many frozen moments from her past. Surely.

"Thank you," Harry said, his hand almost shaking as Abraham handed the package to him.

After that few seconds of awkwardness, Abraham smiled and took Harry's free arm and led him into the study. "Grace will tell me all about her talk with you later, but for now I'd like to talk to you about my son."

"Nora told me...," Harry began, almost defensively, but Abraham waved a finger to quiet him.

"I know everything she told you, and everything you ever told her about yourself. I know about your friend who calls himself a prophet. I know about the girl for whom Dexter cares deeply. I know about Dexter's political plans, which...truth be told...do not upset me as much as they do his mother. She's worried about something bad happening to him, but I assured her that you would take care of him. I told her that I had faith in you, faith that you would look out for him. Am I right, Harry? Will you take care of our son?"

The two men were almost the same age, but Harry suddenly felt much younger, as if he were himself a child, "Mr. Lee, I'm not sure I understand what you're talking about. Dex and I are close, but his doing this is not my idea. All I do is talk to him. This plan was his, not mine, and I'll certainly do my best to help him in his campaign, as hopeless as I think it is, but I don't think there's any real harm that can come to him except losing, and *that* is not really a bad thing."

They were soon sitting across from each other in the study, surrounded by a thousand books and dozens of framed photographs on the paneled walls, of trains and beaches and cemeteries, all of them without a single person in them. Abraham had listened to Harry while looking at the pitcher of water in front of them on a small glass table. "I was assured by the young girl that I could trust you, and your Nora, as well, assured me…"

That was too much for Harry. "That young girl? You mean the mute? The young girl who refuses to talk to me. She *assures* you that I am trustworthy? Why is it that everybody in this goddam town seems to be on her party-line, everybody except me?"

Abraham looked at him with a half-smile, but then looked down at the water again as he almost whispered, "Please don't talk like that in my home. You're a better man than to speak so, and your words should reflect that."

Harry was totally confused, not knowing whether to be angry or embarrassed. He had no idea to what Dexter's father was referring. Was he defending Charlotte Arnold? Was it the tone of his voice? The *goddam?* Surely the man wasn't upset with Harry's profanity? If Dexter's father had known Nora, or Alice, all these years, he had heard much worse. And the world in general? Wasn't it vulgar and profane and crude and angry? Why was he acting like Harry had worn muddy shoes all over his white carpet?

At that moment, he realized that he only had one option. Without understanding why, he apologized. Abraham nodded slightly and closed his eyes for a few seconds before he spoke, "Thank you." Silence, and then, "I suppose we'll get back to the girl soon enough, but I promised Grace that I would talk to you at length about Dexter, how special we think he is. And, of course, I'll apologize for myself now, for seeming to be too prideful about my son. In many ways, it's hard for us to see him as more than just our third, and youngest, child, so perhaps, when the time comes, you can share your own insights with us about his future."

Harry listened for an hour. Dexter's life story began before his birth.

The phone in his apartment rang an hour after he left Abraham's home, but Harry sat on the other side of the room and ignored it. The message machine was broken, but, if it was important, the caller would try again. He was looking at the gift from Abraham Lee and wondering why Nora had suggested it. He had assumed it would be a picture of her in the past, taken by Lee. The matted and framed photo in his hands at that moment, however, had nothing to do with Nora.

A black and white picture of six small children walking behind a man on a dirt road, another small child in front of him, children no older than three or four, all Asian, and Harry assumed that they were Korean. The photographer had to have been behind the group. All of them were look-ing forward, all except the last little girl in line, who was looking to the side. The dirt road was on the edge of a hill, and to the left were small houses down below in the distance. On the road far ahead of the group were two women wearing kimonos. They seemed to be walking into the woods directly in front of them. There was a steep drop-off to the left, and leafy trees to the right, casting their shadows on the road. The man's face was hidden, but Harry thought he was Caucasian. He was wearing what seemed to be khaki pants, a short-sleeved shirt, and suspenders that crossed in the back. In his left arm, he was cradling a tiny child, perhaps a baby, with lots of black hair. The baby had its right arm across the man's back, holding on to one of the suspenders. Something about the scene sug-gested that it had been taken a long time ago, perhaps during the Korean War, the Fifties, but perhaps not? Harry studied every detail, but the gift still made no sense. It had nothing to do with Nora.

The phone rang again. He looked at the caller ID: Fred Tymeson. Harry would call him back. Before then, he wanted someone to help him understand the gift. He called Dexter.

"You said you wanted my expert opinion," Dexter grinned as he came through the door with a carton of yard signs that needed to be folded and stapled to wood sticks. "But this has got to be quick. We have to do some more door-to-door. I'll leave this stuff with you and pick it up later."

Harry had met him at the door and looked over his shoulder to see Charles Yates and Peter Winston waiting in a car. "Isn't it a little late for you to be knocking on doors?"

"No, no. Charlotte arranged all this ahead of time. Prophet had to meet somebody, so we've got time to kill. These people we're seeing are committed supporters. I'm just connecting names and faces."

The mention of Charlotte Arnold was enough to distract Harry into silence. Then, more than distract, to depress. Something about her name merely being mentioned when he had been trying to solve a mystery about Nora—he suddenly wanted to be left alone again. He wanted Nora to be separate from everyone else in his other worlds.

He was about to suggest that Dexter come back another time, to talk unhurried, but he was not quick enough. Dexter had seen the picture propped against the back of his couch across the room. His face went from excitement to frozen wonder. He stared at the picture, and then stared at Harry.

"Where did you get *that*?" he asked, looking back at the picture. Before Harry could answer, Dexter said, "Oh my god, I remember, you met my parents tonight. Harry, did you steal that?"

Harry was stunned. Dexter was serious.

"There is no way my father gives up that picture. No way. That picture has been in my father's house since before I was born. I've heard the story a hundred times."

"But Nora suggested to him…"

Dexter had gone from shock, to suspicion, to incredulity, and then to bemused pleasure in less than a minute. "Oh, the gift, and Nora, and my father, and you…this is rich. Hell, Harry, I want to know why too! My father loves that picture, but as far as I know, it's always been in his private gallery at home. Nobody but our family has ever seen it, I thought, so why Nora would have suggested that my father give it to you is one of the great mysteries of the twenty-first century."

Harry had another mystery. Not why Nora had suggested giving it to him, but why Abraham would have done it for her, especially if it meant so much to him. Even if it was only a copy, it had been personal and private to Abraham.

"Your father didn't take this picture, did he?" Harry asked.

Dexter was in a much better mood, enjoying Harry's confusion. "Not a chance. My grandfather took that picture. It's the first picture ever taken of my father."

Harry was losing track again, and he grabbed for meaning. "Your grandfather took the picture of your father walking with those children?"

Dexter rolled his eyes. "Oh, lord, Harry. My father is the baby that man is carrying." He walked over for a closer look at the picture and then, as a car horn honked outside, turned back to leave. "That's the man who founded the Holt Adoption Agency in Korea where my grandfather found my father and his sister, my Aunt Louise. That man is a saint in our family. My father always said that that picture is the story of how I got here."

"Holt?"

Dexter had pushed open the screen door and waved at the men waiting for him. As he turned back, the apartment phone rang again. He looked at Harry and smiled his mother's smile, "Holt, his name is Harry Holt. Go figure. Small world, isn't it, Harry, a world full of guys named Harry. Now, answer your phone. And let's talk later. See ya."

Ten minutes later, Harry got in his Buick and drove to the address that Fred Tymeson had given him. Before he left, he had looked at the wall calendar in his kitchen. Prophet had said it would happen forty days later. The Child would die. Harry circled the date: November 4th, Election Day. As he drove, he tried not to hear the last words of Dexter's father, *I'm sure you'll take care of my son. His mother and I are depending on you.*

R ST. AUGUSTINE
RECORD

MYSTERIOUS PREACHER MURDERED

September 26, 2008
Web exclusive 8:49 PM
By: Peter Guinta

Those who heard the man who called himself Peter Prophet often heard him predict his own death. That prophecy has been fulfilled.

St. Augustine police were called to Lighthouse Park Thursday to investigate the apparent murder of the man whose followers overwhelmed authorities last year in a surprise appearance at the recently renovated Amphitheatre.

Details are sketchy at this time, including the actual name and age of the murdered man. Initial police reports indicate that the victim was killed by a brutal knife attack. There were no witnesses, but several of his followers are being questioned by authorities.

Charles Yates, one of Prophet's followers, spoke for his group in an exclusive interview. He revealed that Prophet had received many death threats in the past few months. However, Prophet had insisted that no added precautions be taken. "We all knew this was coming," Yates said. "But not this bad. I thought I was prepared, but I was wrong."

Yates also revealed that Prophet had told him that he was to meet another follower in private that afternoon. The identity of that follower is not known.

Prophet had given instructions for when and where to find him to three female followers: sisters Jane and Jean Norville, and Charlotte Arnold. The 911 call was made by Arnold, but she declined a request for an interview.

SAPD LieutenantJeff Carlson said, "We're working under the assumption that the victim knew his assailant. This was not a random act. The intensity of the assault would indicate either a pathological or personal agenda."

Carlson refused further comment until the crime scene investigation was completed.

WWHD radio host Harry Ducharme is the only journalist known to have interviewed Prophet as well as having subsequent contact with him.

Ducharme is also credited with helping alert the public to various appearances by Prophet, but he insisted that, "I don't know him any better than anybody else. All I know for sure is that his people will continue to spread his message because the crowds seem to want to hear more."

Rumors of an unannounced appearance by Prophet at Alltel Stadium in Jacksonville have circulated for

months. Yates would neither confirm
nor deny those rumors. Asked about
his group's plans now that their
leader was dead, Yates' only comment
was, "The Prophet's message was that
a new child of God was coming. That
has not changed."

Neither Yates nor Ducharme knew
of any plans for a memorial service.
Funeral services are pending at the
Croyle Funeral Home.

The Election Countdown
Harry Sees the Big Picture
Life Goes On

Harry and Dexter had an unspoken agreement. Harry assumed that Dexter knew more about Nora's past, when she was Alice, than he would admit. Surely, the pictures in the private gallery of her house would have told Dexter how long she had been involved with his family. Even if he had only known her as Nora, he had to have asked her about the past which was captured in those pictures. Surely, he had talked to his own father about the person in those pictures, the Alice that had disappeared. But Harry did not ask. Dexter did not tell.

Harry told himself that it did not matter, knowing more about Nora. She was gone. Even if he had been able to sleep in her bed for another hundred years, she would not have told him more than Polly had said on the beach. And Polly's wisdom was truer than his own, he finally admitted. The *idea* of Nora was what had seduced him. He accepted the fact that all he would ever know about her…he already knew. Everything else was interpretation.

Life went on, and as much as Harry worked on Dexter's campaign, the more he felt like a spectator. His mind was distracted. He was convinced that Dexter was to be the New Child of God that Prophet had announced. He was also absolutely convinced that Prophet was a fraud. A bigger hoax than the Piltdown Man or a radio invasion of Martians. It had to be a hoax. So why did he believe it?

He would watch Dexter speak to a crowd and marvel at the effect he had on people. All the more odd because the office he was seeking was the proverbial bucket of warm spit. Even if he won, he was merely an independent state representative in a Florida legislature overwhelmingly controlled by Republicans, aided and abetted by the few Democrats. Aligned with neither party, Dexter would be irrelevant. But his crowds got bigger. He talked about changing the system, about helping the poor and infirm, protecting the environment, supporting education. The boilerplate language of every politician in America. State rep or President of the United States, the words were the same. Words without action. And he could even talk about tort levies and bond issues and funding ratios for local schools, the nitty-gritty of local politics. The crowds still got bigger, and Dexter seemed to grow more energized as the campaign progressed, not more tired. He seemed to suck something out of the crowds in front of him, some sort of air and water and bread, and give it back to them. Harry was as impressed as much as he was perplexed. His own life had been wasted before he got to St. Augustine, then briefly saved by Nora, but with her gone all that he had left was a young charismatic, bi-racial man and a dead black Prophet. The connections had to be there, more than a prophecy. But, as hard as he tried to see them, those connections were not totally clear to him.

He was sure of only one thing. Dexter was in danger. Not because he was, or was not, that Child of God. The fact or fable of that role was irrelevant. Harry understood a more important truth because he knew who killed Prophet, and *that* person also believed that Dexter was the Child of God. It was the murderer's faith that mattered, not Harry's lack of it. The murderer had to kill Dexter to make his earlier act complete. Watching Dexter speak to a crowd in Ponte Vedra two weeks before the Election, Harry figured out the last piece of the puzzle. Prophet had insisted that the Child was to die by his own choice. He was to sacrifice himself. That made no sense in relation to Dexter, except for one point. Dexter would not choose to die, but some decision of his would make it possible for someone else to kill him. Harry had told Dexter about his concerns, that

Prophet's killer wanted him dead too, and all that killer needed was the opportunity. And that opportunity would be created by some decision of Dexter's. Regardless of anybody else's skepticism, he insisted that it all made sense to him.

Dexter, however, was not impressed. "Harry, you're worse than my parents. All of you worry too much."

Harry had persisted, "Look, I understand all this because I know who murdered Prophet. I knew as soon as Charles Yates told me that Lincoln Motes had disappeared. You can't ignore this. You can't..."

It was that moment at which Harry became truly afraid. Dexter held his hand up, signalling him to be quiet, and spoke to him like a son calmly explaining to his father why he had to leave home. "I know about Lincoln. Charlie and I have talked. The police know about Lincoln too. They won't tell the public because they don't want him to run away. They want him to make a mistake. And I'm that mistake. Charlie told the police that he thought Motes would come after me too. Motes never liked me from the very beginning, Charlotte told me that. He always thought I was the Child...which, by the way, is not true...and none of us understood why Prophet kept him around. Harry, I'll be fine. The police have undercover people at all my events, and I'm never alone. I'll be fine. I'm as safe as a baby at his mother's breast. How's that for one of your metaphors? A child on its mother's bosom. Or something. I'll let *you* find the right words."

"You're not afraid?" Harry asked.

Dexter shook his head and smiled.

The two men looked at each other, expecting the other to talk, and then Dexter sighed, "Think about it this way, Harry. If I die, then Prophet was right. And if Prophet is right, then there's a god, even if it is a god with some cosmic plan none of us understand. Case closed. If I live, Prophet was not really a prophet, right? You might even call him a phony. And that will prove there's no god. Either way, you'll have an answer to that question you keep asking yourself, Harry, always there in all those conversations between you and me, and threading through your WWHD program. You'll have the proof you need, right?"

"It's not that simple," Harry mumbled, feeling himself un-tethered from the young man he had come to love. The thread was not strong enough to hold.

"You think too much, Harry. Sometimes things *are* simple," Dexter said.

"Well, all I know is that you're awfully damn calm for a man who's just been told that's he's the target of a homicidal maniac. How is that possible, for you to be so calm and optimistic and full of hope, Dex, how is that possible?"

Dexter laughed and stepped toward Harry, gave him a bear hug, almost picking him up off the ground, then he stepped back. "Harry, Harry, you and Aunt Nora *were* made for each other. All I ever heard from her was how life would eventually disappoint me. She'd make fun of my father for his doom and gloom outlook, but she was the same, just like you. But I told her she was wrong. You want to know why I'm calm…optimistic? That's easy. I'm young, Harry, a few years past thirty, in great shape, about to win an election, got a girl who loves me, not a care in the world, and I'm going to live forever, psychos or not. Weren't you ever this way? Like me? Harry, this is the beginning of my life, not the end. I'm never going to die."

As the election approached, Harry had separated himself from everyone else. He felt like he was watching a slow motion train wreck, unable to stop it, but aware of all the small details of the impending crash. The huffing of the engines, the whirl of wheels on an iron track, crew and passengers oblivious to the collision ahead, each of them lost in their own thoughts, thinking about the past or future, asleep in the present.

He went to WWHD and talked to north Florida and south Georgia. The national election was heating up, Republicans preparing for their much deserved eviction from power, Democrats crossing their fingers and hoping that their usual self-inflicted wounds would not be fatal again. They loved their man Obama, but were afraid that the rest of the country wasn't ready for a black man to be President. Harry ignored that world. He even ignored Dexter's political race. He began to read books again. He talked about books. He knew *the* answer was there. He also asked his listeners to call him with their favorite book or poem, and if he had not read those he would look for them. It was not a huge task. Few people actually called him, and he had already read most of the titles they suggested anyway. Sometimes they would ask his opinion about the elections, but he diverted the question. Captain Jack was using high octane rhetoric in the mornings and calling him at night, but Harry wanted to talk about Stephen Crane's poetry. A week before the election, the calls stopped.

He wondered about the people who were out there. People like Dexter and Jack and Polly did not count. He knew them, they were his friends. At first, he still listened to Captain Jack, not everyday, not for the full four hours, but enough to talk about later. Jack invited him for dinner, telling him, "You're starting to sound a little batty, guy. You need my blue plate special." But his offer was declined. Polly wanted to see him at The Blue Goose, but she ended up going alone. Harry's response to both was the same, "Let's get through this election, let the dust settle, and we'll get together." Jack understood, but Harry knew that Polly's feelings had been hurt. Dexter would ask for more help on his campaign, but was rebuffed as well. Charles Yates or Peter Winston would call, not to ask a favor, but merely to see if he was okay. Those two, in particular, would call with specific responses to something that Harry had said on the air. "Did you mean to say…," or "I've been thinking about something you just said…," or "Have you read…?" They were regulars, and Harry looked forward to hearing from them. In the past, there had always been a consistent question from Harry to them, "So, where are you guys going to be this week?" It was routine, as if his program was doing not so subtle product placement. Harry's show had been how most people found out about Prophet's next appearance, without him ever mentioning Prophet explicitly. Yates and Winston never discussed religion when they called, they never invited anybody anywhere, but the code was there, as if Harry was collaborating with sleeper cells in the old Soviet Union, as if his show was the old LP that had to be played backwards to hear that Paul was dead. The crowds grew as if out of nowhere, and Harry would read about them in the newspapers the next day. But with Prophet's death, his role as go-between died too. Yates and Winston still preached, and the crowds actually got bigger, as if the death of Prophet had been proof of his message, but Harry knew better.

When he was not on the air, or reading, he would get in his Buick and drive. Almost like re-reading something he had read before, he drove around St. Augustine and re-absorbed his late-in-life home. Taking in the sights, more like a pilgrim than a tourist, looking for relics and ghosts. He would drive up and down A1A, to Jacksonville and back, cruising that narrow and winding road; the ocean to the East, hidden most of the trip by dunes and marsh grass. He slept less and less, sensing a change in the world that required him to be awake at all times. He walked on the beach, feet bare, flashlight in hand, remembering times with Nora and a time with Polly, who had been gracious in her role as Nora's surrogate: *And now, Harry, we need to talk about the other favor she asked of me. The promise she made me make. And it's okay. She told me that you'd be thinking of her, not me.* Nora knew exactly how it would happen that night, knew before she died how Harry would try to hold on to her. She had been right. Harry had thought of her then, as he thought of her since then. Polly had merely been an angel of mercy, an anodyne for pain. Even more merciful, however, was Polly's explanation of Nora, the insight which allowed him to let Nora go. To let her go because she had never really existed. When the election was over, he told himself, he would thank Polly. It was Polly who would not let him dwell in the past, and the past had always been…a line from somewhere…*possibility?*…dwelling in possibility? Nora would always be a memory, but she would never be real again. Pete had told him at the cemetery, *This here today is for Miss Alice. You're not part of her story.* That was the final truth about Nora James. She had never existed, and that other woman, Alice, was not part of Harry's life. That Alice, she was dead long before he met Nora. And the only man who ever loved Alice was dead too. Harry wished somebody knew enough to write that story, the true story, of Alice and the man who died because of her. The sad how and why of what happened. But their story died untold with them. Mostly, he wished he could have seen them together just once, just to see how they looked at each other.

The Day of Election
November 4, 2008

Faith—is the Pierless Bridge
Supporting what We see
Unto the Scene that we do not—
Too slender for the eye

It bears the Soul as bold
As it were rocked in Steel
With Arms of Steel at either side—
It joins—behind the Veil

To what, could we Presume
The Bridge would cease to be
To Our far, vacillating Feet
A first Necessity.

"You look like death eatin' a cracker, Harry."

He woke up in a sweat, blinking in the dark. He had been dreaming about Nora. She was young again, the girl in those pictures from the past. But he was young too. They were in Iowa, and she was helping him detassle corn in the field near his Springdale home, sweat covering both of them, and she was teasing him about her doing more than he had done. But that was just a scene. The dream was, like all dreams, ultimately incoherent. It was not a story. It made no sense. But it was vivid. Nora became Polly, Polly became his first wife, and Harry heard his father calling him from the front porch at home. Then Nora's voice, but not her body, came back into his dream, her voice mocking him for being so pale and thin. But it was the sound of the corn that was most out of touch with reality. A windy day in Iowa, his eye was level with the top of the stalks, as if his head were barely above some watery wavy surface, and the sway of that corn sounded like the ocean. As if he was floating in a green and golden Atlantic. It was the best part of the dream, until he saw a face arise out of the water. From a distance he had thought that Nora was coming toward him, but he was wrong. It was Charlotte Arnold in a blue cape. And the dream ended.

Harry had slept on his couch. When he woke, still in the clothes from the night before, his back and neck were stiff. He sat up, but did not get up. He would have sat there longer, but the alarm in the bedroom began blaring. To turn it off, he forced himself to rise and limp into the other room. Six in the morning. The polls opened at seven.

He stood in the kitchen, hands on the refrigerator door. *What am I looking for*, he asked himself. He didn't open the refrigerator, but he kept his hand on the handle until he figured out his next move. *Coffee, I want some coffee*, he thought. *Coffee will make me a new man.* He went to his cabinet and found the bag of coffee beans, organic beans from the Manatee Restaurant that Nora had given him a few days before she went away. Harry studied the bag. *How old*, he wondered, *how long do these things last before they lose their flavor, their kick?* It seemed like an essential question. Nora could have answered it, but, then again, so could Polly. Anybody who had paid attention to these sorts of things in their life…they would know the answer. Harry made a leap of faith. The beans would still be magic. He poured some into a grinder and held on as it vibrated and hummed. A simple process. Grind the beans, measure the water, combine them in a coffee press, and wait a few minutes.

Harry had always associated coffee and voting. He began both at the same age, forever linking Hubert Humphrey and Folgers as concurrent memories for him. He had volunteered for Humphrey's campaign, a bitter pill to swallow after the sweetness of Bobby Kennedy, and a young woman had insisted that he accept her offer of coffee as they worked late at night. She was his *first* for more than coffee.

I haven't thought about her for years, he said to himself as he sat at his kitchen table reading the morning *St. Augustine Record. I wonder what happened to her. And her name? I should remember her name, but I don't. Someone like that, I should remember.* He checked the weather forecast. A good day was ahead. Turnout would be heavy. For the briefest of moments, sitting there as the old coffee began surging through him, he forgot what was also going to happen today. Or not. Whatever it was, he had still come to an irrevocable decision. Prophet and his prophecy be damned. The big picture be damned. He was going to make sure that Dexter King Lee did not die today. If that upset the apple cart of God, then God be damned himself. Abraham and Grace would not lose their son. Harry had promised them that. Dexter was their child, not God's. Get the young man through today, win or lose, and he would be safe for a long time. There was only one problem, he knew, *How the hell am I supposed to do it?*

The schedule had already been set. Dexter had spent the night with his parents, and Harry knew he would be safe there until he left the grounds. Charles Yates had promised Harry that he would be side by side with Dexter for the rest of the day, along with the undercover St. Augustine cops. Harry would join them at the campaign headquarters in the Vilano Beach town-square. He would be the oldest of the bunch. He could almost hear Nora's voice, "*You* playing Secret Service, Harry Ducharme? That oughta be a *great* comfort to his folks."

Harry tuned in to WWHD and listened to Captain Jack make his frenetic pitch for John McCain, warning his listeners that the Democrats were a Death Star of socialized medicine. But then, to Harry's amazement, he heard Dexter's voice. The Captain was interviewing him in the studio. Although there was no explicit endorsement from Tunnel, the message was obvious: *This is MY man.* Harry tried to call the studio, but the lines were all busy. He tried again, still busy, odd because Tunnel was obviously not taking calls on-air at that time. He was shutting the public out, giving Dexter all his attention. Still, Harry felt good. Dexter and Yates were nearby. All he had to do was walk over to the station. The morning interview with Tunnel was not on the schedule, but it was safe. Everything else would go as planned. And then somebody knocked on his door.

Charles Yates was frantic, "Have you talked to him this morning? I've called, but he never answers. I leave messages. And more messages. So, please, tell me that you know where he is."

Harry looked at the trembling man and shook his own head. "He's just around the corner, isn't he? At the station, on Jack's show. Listen…," and he walked over to the radio and turned up the volume. Dexter was still talking to Jack Tunnel. "See, it's okay. Give me a minute to finish cleaning up, and we'll walk over there." But then he stopped himself and looked back at Yates. "You were supposed to pick him up. You were supposed to be with him."

Yates was gritting his teeth, "Harry, that program is taped. I heard it too, and I called the station, couldn't get through, so I called the office line. The Station Manager was there, cussing at some bird in the background, and he told me that Jack had come in early this morning with a tape and then left, something about helping on a campaign."

Harry stopped him, "But you were supposed to pick him up this morning."

Yates looked down, and Harry watched him clench his fists before he spoke, "He called me at six, told me that he had changed the plans, told me that Charlotte was coming to get him, and that he and her would be doing more door to door knocking, some calling, trying to get some last minute media attention. Told me not to worry, said it was his decision. Told me to work on my own plans, that he would see me tonight before the polls closed. Said that he had cleared it with you, which, I guess, was not true."

Harry was about to ask about the police protection, how Dexter had managed to elude them, but then he realized that Yates had revealed something else. "You said something about him telling you to go work on your *own plans*. What does that mean?"

Yates looked at Harry like he was seeing a parent's first sign of dementia. "I thought you knew. I mean, I just assumed that you knew."

Harry sat on the couch while Yates remained standing. "Charlie, I sometimes feel like I am unlearning everything I thought I knew. So I have no idea what you're talking about."

"The meeting. Tonight's the night, up in Jacksonville, at the stadium. We're all going to be there. I'm speaking. And Charlotte said that Dexter would be there to speak too. First up, nothing political, and then he was heading back to Vilano to be at his party when the results come in. We got the word from Prophet the day before he died. He told us that it was going to be the biggest crowd ever, that the Child would appear then and there. And the future would begin."

Harry looked up and beyond Yates, to the wall behind, where the picture that Dexter's father had given him was hanging. Harry Holt was still walking up the road in Korea, carrying Abraham in his arms, with two women in kimonos ahead in the distance.

Who was I when that picture was taken? I was born. I was alive. I was just a kid, probably three or four, but I wasn't the son of my parents yet. I was somebody else's child. I don't know who I was. Nora was right. I could have found out, but I didn't, and now it's too late. She made him give me the picture. She had to have a reason. The only Harry in that picture is Harry Holt, not me. Where was I then? Who was I?

"Harry?"

He focused on Yates again.

"Harry? I thought you knew. I'm sorry. I guess I should have told you on my own. But the thing we need to do right now is get hold of Dexter and make sure he's okay. Right?"

Harry nodded, his mind a blank, as if erased. Yates extended his hand to help him get off the couch, and then Harry put words to an emerging question, "You know who that child is, don't you? You've known all along, haven't you? He told you, didn't he?"

Yates grasped his hand and pulled him up, but still shaking his own head, "No, Harry. I don't. I thought I did at one time, years ago, but I was wrong. I actually thought it was Lincoln, but...well, so much for my intuition. All I know for sure is that it definitely is *not* him."

"Prophet didn't tell you before he died? Surely he told you. Surely."

"I wish I knew, Harry. But, you see, it doesn't matter if I know or not. It's going to happen regardless. You and me are irrelevant to it happening. Only Prophet knew then, and only...," he paused, sensing the weight of his words as they approached being spoken, "...and only Charlotte knows now. She's the only one that Prophet told."

The parking lot filled slowly, beginning at noon with a 1998 maroon, Nissan Sentra driven by Tara Prescott from California. She had packed for a long trip and told her classes back at UCLA that she was taking a *sabbatical*. It was a joke her students did not understand. Tara was a Teaching Assistant, with no job protection at all. She told her Chair, who told her to forget about a future in academia, that she was making a mistake leaving in mid-term, going to a revival that nobody knew about. But she went anyway, sleeping in the back seat every night, spending money on gas but not food, seeing America courtesy of the interstate highway system, finally reaching Florida just as her Sentra's odometer passed 100,000 miles. Seeing the empty lot, she had hesitated before stopping. But she had come this far. It was time to rest. Her only regret was that she had forgotten to vote back in California before she left.

By two o'clock, Tara was one of hundreds. By sundown, one of thousands. Music was playing, Frisbees flying, and everyone seemed in a good mood, but nobody knew what to do. The police had come and threatened them, but their discretion was admirable. Nobody was arrested, nobody was towed, and then WJXX and WJCC showed up. Somehow, somebody who had arrived after somebody who had arrived after Tara Prescott led the reporters to her, and for the first time in her life she spoke in front of a television camera. She resisted the temptation to say hello to her Chair. After a cursory introduction for the viewers, she was asked the obvious question: *Why are you here?*

Sitting at the counter of The Tavern in St. Augustine, Harry watched the young woman's face on the overhead television. Michelle was tending bar, watching Harry's face. "You making any predictions about the election?" He did not answer. "Planet Tavern to Harry," she said, tapping his water glass with a spoon, "You here or somewhere else?"

He looked down to find himself eye level with Michelle's chest escaping the confines of a button-challenged blouse. He looked at her breathe for a few seconds, and then he looked up at her face, comforted by her smile, and said, "I think this is how we met, Michelle, but I'm not sure. I was either drunk or hung-over at the time."

"You were yourself, Harry," she winked at him, "And we're both still here. I'm not sure about you, but I'm guessing that I'll still be here until they put me in a box and drop me in the ground. I asked Clint if he'd have me stuffed and propped up in a corner, told him that most of the regulars here wouldn't know the difference after the third round, but he wasn't keen on that idea. Some bullshit about health codes. So I told him…"

Harry's cell phone started vibrating on the counter. He looked at the number: Dexter. He did not answer. Michelle looked him in the eye and tilted her head to point to the phone. "You gonna get that?" He hesitated, so she reached for it. He quickly picked it up and flipped open the cover.

"Charlie says you've been looking for me," Dexter said, and Harry could hear voices in the background. "Him and you are like mother hens…"

"Dexter, stop it!" Harry interrupted him. "Where are you, and why are you *trying* to make this difficult for us? Who are you with? Did the cops find you? Can you at least let us try to protect you, at least for today?"

Michelle was frozen in place, hearing a conversation she had not expected. As she listened, her right hand slowly moved back and forth on the counter between her and Harry, a damp rag in it, back and forth as if in a spell. Harry looked at her, realized she was listening, and turned his back to her. When he turned back around a minute later, she was still there, her hand motionless again. He stopped talking, put his hand over the phone, and whispered to her, "I'm sorry. I didn't mean to be rude."

She shrugged and shook her head, her thick hair bouncing, "No big deal. I was just sorta worried about you."

Harry felt it again, how much he liked Michelle, just as a person who was always there and had seen him on many less-than-good days for the past few years. He kept his hand over the phone, pointing his other forefinger at it as he smiled, "This is the guy you ought to worry about. Trust me." He put the phone back to his ear, but Dexter was gone. Just as he was about to speed dial him back, Harry looked at Michelle again. Her attention was focused on something behind him. Harry slowly swirled around on his bar stool.

Charles Yates, Peter Winston, Jean and Jane Norville were standing in The Tavern doorway, dressed in their Sunday best. Yates spoke, "Harry, will you take us to Jacksonville? We need a ride. The van is finally dead."

Harry looked around for the clock on the wall. Four o'clock, the traffic would be murder between St. Augustine and Jacksonville. What should be a one hour trip would probably take two. He felt Michelle's eyes boring into the back of his head. But he already knew he would do it because he knew that Dexter would be in Jacksonville too. The fortieth day was almost over. Harry stood up and reached into his pocket and pulled out the keys to his Buick, then he turned around to Michelle and said, "Anybody asks, *this* is my seat. I'll see you tomorrow. And do me a favor. Call Polly and tell her that I'll see her tomorrow too."

Michelle nodded, "Sure. And I'll take care of your laundry too. Me and Polly, we'll….," She paused, and then, still clutching the bar towel, she raised her hand and waved it at him. "Good-bye, Harry. You take care."

Yates had suggested that they take I-95 to Jacksonville, but Harry ignored him and took the A1A route. Nora had told him once, as they were on A1A, "You're a man of routine, Harry. You like it when things don't change." But it was more than a routine this afternoon. He wanted to see something specific before he got to Alltel in Jacksonville. If he had been alone, he would have stopped, but, with passengers and a timetable, all he could do was slow down as they neared the wide curve in the road.

Yates was in the front passenger seat, Winston was between the sleeping sisters in the back. The Buick was, indeed, a smooth ride. Yates noticed Harry looking to his left and then to his right as they cruised slowly around the curve. "You okay, Harry?" he asked. Harry nodded but did not speak. When he turned, his eyes were looking past Yates and toward the ocean. Yates turned in the same direction. The Atlantic was as blue as the cloudless sky.

Harry finally spoke, "He's going to be there, you know that, don't you."

"Dexter?"

Harry exhaled, "No, you know who I mean." Yates, still looking at the ocean, did not respond. A1A had straightened out again, and the Buick was floating past beach-houses crowded together on both sides of the road. Up ahead, Harry could see that traffic was almost bumper to bumper. He slowed down, in no hurry. "You know," he said again.

Yates looked back at Winston, who shrugged, and then he turned to Harry, "*All* of us are going to be there. You and me, all of us. I've been waiting for this day for a long time, Harry, a long time. And he has to be there too. That's all I understand. He has to be there too."

"Well, at least you understand *something*," Harry sighed. *All I understand,* he thought, *is that I promised the boy's father that I would take care of him.*

The Alltel managers had been more prepared than the Amphitheatre managers the previous year. With the first clear signs that the revival rumors were true and that it was going to happen that day, they had private security personnel on hand to back up the Jacksonville police. Their plan was simple. Deny access to the stadium itself, but allow them to congregate in the parking lot. Any preaching logistics would have to be improvised on the spot. Whoever spoke, chances were that they would not be seen by most of the crowd. As one manager told the Mayor, watching a television crew interview a young woman from California, "Thank God these people don't seem to be drinkers, or else we'd really have hell to pay when they figured out we aren't letting them inside."

The sun was setting by the time the Buick got to the Mathews Bridge. As soon as they got to the top of the narrow bridge they could see the Stadium. Yates leaned forward and pointed, "Look at the cars. Look at how packed they are." From the backseat, Peter Winston was less excited, "How are we going to find them in that crowd?"

Harry was concentrating on his driving. The Mathews was an old steel bridge, always being repaired, but it was the most direct route to the stadium. As soon as he crossed the high center point and began his descent, he glanced toward the stadium. Yates was right, the lot was packed, but Harry knew that Winston was wrong. Finding Dexter would be easy.

The lot was full by the time they got to the first entrance, and the cop at the corner waved them toward a side street. They had to park and walk a mile back to the stadium. The Norville sisters asked Harry if he thought the Buick would be safe in that neighborhood, but he assured them that his car had been through much worse, including a tornado, than being left alone in a run-down neighborhood. Winston kept insisting that it would be a miracle if they were able to find Dexter.

Harry was leading the group. When he heard Winston, he turned and walked backwards for a few steps, laughing, "The real miracle will be Dexter getting back to his campaign headquarters in Vilano Beach before the polls close." Yates was the last in line, but an obvious second in command. Just as he was about to say "amen to that" in response to Harry's prioritizing of miracles, the newly dark night exploded in light up in front of them, followed by a roar from the parking lot crowd. An Alltel manager had given permission for all the parking lot lights to be turned on as a concession to the crowd's safety. It was not quite the light of day, but it was much more light than dark.

The closer they go to the parking lot, the more they were absorbed into the mass of new arrivals coming from all the other side streets. Harry had set a fast pace as they were walking, and as soon as he crossed the final street and got into the lot itself he stopped to catch his breath. He almost laughed to himself as he paused and closed his eyes, *I am too damn old to be leading anybody on a hike.*

Everything went quiet. He opened his eyes and blinked. He was alone. Yates and the others were gone. The lot was empty. The stadium itself was gone. The bridge he had just driven over was gone. The air was cool, and the only thing he heard was his own breathing. He closed his eyes and listened.

"Harry?"

He opened his eyes.

"Harry, where do we go from here?" Yates was in front of him, and he was surrounded by three thousand cars and ten thousand people. Nobody seemed to be in a hurry, but, then again, everybody seemed to be going in different directions.

Harry suggested that they separate and mingle with the crowd. If anybody saw Dexter, they could use their cell phone to call the others. He had called Dexter as soon as they got to the lot, but had gotten no answer. Yates had a better idea. "I should have thought of this earlier. All we have to do is call Charlotte. She'll be with him." The others nodded. Getting no response from Harry, Yates asked, "You okay with that?"

Harry merely shrugged and said, "Sure. Let me know if you get any-thing from her." And then he walked away. After tonight, he told himself, she won't matter. All he had to do was get Dexter into tomorrow. He walked through the crowd, sometimes imagining someone pointing to him and whispering, or looking at him and reacting as if they had seen a ghost from their past. Or perhaps not. He might have been over-interpreting. All he knew was that he saw a lot of people whose happy expression seemed to turn serious when they saw him.

It was Election Day. The people were a mix of the secular and tem-poral. Harry noticed the buttons and signs. *Somewhere, a village is about to get its idiot back* had started showing up on shirts a few months earlier.

Tonight he was surprised by the number of *Our Long National Nightmare is Almost Over* buttons worn by the same people who had a *Support the Troops* button. And then he realized that a lot of the people were wearing a white button with blue lettering: *11/04/08: The Beginning*. Old and young, man and woman, the date was on everyone's chest. If somebody was selling the button for a dollar, tonight was a lucrative gusher for them.

His cell phone rang. Dexter was calling him. The first thing he heard when he answered was Dexter laughing, "Harry, you are as blind as a bat. You walked right past us. Turn around. We're looking right at you."

Harry turned around, still connected to Dexter's voice, and saw him through the crowd, about twenty yards away. "I see you...I'll," and then his view was blocked by the milling crowd. "Wave at me, or something," he said as he walked toward the spot where he had first seen him. The crowd parted again, but all he saw was the back of a royal blue cape, topped by wavy silver hair. The blue cape swirled around and Harry looked into the face of Charlotte Arnold. She actually smiled at him, and then the cape whirled around again and she stepped aside into the crowd, leaving Dexter in clear view.

"Now do you see me?" Dexter said, waving at Harry. "Get over here. We've been waiting for you."

The crowd parted as Harry walked toward him. As soon as he was close enough, the crowd came back together and encircled them. Harry remembered something Nora had told him the first day they met, after Dexter had shown him into her kitchen, "He's a big baby, that boy is, still living with his mama and daddy, like he wasn't even born yet." At that moment, in the shadow of Alltel Stadium, Harry thought that the crowd had become a womb, and Dexter was a yet to be born baby, safe and nourished and whose eyes had not yet opened. That was Harry's first thought as he accepted Dexter's outstretched hand, *You look like you don't have a care in the world. And all I can do is make silly comparisons. You and me in a womb of ten thousand people desperate to believe in something, anything, even if it's only the end of something else.*

"You're going to miss your victory party," Harry said.

"Oh, they'll wait. I mean, it's not like NBC is going to be there broadcasting my speech or anything. I'm not exactly the big news tonight," Dexter laughed again.

Harry felt a blue swirl behind him, but he did not turn around. He looked at Dexter, whose eyes were staring past him, and he recognized the look. It was the same one he had seen at Nora's last dinner party.

"Let's take a walk," Dexter said suddenly, grabbing Harry's arm and leading him through the parting crowd. "I've got a favor to ask of you."

Dexter talked as they walked, but Harry was not paying attention. Words about how much he appreciated Harry's help and guidance, about how he learned so much from him, and how his parents had come to trust and respect him, but Harry caught only individual words, not the thoughts. He was looking for Lincoln Motes.

He knew that Motes was in the crowd. He knew that Motes would have to confront Dexter face to face. He knew that Motes would not look like the Motes of a month ago, that he could be anybody in this crowd tonight. Harry also knew that he had not been smart about all this. If he had been smart, he would have called the St. Augustine police as soon as he found Dexter, would have made him wait until they arrived or they had the Jacksonville police find them. Or he should have called Yates and the others, telling them where he was and that they had to come there immediately to surround Dexter until help arrived. Better yet, he should have made Dexter leave immediately, go with Harry to the Buick and drive away from Prophet's assignment.

"Harry?"

They were at the center of the parking lot, surrounded by a motionless crowd, and Harry suddenly realized, *These people are here to see a promise fulfilled. They all know what Prophet said. A new Child of God would appear forty days after his own death, but that Child would also die at that time. A second death was required to make these people happy. For them to have truth revealed, Dexter Lee would have to die.*

He looked around, sure he had seen Charlotte's blue cape in the crowd, but she was not there, and then his final question, *What kind of people are these?*

"Harry, have you been listening to a word I've said?"

"I'm sorry, Dex," he said, still scanning the crowd. "Tell me again."

"I said that I want you to do me a favor."

Harry turned and looked directly at him. "A favor? Okay, ask me again."

Dexter took a deep breath, as if his adult patience was being tested by a child, exhaled, and said kindly, "Charlie and his people need another car. Their van is useless, and even if it ran I know that the Norville sisters don't want to ride it again, considering…well…considering it was where Prophet died, and those stains just won't come out. So I want you…"

Harry sensed the presence before he saw it. Motes was bearded, and gauntly thin, but it was him, in the crowd off to Dexter's right. Far enough away so that all Harry had to do was yell to the crowd to *stop that man*, to tell them that a murderer was among them, far enough away for him and Dexter to escape. All he had to do was speak.

Keeping his eyes on Motes, Harry finished Dexter's request as he slowly turned back to the young man, "You want me to give them my Buick, don't you."

Dexter nodded, as if embarrassed, and his smile reminded Harry of the boy's mother, her smile, but his father's face was there too.

"I love that car," Harry said.

"Let it go, Harry. For me, let it go."

Lines from a book floated by, lines from a song, lines from a poem, a stream of words, and Harry chose one. "Okay," he said. With that renunciation, Harry took Dexter's arm and gently turned him around to face the man emerging from the crowd.

Harry had made his choice.

Lincoln Motes walked toward them, but Dexter did not move, as if innocence were a defense. Then, as Motes pulled the serrated knife from under his jacket, Harry calmly stepped around in front and accepted the embrace meant for Abraham's son.

With an upward motion of his hand, Motes plunged the knife into Harry's chest. The two men locked on to each other as Harry gripped his hands around Motes' hands, refusing to let him step back. A few seconds, that was Harry's goal, a few seconds to let the crowd react, for Dexter to be safe. A few seconds of torching pain, and it would end. He felt himself falling backwards as Motes loosened his grip on the knife handle. The hands of strangers began pulling Motes away and holding him down, and Harry felt Dexter's hands gently lower him to the ground.

"Harry?"

His eyes were wide open, but he saw nothing.

"Harry, hold on. Don't move. Help is on the way."

He heard voices, and screams too, but far away. He was cold, and he raised his hand to touch the hardness he felt in his chest, but another hand stopped him. A wail sounded in the distance, like a siren, but faded to a low moan. More voices, but from his past, and he was in a field in Iowa. He felt his father's arm across his shoulder as they looked for John Brown. He was dizzy, and the hardness in his chest had turned into a razor stroke. *I'm cold*, he wanted somebody to hear him, *I'm cold*. Above him was a blue sky, and the world was spinning. He closed his eyes and felt the girl settle over him, straddling him like a lover, the two of them hidden under her blue cape. She leaned forward and gently kissed his forehead. Then, after her lips barely touched his, and her breath flowed into him, she moved to whisper into his left ear, "It was you, Harry," and then into the other, "It was always you." The only words she would ever say to him, and then she pulled the blade out of his heart.

Harry Ducharme was a child again, walking on a beach with his father, who was holding his hand and looking down at him. The sky was postcard blue. The beach then became a tree-lined river's edge, and he was alone. He stepped into the cool water of the river, flowing back to the ocean, and he finally saw the words that someone else had prepared for him, those words he had read a long time ago, always there to return at the end. He plunged under, and the waiting current caught him like a long gentle hand and pulled him swiftly forward and down so that he began to drop backwards into the immense design of things. For an instant he was overcome with surprise. Then, since he was moving quickly and knew that he was getting somewhere, all his fury and fear left him.

Larry Baker started writing short stories at the age of fourteen and had his first one published when he was fifteen. His second was published 18 years later. He was, of course, honing his craft.

In between his first and second stories, he was (in no particular order) married and divorced, a theatre manager in Texas and Oklahoma and later the owner of the Hollywood Theatre in Norman (OK), a Pizza Inn manager, a Pinkerton security guard, did publicity and promotion for an advertising agency, was a master of ceremonies in a strip club, sports reporter, janitor, waiter, and had other even more humble jobs.

He moved to Iowa City in 1980 and was eventually elected to the City Council twice. He was also defeated three times, but he doesn't talk about those times.

He is the author of two novels: *The Flamingo Rising* (Knopf), which was adapted by Hallmark for a television movie, and *Athens, America*.